I0662604

SOMEONE'S LISTENING

A NOVEL

Susan Mimram

Published in Australia by
DreamMaker Press
Neutral Bay, Sydney, NSW, Australia.
Email: susanmimram@gmail.com
Web: www.susanmimram.com

First published in Australia 2018
Copyright © Susan Mimram 2018

All rights reserved. No part of this publication may be reproduced, stored in a retrieval system, or transmitted, in any form or by any means without the prior written permission of the publisher, nor be otherwise circulated in any form of binding or cover other than that in which it is published and without a similar condition being imposed on the subsequent purchaser.

A catalogue record for this book is available from the National Library of Australia

NATIONAL LIBRARY OF AUSTRALIA

National Library of Australia Cataloguing-in-Publication entry
Creator: Mimram, Susan, author.
Title: Someone's Listening / Susan Mimram.

ISBN: 978-0-6483101-1-2 (Paperback)
ISBN: 978-0-6483101-2-9 (epub)

Cover layout and design by DreamMaker Press
Interior typesetting by Standoutdesign

Printed by Createspace

Disclaimer
This is a work of fiction. Apart from the time spent with the author's father, names, characters, businesses, places, events and incidents are either the products of the author's imagination or used in a fictitious manner. Any resemblance to actual persons, living or dead, or actual events is purely coincidental.

Dedicated to my father
Forever young

'You are my sunshine
My only sunshine
You make me happy when skies are grey
You'll never know dear how much I love you
Please don't take my sunshine away...'

Jimmie Davis

SUSAN MIMRAM

Prologue

Murrae... November 2010

'How long have I got?'

'Maximum six months.'

Dad slowly nodded. 'That's what you reckon, Doc?'

'Afraid so, Mr Henderson.'

'Well this bugger has picked the wrong fellow. I'm not going down without a fight.'

The doctor smiled. No doubt it was something he had heard before, but then again he didn't know my father.

'We can start the chemotherapy next week and it will give you extra time.'

'No, I don't need that stuff,' said Dad.

In December 2010 I flew out of Sydney and moved back into my parents' home in Auckland for the expected duration of the illness. Christmas came and we did our best to ignore the truth. It would be the last one as we knew it.

We visited our old home and the farm. We walked along Takapuna beach, along Milford beach and strolled the Devonport wharf. Dad was from farming stock but the sea was where he came to be. We talked, we were silent, and we were together. With my camera always ready to discreetly capture the fleeting moments and little video snippets of him before he became something else.

February.

'How are things going?' asked Lidia.

She never let it too long before calling me from Sydney to check in.

'Not great,' I said. 'We've shortened our stroll around the neighbourhood to a shuffle down the drive and a shuffle two doors up.'

Lidia and I had backgrounds and statures at opposite ends of the spectrum. We had worked together in a North Sydney drawing office. She was from Bulgaria and I from New Zealand but it was a friendship we knew would be with us to the end. I was aware Bulgaria had been part of the Soviet Block. And I vaguely recalled reading about the assassination of a Bulgarian defector poisoned by a jab in the thigh with an umbrella tip but that was the extent of my knowledge. Getting to know Lidia sparked my interest and I was keen to learn more.

On hanging up I went to the sunroom but Dad was not to be

found. The next best option was the downstairs garage. That was where he liked to spend his retirement, at his bench restoring his fleet of vintage cars. I found him with a patch of sandpaper and a small rusty car part in his hand. I sat next to him and placed my arm over his shoulder.

'What are you up to?'

'Tinkering,' he said as he scrubbed the folded piece of sand paper back and forth along the edge of the worn metal.

But he sat on the running board of the old Buick and it could hardly be said he was tinkering. It was more like a battle of his will to continue life as normal in a day taken up with red morphine in little paper cups followed by pulped kiwi fruit.

'Tell me a story,' he said.

I gave his shoulder a squeeze. 'That's a turn-around for us. You were always the storyteller.' He smiled back. 'It's your turn.'

'All right. What about?'

'I don't know. Make something up.'

At that moment I was at a loss to think of anything, but having spoken to Lidia I decided Bulgaria might be a good place to start. And so I began conjuring up a world to distract him from that taking over his own. In the months to follow my nights were spent in the darkness of the sunroom and as the neighbourhood slept I wrote.

Every day he asked the same question. 'I wonder what will happen tomorrow?'

And every afternoon I gave him the same reply, 'I don't know, Dad, but I'll think of something.'

Once upon a time

Bulgaria between 1944 to 1989
- Deportations, withdrawal of free movement in the country and abroad.
- No right to religious denomination and racial equality.
- Thousands of people imprisoned without trial, missing and murdered.
- Repression of accused families and relocation.
- Children of accused unable to graduate from high school.

Romania

Belene
Persin Island

Porgovo
(village fictitious)

Train route

Serbia

Veliko Tarnovo

BULGARIA

SOFIA
(Capital)

Balkan Mountain Range

Tundzha River

Black Sea

Mt Vitosha

Stara Zagora

Plovdiv

Sakar
Mountain

Elhovo

Rhodope
Mountain
Range

Haskovo

Border crossing

Macedonia

Edirne Kirklareli

Turkey

Greece

Between November 1943 and April 1944, 200 Allied bombers pummeled Bulgaria's capital. By Black Easter a quarter of Sofia's buildings were leveled and two thousand people lay dead. Five months later the Red Army crossed Bulgaria's northern border and strengthened the Communist fist.

4

CHAPTER 1

IT WAS EASTER SUNDAY and one hour before midnight. It wasn't the painting of the eggs I remember but the noise and the shaking of the earth when the hole in Slavinkov Street appeared. Most of the neighbourhood was in church but in seconds everyone was huddled in the corners hoping to God the domed roof didn't fall in. And rather than celebrating the resurrection, the only thing rising out of that night was fire and dust. A once dark sky had turned amber. Fearful folks rallied around my father and when the bombers left he led us out. In the street everything was in place save for the looks of bewilderment on locals venturing out. Though a block away Slavinkov Street had taken a hit. We rounded the corner and shocked gasps sucked the conversation out. Then came the screams, the staggering shadows and the wailing of the injured.

Fortunately for us our big old building stood strong. Its baroque façade still had the appearance of an iced wedding cake though the cherubs were sooty and the double-bay windows had glass panels missing. But two doors down was a different story. In fact there were no storeys left. My mother splayed open the side of her coat to shield me from the human mess left behind as the dust settled. She bustled my brother and I into the apartment and *Tatko went about the business of tending the injured.

At six years old that is what I remember of the Easter that became Black Easter. But after that my friends and the other local children had a whole new place to play. Broken walls and rubble piled high became medieval castles and when it rained, moats filled and streams flowed. You could look up at the missing bricks at the top of a wall and suddenly there were turrets and battlements where bows made of sticks and string could fire at the enemy. We were never quite sure who was the enemy, be they Germans, Americans, or Turks but it did not matter for we were always victorious. And as for the neighbours who lived two doors down, before it was a hole, my father said they didn't like living there anymore and had moved away. He said the only thing holding up their apartment were the wardrobes, so when they moved out the whole building tumbled to the ground.

Tatko was a good ten years older than most of my friends' fathers but a good deal more fun. Head and shoulders above the rest he could appear imposing but his deep, soft voice delivered sound advice, be it to a neighbourhood dispute or comforting words to the dying. I guess he didn't fit the mould of doctor, with hands more suitable to holding a spanner than a scalpel, and a sense of humour that could take the sting out of a gravel rash or a painful situation. And as was his habit, a few freshly-baked treats hidden from Mama in the lower drawer of his desk made a child's

Tatko: Bulgarian name given to father, as in Dad

visit to the surgery less traumatic. I'm sure she knew she'd baked twelve and not ten but for that she came to accept. It shortened a squeal from the front room when a needle jab into a little plump arm was necessary.

There were two things he couldn't abide —fools and bullies, and usually they went hand in hand. He was a member of the Country Party as my grandfather was before, so being made to join the Communists was something he found hard to accept.

Three years after the war ended, the buildings stopped falling and our country had a brand new set of leaders.

Tatko hit the newspaper with the back of his large hand. 'Who do they think they are, nominating themselves as our leaders? They're just a bunch of lowbrow blockheads with barely enough brains to wield mops around a latrine.'

'Sshh...Keep your voice down,' said my mother. 'You'll have every tongue in the neighbourhood wagging.'

His eyes flicked to her then back to the paper and he muttered something under his breath and read on.

Mama let out a long sigh and looked across to me. 'It's time you were in bed.'

'But it's not late.'

'Did you hear me?'

I slid the jigsaw puzzle back into the box, kissed them goodnight and dragged my feet to the bathroom.

'Make sure to clean your teeth,' she called.

I did but I decided to forego the usual two-minute humming that accompanied my teeth brushing session. Tatko said that if you hummed when you cleaned your teeth the vibration loosened the germs. But tonight they got a reprieve and soon enough my ear was pressed to the bathroom door. I hated to be banished when they were about to have one of those adult conversations. It only served to make it more alluring to listen in.

'They just don't know when to back off,' he said.

'For goodness sake, Aleksi, just join the party. Stop making such a big issue out of it. Life would be easier if you weren't so stubborn.'

'I'll be darned if they're going to take away my freedom to have an opinion,' he said.

'Aleksander, stop it. I'm tired of hearing this.'

'You think I should roll over? Give in! I'm telling you, not without a fight.'

'And what do you mean by that?'

There was a pause then he continued in a softer tone. 'It's the principle of the matter. I'm not the only one who feels this way. There are others at the Faculty who feel the same.'

'I don't care what they think,' she said. 'I care about us. Your principles will be the death of you.'

The chair legs screeched across the floor and soon after, cutlery was fired into drawers and cupboards were slammed. If Mama was upset the kitchen was the place that took a battering. I tiptoed out of the bathroom and into the bedroom where my brother lay cramming for his high school exam. He looked over and feigned disinterest but I felt sure he was as disturbed as I by the din coming from the kitchen. Ten minutes later he turned off the lamp and we lay listening. I rolled to the wall and pulled the blanket over my ear, but the temptation to listen was great and I rolled back. An icy silence had descended on the other side. I looked across to the dark hump of Raphael curled in the bed opposite and took comfort we shared a room.

Tatko lowered his voice. 'Come on, he said. Stop all this worry.'

'I'm sick of hearing your constant rants. And I'm sick of listening to that broadcast, too. All you seem to do lately is twiddle the nob on that radio. It's not a good thing and the children shouldn't be exposed to it,' she said.

'They don't understand.'

'They understand enough. Plus that's not the only thing.'

'What... don't tell me there's more?'

'Yes. Stop attending to the mishaps of the neighbours. They should go to the hospital. It's only inviting trouble.'

'Huh! That's the problem,' he replied. 'People are too afraid to stand up for what they believe in. I'm a doctor for heavens sake. I didn't go to University for seven years to be treated this way!'

'That's not so. You know very well you are respected. There's not one doctor who doesn't admire you.'

'Being acknowledged by your colleagues means nothing. We're treated with disdain! They can shove official dogma down my throat but I'm never going to swallow it.'

It was rare to hear them argue. Mostly their disputes were more akin to lively discussions, but on that night Mama's voice hovered just below shrill. The only comfort gained was it had not escalated to the level of our neighbours Mr and Mrs Lolovi. Their disputes often left one wondering if all that was left was hair tufts and skin scraps.

'Tell me,' he said. 'On a scale of one to ten where would you say I rank in the intelligence stakes?'

'Don't be ridiculous. You're not taking this seriously.'

'Answer me.'

There was a short pause till she replied. 'An eight.'

'Then, you don't have to keep telling me the same thing over and over. I got it the first time.'

The orange stripe in the middle of the rug between our beds was the demarcation line but in recent days I felt compelled to cross it and climb onto Raphael's bed.

I nudged him in the ribs. 'Are you awake?'

'Yes.'

'Why do you think she's crying?'

'Don't worry. Things will be ok in the morning,' he said and he rolled over and placed the pillow over his head.

'But I don't understand?'

He lifted the pillow up and rolled back.

'I've got stuff I have to remember tomorrow. Go to sleep.'

With that said, he gave me a firm push. I slid from his bed and begrudgingly returned to mine. He was right. The following morning the night's argument had been laid to rest and things returned to normal.

In the corner of the bedroom was my museum, a rosewood china cabinet that once belonged to my grandmother. After her death Mama thought it too old fashioned to be in the lounge, so it was shunted into our bedroom. Despite Raphael ribbing me over my collection I was very particular about what I displayed, be it a shiny bottle top, a dried bug skewered to the back of an empty matchbox or a feather. My most treasured possession was a vivid blue butterfly with wings that spanned eight centimetres, edged in a frill of white. On finding it I named it "Freedom", for butterflies were free to fly to wherever the wind would take them. I placed it in a glass jar, positioned it pride of place and relocated the butcher's finger to one shelf down. The day that finger departed the hand of Yanko was the day that saw him wildly running down Slavinkov Street with a bloodied tea towel wrapped around his hand, and his chubby wife hard on his heels holding a china bowl with the severed digit. Alas there was no possibility of re-attachment and Yanko's loss was my gain.

With a lot of pleading, Tatko allowed me to keep it for anatomical reasons. It was submerged in a jar of formaldehyde with a screw top lid and I covered it with a lace edged handkerchief to keep the dust off. For a long while it was the star of my museum. Yanko never knew that a small part of him was famous amongst the local children. He retrained his trembling hand to clutch the meaty joints but never with the same dexterity.

Time slipped past, the museum filled to capacity and by the time I'd reached twelve my interest in the encased curiosities waned. Brushing hair was no longer a chore and things once considered sissy were now more interesting. It came as a relief to Mama as my scruffy appearance was something she couldn't abide. Patching knees and discouraging my pursuit to beat the boys was not what she had envisioned. I guess she had her reasons. Everyone always said that I had the prettiest mother in the neighbourhood and Mama lived up to that. You'd never see my mother in a little handkerchief headscarf and thick grey stockings. She wasn't a short woman but under Tatko's arm she appeared smaller despite the stretch in her graceful neck.

They were an odd match in many ways. Probably it was a case that what one lacked the other filled, like the pieces of a jigsaw fitting snuggly to form the complete picture. She kept an ordered house, and had a busy-ness that continued even when the household chores appeared to be over. Tatko on the other hand was less concerned. At work he was meticulous but home was a different story. Certainly things had a place but it did not mean that was in a drawer or a cupboard. As long as the item ended up in the right room it didn't worry him if it hung from a door handle or was flung to the floor. He was a free thinker and when he left the rigors of the hospital, home life was to be treasured. On the occasion he managed to listen to the new-fangled western jazz, he would let loose a flurry of cheery movement, flicking fingers to the rhythm coming from our old gramophone speaker. It wasn't that

Mama protested but a disapproving look could sometimes hinder that little part of his spirit that liked to take flight every now and again.

It was Sunday night. The table cleared, the dishes done. Mama positioned the sewing machine and draped the table in eight metres of red velvet. It was a gift from a former patient and she was eager for it to grace the living room windows. Soon the needle was thumping a line of stitches and gathers in competition with the piercing whistles and white noise coming from the radio. It was hard to understand why Tatko bothered as tuning into the Radio Free Europe took patience and determination.

Mama looked up as she turned the sewing machine wheel. 'What about some music instead of letting us suffer all that noise?'

His soft brown eyes met hers. 'In a few seconds it will stop.'

She raised her eyes to the ceiling then looked at me with a disapproving shake of her head. 'Don't tell anyone your father listens to that silly station,' she said.

'Why would I? It's boring.'

I lay stomach down on the rug turning the pages of the encyclopedia at his feet till settling on *The Planets of Our Universe*, and I looked up puzzled. 'How many?'

'Ssh... One moment,' he said. 'I just want to listen to this.' And he drew his ear closer to the radio set.

Raphael looked over from his studies and Mama did her best to switch off from the foreign report. Radio Free Europe had outsmarted its opponents and through the speaker the tones of a West German announcer crackled.

"Friends of freedom... A new way of reaching you... the free world... Look to the skies tomorrow. Hundreds of balloons with messages of... we have not forgotten you."

Tatko had studied medicine in Vienna before the war leaving him with a love of the German language and he liked to impart this on us. I had caught most of what had been said and was curious. Especially on seeing his stony expression accompanied by an approving nod.

'What were they talking about?' I asked.

'Nothing,' he said and immediately changed the channel.

But "nothing" often meant "everything", and I was old

enough to know that "a nothing" accompanied by an adult frown meant trouble was brewing.

'Sometimes you treat me like a child,' I said.

He nodded and smiled. 'You are.'

'I'm twelve,' I said tightening my folded arms.

'Yes,' he said. 'And you've a few years before you're a grown up.' He reached over to tickle me but I gently pushed his hand aside.

'What did the man say?'

Mama shot him a look and cleared her throat, causing him to straighten in his chair. He smiled. 'What were you going to ask?'

But it was too late. I had flicked past the pictures of the planets and momentarily lost interest in the Universe. I closed the book.

'Come on, don't be silly. What was it?'

Two could play that game.

'Nothing.' I said.

Tatko and I talked of many things but sometimes there were conversations out of bounds and this was one of them. He gathered his trouser at the knee and folded his straight legs. His eyebrows joined and his sharp nose appeared to guide his eyes along the printed line in an effort to dissuade further questioning.

The following morning he sat dressed in his grey flannel suit, eating breakfast and dunking sourdough into his yogurt. He raised his napkin to his moustache, gave it a vigorous rub then walked over to Mama.

'I'll be back for lunch around one,' he said and he placed his hand against her cheek. 'Stop worrying.'

'Be careful,' she said.

'Of what?'

'I just feel today's different,' she said patting down the lapels of his suit.

'You worry too much.'

He raised his hand to her cheek and pulled down the lower rim of her eye. 'Anaemia. You need iron.'

'My friend's sister has an iron deficiency.' I interjected.

'Does she now.'

'Yes and I told her she should suck on nails?'

He laughed. 'I haven't heard of that approach. It can't be too good for your teeth.'

He ruffled my hair and kissed Mama. From the hallstand he pinched the front of his felt hat, placed it slightly forward on his head and checked himself in the mirror. With a slight re-adjustment of the brim he picked up his small leather case and waved goodbye. Unbeknown at the time, the image of that farewell would leave an indelible mark on Mama, Raphael, and me.

CHAPTER 2

WE STOOD UNDER a cool sun in ordered rows, ready for compulsory school warm ups before class. Between star jumps and side bends my eyes scanned the sky. Soon balloons from a foreign land would be floating high on a westerly breeze. Our teacher was in her late thirties and held in her breast a pride that she was somehow related to the president. Something I never told Tatko for he wasn't keen on the President. He liked to refer to him as "Little Stalin."

Class was run under Comrade Chervenkova's strict guidance and the thought that a misdemeanour could reach all the way to the top was more effective than a rap over the knuckles with the cane. She received a lot of attention but not the attention for which she longed. Her didactic instruction could keep a fidgety class stuck eyed and ridged but behind her wide brassiere-strapped back, small faces twisted, and muffled titters played out. We filed into a line as straight as an arrow and she led us into class. There were four two-seater desks across and five rows deep. We scrambled to be seated. Timber flip-top lids were raised, textbooks and pencils gathered. Comrade Chervenkova brought the class to order with a firm clap of her hands.

'Good morning. Today we will start our lesson with current events. Is there anyone who has news they would like to share with us this morning?'

My hand shot up with a pointed finger.

'Yes Lidia, do you have something to tell us?'

'I do, Comrade.'

'Come up then.'

Every head turned. This was my moment. I stood up, brushed down my skirt and walked to the front. I picked up the white chalk in the wooden trough at the base of the blackboard and drew a large circle with a wiggly line at the bottom then turned to face the class.

Comrade Chervenkova smiled. 'What's this all about?' she asked.

'Today hundreds of balloons shall be floating across the sky.'

'Really? And where did you hear that?'

'I heard it on the radio last night Comrade.'

She leaned forward in her chair. 'Now that is interesting,' she said and she turned her thick neck to scan the class with a keen eye.

'Are there any other pupils who have heard such a thing?'

The class fell silent. Hands were firmly on the desks and mouths firmly shut. I looked about certain others had heard it too. On realising this was not the case it gave me a sense of pride to think I was the only one privy to the exciting news.

'That's an interesting snippet of information,' she said and she pushed her tortoiseshell glasses further up the bridge of her nose. 'Is there anything else you can tell us?'

'No Comrade.'

'Very well, sit down.'

I walked back without the anticipated class response but confidant that by the end of the day I would be proven right.

Since the closure of the surgery, Tatko and Mama had been sent to work at the hospital. It was common for us to have lunch together due to the close proximity of our apartment to the school and the hospital. It was unheard of to start eating before Tatko sat down but that day things were different.

'Eat up,' said Mama placing the steamy bowl of vegetable soup on the table.

I looked at the tall seat firmly tucked under the head of the table but before I could ask she said, 'He'll be back later.' And she unscrewed a little bottle of painkillers and swallowed two tablets.

'Are you ok?' asked Raphael.

'Yes. Just a little headache. Now eat up.'

Raphael shrugged and spooned up his soup but I got the feeling there was more to it than that.

'He said he was coming home for lunch.'

'Something came up,' she replied.

We ate in silence and without having finished she rose from the table and poured the other half down the sink. Mama's soup was always a challenge but it struck me as odd because her Russian background saw no food ever wasted. Many were the times my left- over portion became a battle of wills. I was not allowed to leave the table until every spoonful was eaten. It was a losing battle. I'd force it down on the third count, raise my eyes to the ceiling and gulp hard. This time I made sure I ate it all but she seemed not to notice.

Senior school was in the afternoon and junior school the morning, so when lunch was over I was left with the cleanup. Raphael returned to school and Mama to the hospital dispensary.

'Hurry up,' she said, tucking in the tail of his shirt. 'Take some pride in your appearance.'

He grimaced and bent down to tie his shoelace. His teenage years saw fewer asthma attacks but his bony frame had yet to acquire a good amount of muscle. He had reached the age when to be seen walking with a parent caused maximum embarrassment and Mama's fussing did not make it easy. He stood and flung his school bag on his back then tugged at his shirt. To appear a little rough around the edges was preferable to looking like Mama had dressed him. I smirked and he rolled his eyes and hurried ahead. He could be a tease at times but I made sure I gave as good as I got and as far as a brother went he would do. There was no mistaking he was Tatko's son. His hair was dark and slicked back to the crown of his head, the shaven sides emphasizing ears that stood out a little more than he would have liked. Nevertheless he was handsome despite the awkwardness of youth.

I cleared the lunch dishes and stood at the sink frothing the wire soap holder into hot water. Looking out through the kitchen window I stared up at a strip of dirty white sky between our building and the next. It was disappointing to see a sky full of swallows and not a balloon in sight but there was still a few hours of daylight to go. When everything was cleared away I set myself up in the front room next to the window facing the street. There I sat with my chin cupped in my hands and my elbows on the window ledge, mulling over the recent day's events. It was not until I caught sight of Mama walking quickly up the street that I leaped off their bed and scurried into my own room. I snatched my homework from my satchel, jumped on the bed and opened my schoolbook at random. Seconds later she walked in.

'You're home early,' I said as she poked her head in through the bedroom door.

'Yes, but I have to go out again.'

'Why?'

'Your father and I have some business to do.'

'What?'

'Just business. We'll be home a little later.'

And she walked quickly into her bedroom.

'When Raphael comes back you can share the Reyane cake,' she called.

Shortly after she was out the door with her brown hair in a tight French roll and her fur collar hiding a tight jaw. It was confusing and I watched her hurry up the street but soon my thoughts turned to the cake and I eagerly waited for Raphael. A good half hour went by before I spotted his lanky swagger. Lately I had seen his lingering glances at Katia's sister and watching him talking with her was confirmation enough, I smiled, and by the time he'd opened the front door I was ready.

'Raphael loves Anna, Raphael loves Annnnna.'

'I do not,' he said elbowing me in the ribs. 'Where's Mama?'

'Gone to meet Tatko.'

'What for?'

'Don't know. But she said we could eat the cake.'

'Great!'

Down went his school bag and we raced to the kitchen as if we had to catch the cake rather than rip the lid off the tin. He took the knife and sliced through the dense chocolate. I looked on making sure my share was of equal measure. But by the forth cutting most was eaten and we were in no mood for more. Three hours later our parent's absence was telling us all was not right. We stood at the front window with the curtain pulled back and watched the street lights come on. Occasionally someone hurried along the sidewalk causing our hearts to quicken but footsteps came and footsteps went. When dusk arrived Raphael wrote a short note explaining where we were and placed it on the floor in the hallway so it could be clearly seen.

'Come on,' he said. 'Let's go.'

We ran full speed up the street and around the corner. A strip of yellow light shone below the apartment door and we could hear Uncle Boyko scuff his way across the room. I jiggled about in the hallway with my hands tightly clutching my woollen scarf. The moment the door opened we rushed him.

'Mama went to get Tatko,' said Raphael. 'They haven't come back.'

Uncle Boyko raised a halting hand.

'Goodness me. Calm down and tell me slowly what's happened.'

His generous moustache and imposing frame gave him the

appearance of a walrus and it was comforting to feel his thick hand on my shoulder. In the lounge Aunt Iva, cousins Yana and Marko sat wide-eyed with shredded cabbage dangling from their forks.

Aunt Iva and Mama were as different as two sisters could be. Although she was lean her thickened waist and short brown hair chewed up any femininity and gave her a slight masculine edge. Being older and the least attractive, Aunt Iva let it be known that she may not have been blessed with beauty but she was certainly blessed with the brains. And between the two of them there was a quiet rivalry.

Despite their differences our families lived within a block of one another. Social events and holidays were always taken together. Though the last camping trip to the mountains had not been the two week adventure intended. Uncle Boyko's Russian tent turned out to be a challenge and even Aunt Iva was at a loss to decipher the instructions. After spending four hours assembling poles, canvas and pegs we were shamed by an East German couple who pitched their tent in fifteen minutes and were sipping beers between smug smiles as they watched us struggle. For Aunt Iva it was no laughing matter but the longer it took, and the tighter her mouth became as Tatko and Uncle Boyko fell into belly aching giggles.

Now Aunt Iva's mouth was pressed firm once more but more from a deep concern. She pushed her plate away, got up and walked over to me. 'What's happened?' she said.

That was all that was needed for me to burst into tears. Uncle Boyko walked to the gramophone and lifted the needle. The vinyl record came to a stop and my jaw began to chatter.

'I'll make a hot drink and you can tell us all about it,' said Aunt Iva.

Uncle Boyko leaned forward resting his chin in one hand with his other hand on his hip. There wasn't much to tell. Just that for reasons unbeknown to us our parents had not come home. On hearing the news the legs of his chair made a low screech backwards across the vinyl floor and he stood.

'It'll be ok, I'll take you home and we'll wait together. I'm sure there's nothing the matter. These things can happen especially with the weather as it is. Your mother and father have probably missed the tram,' he said.

But his soothing words were in stark contrast to his furrowed brow.

December clouds rolled in from the Vitosha Mountain Range sending icy gusts and stinging rain. We hurried past doorways and shaky power lines as the street took a battering. The building came into view but no light shone from the first floor front window. On the landing Uncle Boyko shook the rain from his umbrella, we removed raincoats and opened the door to the cold apartment.

'Hello,' he called, but there was no crackle from the radio or thump from the sewing machine treadle, only a morose silence. They we're not sleeping. They were not there.

'Go wash and change out of your school uniforms,' he said taking a pack of well-thumbed cards from his pocket. 'When you're ready I will show you some tricks.'

Under normal circumstances this would call for cries of glee but tonight was far from normal. After an hour of card shuffles one slipped from his fingers and the predicted King of Hearts was replaced by the Ace of Clubs. He had all but exhausted his repertoire when the front door opened. Darkness entered the house along with my mauled mother. We jumped to our feet, horrified to see her disheveled state. A sopping wet yoke covered her shoulders and half her unpinned hair hung lank like black rope. I threw my arms around her and she held me tight to her chest and the world fell to bits on that one winter's night.

'What's happened?' said Uncle Boyko.

Her head shook from side to side and she dragged her feet to the kitchen sink and she gripped the edge of the bench.

'He's gone,' she sobbed. 'They've taken him.'

Suddenly my mother's words seemed to suck all the air from the room. My breath up and left me and Raphael stood in mute shock. She tugged at her necklace as if to free her neck. The string broke and pearls scattered across the kitchen floor.

'Who's taken him?' said Uncle Boyko.

'The *Darzhavna.' He pulled his chin in. 'What for?'

Her hands covered her face. 'I don't know.'

'There must be a mistake,' he said. 'Did they say what he's accused of?'

She did not reply, but shook her head and wept. He took her elbow and guided her to sit at the table. Her once upright shoulders slumped in. She took the tea cloth and wiped her face. The leftover lipstick smeared across her cheek in a macabre grin.

'Did you see him?'

'No. No one at the hospital had seen him either. He wasn't

* Darzhavna were the Bulgarian Secret Police.

home for lunch and when I got to work I ran into Rita Lovech. She was waiting for the tram and saw him pushed into a car at the corner of Donkov and Radost Lane.'

She stopped and ran her hand across her forehead, then shook her head. 'I had a bad feeling this morning and the moment she told me I felt sick to my stomach. I left and came home. I figured I would go to the police and find out what happened.'

'What did they say?' asked Uncle Boyko.

'He's to be tried by the Peoples Tribunal.'

'That's crazy. There must be a mix-up.'

'No. They took me in for questioning. Wanted to know if I knew anything about his anti-government activities.'

'Aleksi hasn't done anything. Has he?'

I felt her back stiffen. 'Of course not.'

'Sorry. I'm just trying to understand what's going on.'

'I don't know what's going on. They wouldn't even let me see him. They said if I didn't leave I could expect the same. Oh God, Boyko what am I going to do! What am I going to do!'

'There, there,' he said.

I looked from Uncle Boyko, to Mama, to Raphael but no one had an answer. All the predictability of the world, the guidance and the protection of my loving father had gone. We were left to float on an uncertain sea with no warning of what was to come and no way back to what was before. I did not understand.

'Go get your mother a blanket,' said Uncle Boyko.

Raphael returned with a blanket and wrapped it around her shoulders. Uncle Boyko placed the kettle on the stove and soon the steamy whistle was squealing into the sober atmosphere.

'I'll make enquiries tomorrow,' he said. 'You'll come home with us tonight. I'll call Iva.'

'No, we'll stay here.'

'Why not?'

'Because if they release him I want to be here,' she said.

'All right but I'll get Iva. You need your sister.'

'No, Iva must stay away. I've no idea what will happen. I don't want her involved,' said Mama and she looked at me with an expression that left me doubly anxious.

'Can you bring a change of clothes for Lidia? Marko's would fit.'

'Why?'

'It's a just a precaution.'

'Precaution against what?' I asked.

She gave him a look that was baffling and I was left wondering why adults sometimes had the need to talk in riddles. There was no telling where all this was going but it did not bode well. He shook his head and his horn-rimmed glasses appeared to hold tight to his temples and rage coloured his cheeks. He could offer us no more protection than a crepe umbrella in a hurricane.

'Dear God, what has become of our nation?' he said.

She blew her nose and looked up at him. 'Promise me, Boyko. Keep Iva away tonight.'

'All right then. But she will be here first thing in the morning and I'll go to the police station to sort this mess out.'

He grabbed his trench coat and battled to place his arm into an inverted sleeve, all the while cursing under his breath. With cap and umbrella in hand he shut the front door.

The dim light cast ghostly shadows on Mama's fine face, and childhood dreams disappeared on that fateful night. Our names and photographs were now on the authorities list and doom was slamming down onto once hopeful hearts. Twenty minutes went by before he returned with a small tan leather suitcase in one hand and a pot of leftovers in the other.

'Iva is very worried about you. There's stew in this pot. I'm sure you'll feel a little better having eaten something.'

He placed the case on the table and unbuckled the two leather straps. One small white shirt, one pair of heavy trousers, a brown home-knitted pullover, a thick gabardine coat plus one well-worn cap.

'These should fit,' he said looking at me.

My school blouse just camouflaged impending adulthood and my slender legs could outrun most of the boys but putting on boy's trousers was another matter entirely.

'Why? I don't understand.'

He closed the suitcase. 'You don't need to understand. It's what your mother wants and if, God forbid, there's a visit from the Darzhana* you must put them on.'

'I don't want to. I want Tatko to come home.'

'He will,' he said. 'And tomorrow I shall go with your mother to the Town Hall to sort things out.' He patted Mama on the shoulder. 'I don't like leaving you like this. Eat some food and try to get some sleep.'

'What's going to happen?' asked Raphael, with his adolescent voice breaking.

'I don't know, Raphe. But right now you're the man of the house. Look after them,' he said with a nod in our direction. 'I'm going now but we'll be back first thing.'

The stew sat untouched on the cold stove top.

'You'll sleep with me tonight,' said Mama and silently we made our way to bed.

The question surrounding her disheveled state was not asked. Nothing more was said, for some things are best left unsaid. The only one who could truly comfort us had vanished.

CHAPTER 3

2:00am

ALL WAS QUIET in the neighbourhood until the groan of an engine and a set of white headlights shone down Slavinkov Street. One door slammed, then another and very soon there was heavy pounding on our door.

'Open up! Milizia*. Open up!'

Mama leaped out of bed. She stood in the centre of the room with a crazy expression and her hand to her mouth. A paralyzing fear glued me to the mattress. I could barely breath, as if a large block of lead had landed on my chest.

'Get up!' she yelled.

Raphael tore into the room with arms in the air. 'What's going on?'

'I don't know. Quick, go to your room.'

I sprang to my feet and the pounding on the door matched

the terror in my heart. We ran out of the master bedroom knocking the pot of violets from the wooden stand. Black tarry soil and china pieces smashed to the floor.

'Stay there,' she hollered.

But before she reached the door a shoulder charge from the other side sent it slamming against the wall. Two men barged in and a large hand pushed her aside.

'What do you want?'

'Vacancy!'

There was no disguising the fact they were the secret police despite civilian clothes. The shorter man yelled orders while the other stood with his bulky arms folded across his double-breasted suit. His large shape projected a foreboding shadow over the wall and ceiling of our living room.

Down the hall and behind the door Raphael and I cowered.

'Malina Petrova Ivanova?' said the short man.

'Yes.'

'You have fifteen minutes to collect your belongings.'

'There must be some mistake?'

'No mistake. It's right here,' he said and he waved the list of names in her face. 'You are to be relocated.'

She took a backward step and clutched her chest. 'Don't do this. Please, I beg you. We've done nothing wrong.'

He looked at her with a flat expression and placed the list back in his top pocket. His gaze moved to the mantel piece and he walked over and picked up the vase. 'Nice,' he said as he turned it in his hand.

'Take it… Take anything. Don't take us away,' said Mama

tugging at his coat sleeve.

'Get your hands off me!' He jerked his arm free and in one action he tossed our family heirloom over his shoulder. It shattered into an array of coloured chips.

'That's one less thing you need worry about.' He tapped his watch face. 'Fifteen minutes starting from now.'

I stood frozen in the middle of our bedroom.

'Get dressed!' yelled Raphael. He ripped open the lid of the suitcase and tossed Marko's clothes at me. I heaved the trousers over my pajamas, buckled the belt, buttoned the jacket, pulled on socks and cap. My feet scuffed into my black school shoes and the heels collapsed inwards. Out in the lounge the red velvet, soon to embellish the living room window was thrown to the floor. Somehow in the face of fear Mama found the presence of mind to gather the basic necessities.

'Time's up,' said the skinny man. He grabbed the photo from her hand and tossed it away. 'Move!'

Mr and Mrs Lolovi peered through the crack in their apartment door watching us shuffle down the hall. All that could fit in the curtain was bundled and knotted, and between them Raphael and Mama carried it out. I followed closely with wet eyes wide and nose streaming. In one hand I carried a pillow and in the other, Uncle Boyko's suitcase. Inside was a jumble of clothing and buried within was the screw top jar containing my "Freedom butterfly".

Out into the black night we moved. Mama climbed the step at the rear of the truck and two people stepped forward to help haul us aboard. We shunted our possessions across the floor and three families moved aside. The man in charge stood on the tray and through his thin lips said, 'Enjoy the ride, folks.'

The tailgate slammed and the bolts slid into position. Under the canopy and in the cold darkness families huddled together and children whimpered. A half a kilometre down the street at Georgi's Bakery the shop door flew open and they burst in. Angry protests could be heard, followed by a thud and a wail. Minutes later the bakers with their flustered cheeks and floured brows appeared. They tumbled into the back with no baggage allowed other than their thick coats and sticky aprons. In the darkness they slid to the floor next to us. It was apparent we had fared better for our hoard was larger than most. It never occurred to me that perhaps my mother's fine features might have given us a more lenient allowance.

The truck made its way towards the outer suburbs where another vehicle with additional guards slipped in behind. We were headed to a train station on the outskirts of Sofia so as to raise the least amount of public attention. For the first hour concerned conversation filled the dark interior but by the time the city lights were a distant glimmer, bewilderment laid claim to eighteen of us. We clung to our coat openings as the icy air bit through the canvas and Mama's arms wrapped firmly around me. From the south, the east and the west, trucks converged on the northern most reaches of the city. Along the street vehicles lined up and people spilled onto the sidewalk, to be herded through the gates of the railway station.

The train veered north and crossed the Yantra River where the old city of Veliko Tarnovo clung to the hillside. The conversations had run out. It was a long night with three stops at which groups of people were off-loaded. We sped across the plains stretching out beneath the Balkan Mountains. I woke to the sound of squealing brakes and a steady decrease of speed. I peered out through the timber slats. It was early and the light was mellow but men in thick coats were moving about. The train slipped alongside the platform.

'Pull the hat down,' whispered Mama and she tucked a strand of hair back under my cap.

'What are they going to do with us?' I asked.

She shook her head. 'Keep quiet and just do as they say.'

'Where do you think we are?' said a voice in the dark.

'The last station was Tsareva Livada. The Romanian border can't be far,' replied another.

Moments later the steel wheels on the weighty door tracked back and the murky darkness in the carriage gave way to morning.

'Out!' cried a guard.

We struggled to our feet and one by one climbed down. Men stood either side of the opening watching our group spew out. Families moved off the short platform, past the railway hoarding and across the road to a clearing. Large tarpaulins were thrown over the sleet-covered ground. We sat down and dry sausages and stale bread were dished out.

As two guards approached, Mama called out. 'Excuse me, Comrades, we need to use a toilet.'

Their heads turned. 'Who's we?' said the young man.

'My children Comrade.'

'What do you reckon, Vlad? Fancy a bit of sugar on your

breakfast?' he said as he circled us like a hyena. His eyes flicked between Mama and me.

'All right. You and you stand up. Not you pimple face,' he said, pushing Raphael in the collarbone.

'Do as he says,' said Mama.Raphael hesitated then knelt next to my legs. The man lifted Mama's chin with his left hand while his right groped her breast and squeezed. She didn't flinch but stared straight ahead. The other man stood shielding us from their superior's view.

'No, too old. But this one's a beauty.'

His face was close and menacing and his steamy breath held the remnants of stale tobacco. His narrow eyes scrutinised and slipped across my scarlet cheeks, down my scarlet neck and over the pounding chest pockets of Marko's coat. He looked straight into me and I stood as if made of stone. Fear made his face appear a quivering wet blur. I was sure the world could hear the thump of my heart and the drone in my temples. As I stood beside with Mama, I could feel the terrifying rhythm shaking her body.

Should I hold my nerve? Should I look into his eyes? Should I say, no you're wrong, I'm a girl? Then would he leave me alone? When the tears fell down my cheeks his stare punctured my soul. What he wanted, I had no idea but he was no fool. His sharp eyes flashed back and forth, up and down. And his nostrils flared like a black bear sniffing the air of its prey. Mama's hand slipped into mine and gripped tight.

'He's just a boy,' she said.

'He's a girly boy. Fucking pretty if you ask me.'

His friend burst into laughter, ending with a snort. 'You

34

desperate bastard,' he said.

'A boy who cries lie a girl, I like that,' said the man with his face a fist-space away.

Slowly his hands reached between Mama and I and one finger at a time he unlocked our hands.

'Don't worry Mama,' he said. 'I'll take your boy to the toilet. I'll show him how to piss.'

Suddenly behind us a man hummed. A song we all knew. A song to touch the heart of the nation. Then a voice came and then another until the whole group joined. Raphael rose to his feet and they all followed. And with guts and gusto they sang the national anthem.

'...*Countless fighters died, for our beloved people, mother, give us manly strength to continue ...*'

Their compelling dignity held the attention of evil and the guard stepped back.

'Shut up,' yelled the guard and his backhanded slap crossed Raphael's cheek, knocking him to the ground.

'That'll keep your jaw from clacking,' he said and he looked back at me.

'Come on,' said his friend. He grabbed his elbow. 'I wouldn't dip my cock in this filth.'

They sauntered off. Shaken we sat down. Nine hours later we were rounded up and loaded onto another truck. The engine roared and the floorboards clattered as we drove along an unsealed road. Our destination was a small village in the province of Pleven. By morning we rolled into the center of Polgovo, increasing the population by eighteen. Blurry-eyed folk watched the unfolding event from behind parted curtains.

It was not the first time village life had been disrupted. For some years a future reservoir had been mooted and was the cause for a serious discussion at the local bar. The village put up a hardy protest till common sense prevailed and another site was identified. The community took a collective sigh and the fields continued to yield bumper sugar beet harvests. Now there was a load of city folk dumped at the village doorstep and the locals were suspicious. Word spread quickly and people gathered in groups at the edges of the square to watch. We climbed out and re-assembled in front of a stout man with a clipboard.

'Good morning,' he said. 'This is your new home. You will be allocated accommodation. When I call out your name step forward... Georgi Nikolov Markov, Ivanka Stoianova Markova, Gergina Georgieva Markova, Malina Petrova Ivanova, Raphael Alexandrov Ivanov, Lidia Alexandrova Ivanova!'

What had happened was beyond our understanding. We stepped forward. Pots, pans, and various items clanged together. Each family peeled off in different directions. We were led across the square and away from the village centre, accompanied by two men. Every now and then the weight of the curtain caused Mama and Raphael to stop, catch their breath then stumble along the uneven lane. At the end we arrived at an abandoned house.

'Welcome home,' said the guard.

He climbed the steps of the house and unbuttoned his fly. With an exaggerated arch in his back he urinated on the front door then gestured widely and bowed. 'You can move in now. It's christened.'

The house stood on the outskirts of the village, like an outcast. The orange roof tiles were the one part that appeared unbroken. Two front windows were boarded up with packing-case timber. Through the weeds chickens, lucky to escape the dinner plate, bobbed their heads from left to right pecking between bits of rusty machinery. A black dog too lazy to bark lay in a wheelbarrow.

Raphael stepped over the puddle and led the way into the house. The floor groaned and the doors creaked as the house adjusted to the shifting weight on its floor. We moved ahead cautiously and the musty front room seemed to breathe in new life. Most of the furniture remained, though the vinyl couch was now a rat's paradise. Fluffy kapok was strewn about, peppered in droppings and in the kitchen stood a sturdy table with two chairs.

Mama's face grew pale. She steadied herself at the door but soon after her legs buckled and she slid to the floor. We sat her up and her head hung between her knees.

'I'll be all right,' she said. 'I just need some air.'

'I'll fix this place up,' said Raphael. 'Take her outside.'

I took her out and together we sat with our backs to the wall staring at a foreign landscape. Stretching out in front was a network of black, brown and green patches. To the right and rising up, rugged hills with a thin white goat trail winding back and forth like a crack in a pot. To the left was a gully where spinney pines followed a stream that cut a slippery path through the fields, tunnelling a way under a stone bridge that led to the village. No building was taller than two storeys and the sky could be seen from every corner. Through happy eyes it was a scene to free the spirit. The vibrancy of the greens, the wavering grasses that shimmered and danced and the scent of freshly-ploughed earth could make one believe all was right with the world. But to sad city eyes it was a wasteland where distant hills horseshoed the valley like giant claws creeping in on patchy plains.

Raphael dragged the mattresses into the yard and heaved them up onto the cart. He took the challenge onto his skinny shoulders with a determination never before seen. The injection of activity caused the dog to spring into action and his bark was waging war with his wagging tail. Pent up anger was vented out on the mattress aided by the end of a broomstick. The chickens ran for cover, alarmed by a flurry of kapok and feathers rising into the air. When he was certain all life had left the nest he dragged the bedding back inside. And in the grass at the side of the house he found a bicycle with flat tires, stiff gears and a rusty chain. It was mid-morning and there was a lot to be done before nightfall.

The colour seeped back into Mama's cheeks. She pushed onto my shoulder and lifted herself up. Hot embers had not warmed the belly of the wood oven for some time but thick ash remained. With a piece of cardboard I cleared it away while she searched the cupboards. Above the rusty cooktop was a shelf of dusty pots and tall bottles of grey peach preserves. Her fingers ferreted along finding matches between a vinegar bottle and a saucepan. We mopped floors, wiped benches and scoured for food. Raphael gathered arm loads of pinecones from the tree in the front yard and hours later a minimal amount of domesticity was restored to the rooms. To the rear of the yard was an overgrown vegetable garden. Amongst the weeds poking through the net canopy, a patch of moth-eaten cabbages struggled to exist. We leaped around the yard with the determination and agility that accompanies pangs of hunger as the lifestyle of the five chickens and stately rooster came under threat. They dashed and squawked with wings out-stretched.

As the sun cooled, giving way to late afternoon, the fire spat and crackled. It flushed warmth into the musty walls but the bone-deadening cold clung low in the bedrooms and we dragged the mattresses to the kitchen. Come the evening the slowest of the feathered quintet morphed into a meal for three. Its bones and feet picked clean and placed in a pot of water, extending the meal into humble cabbage soup. From that day the chickens were given a reprieve. Their life was guaranteed depending on how well they laid. We repaired the hole in the wire and placed them back in the coop.

At night we curled together near the heat and silently wept. The broken catch on the unsecured bathroom window clanged against the frame and high in the pine tree an owl hooted at the moon. What had come to pass was beyond discussion. As if we had been drawn into a black void with no way up and no way out.

We rose early to the sounds of the countryside waking and at eight o'clock we stood outside the town hall. In front was a man whose clothing suggested he was not someone who worked the fields but whose preference was to hand out orders and stamp documents.

His eyes flicked over us then he looked straight at me. 'It says here you're a girl. Remove the cap,' he said pointing.

My two plaits fell to my shoulders and I gripped the cap

tightly to my chest.

'What's your name?'

'Lidia Ivanova.'

He looked me up and down. 'Can't you decide whether you're a buck or a doe, Lidia?'

My cheeks flushed and he continued.

'You will go to the school. Make sure you're not late for lessons tomorrow. Understand?'

'Yes Comrade.'

His attention moved to Raphael. 'You boy will be picked up at 6:30am.'

'He's still at school,' protested Mama.

'Not anymore. A boy can do the work of a man. As for you, report back here tomorrow at 7:00am with the other women for the bus to the garment factory.'

The village had a population of fifteen hundred not including goats and geese that were given free rein to wander the laneways and community square. It was rare to own a motor vehicle so transport was the horse and cart. Next day a low mist hovered outside and we hurried to dress. By 6:30a.m. a young man with hair the colour of molasses, knocked on the door. The transport stood at attention beyond the gate pushing fog from its nostrils and shaking its mane.

'Morning, I'm Petar,' he said. 'Are you ready?'

Raphael nodded and the man dropped a pair of rubber boots, one size too big, to the floor.

'Put em on.'

He changed shoes and buttoned the top of his coat and we

watched him climb into the back of the cart. The man took hold
of the reins and turned back.

'Sit up here. I've two others to pick up.' Then he laughed.
'Relax; it's not so bad. All you have to do is shovel shit and keep
your mouth shut.'

Raphael clambered forward and with a flick of the whip the
horse moved off down the lane.

The bumper harvest had ended. It was time to prepare the
fields to repeat the yield. Manure was hauled by horse-drawn
wagons where men pitched it off. In the coming weeks Raphael
returned home exhausted but as his shovel technique improved he
increased his capacity and his shoulders widened.

Seven new students boosted the class at the village school.
Our introduction was brief and met with whispers behind cupped
hands. Next to me sat a new boy whose endless nose stream
spread a slippery path along his jumper sleeve. We sat together
like a couple of junkyard throw-outs. My forehead rested on my
hands and my eyes were fixed on the white page of the school
exercise book. Focused on nothing, because nothing was the only
thing left.

In Slavinkov Street everyone knew me. Here everyone
was curious but no one wanted to know. The change had been
swift and brutal. I sat unable to remember the day before or
the day before that, and when I did recall the results were
incomprehensible and crushing. We would not be going home

and there was no trace of Tatko. I felt as if I stood at the edge of the Earth, nowhere to go, nothing more to see.

Two feet appeared directly in front of me. I had not noticed her in my class but then again I hadn't noticed anything that morning. She was smaller than the other students in the year, with apricot freckles and straight orange hair that finished at her chin. She stood with her arms folded and face screwed up.

'Are you a prisoner from Sofia?'

Her comment was enough to drag me back. 'No!'

'Then why are you here?'

I did not answer and she paused a moment and shrugged.

'Do you want to be my friend?' she said and undeterred by my lack of response she plunked herself down next to me.

'My mum said you shouldn't sit on the cement it'll freeze your ovaries.' She nudged me in my ribs. 'What's your name? '

I looked over. 'Lidia.'

She reached into her pocket and produced a white rat. 'I'm Anna and this is Captain Snowy. As you can see he's a bit sleepy. I have to bring him with me because he tends to get depressed if I leave him at home.'

His little red eyes opened and he chipped his front teeth together as she stroked him.

'You know he might be small but he's very intelligent. Do you want to see?'

She placed him on the ground and with her right hand stiffly planted in front of him, she whistled. Captain Snowy leaped into action and hurdled over her fingers. Another whistle bought about a reverse performance.

It did not matter that she was a year younger. I was grateful for her friendship. I soon learnt she was different from the other children and excluded from their games. That was unless she was the butt of their jokes. Having one eye look straight ahead and the other slightly turned was reason enough. But it did not seem to bother her nor the fact that her mother, Mrs Stoeva prided herself on her hairdressing abilities where the outcome was 'hit and miss'.

That afternoon we walked home together. She held back from any more questions and seemed happy to have another's company besides Captain Snowy. From that day on she considered me her "second best friend".

'See you tomorrow,' she said, and she skipped across the square.

Her family ran the store that was the bank, the post office and the bar. It was a place where locals went to shuffle cards and down shots, and a place I came to visit daily. It was also frequented by a retarded boy, who sat on the bench at the front no matter what the weather. Anna said he was fifteen but with his drooling chin and loose grin he appeared much younger. On the second day, Anna took me into the store to meet her mother.

'So you're Anna's new friend?' said Mrs Stoeva patting the back of her homemade perm.

I nodded.

'One moment,' she said and she reached down below the counter and produced a cardboard box in which she placed a selection of groceries. Her head popped up and she slid the box across the counter.

'Take these to your mother. Anna tells me there's an old bike at the house so there's a packet of tire patches and the loan of a pump. Give it back when you're done with it.'

I thanked her and with arms full I returned to the house with an element of faith that perhaps all was not lost. That night we patched the tires, coated the chain in vegetable oil and it was road worthy. Over the following weeks I peddled back to the store each afternoon to prop the bike against the stucco wall.

'Any mail for Ivanova?' I would ask.

'No dear,' came her reply.

It was always the same. I never left with the speed at which I had arrived. Common sense was telling me there would be no letter but hope refused to give in.

Six weeks later I slung my leg over the cross bar and rode across the square at speed. My heart was pumping. Outside the store the drooling fat boy sat hunched with his elbows on his knees. Today he seemed to sense my excitement as he watched me peddle off. I was careful to stay in the centre of the road to avoid the stony build-up on the shoulder. I crossed the stone bridge and down the other side with the spokes clanging against the bracing bracket of the rear wheel. In my pocket was Uncle Boyko's letter. The flap of the envelope had been tampered with but resealed. His cautious reply meant the content of his letter had got through. I handed it to Mama. Craggy claws etched away across her cheeks and her eyes slipped along every line.

Uncle Boyko had written back immediately on receiving the news from Mama, but the interception of the letter meant it arrived a month later. Apparently he had not learnt of our relocation until Aunt Iva turned up at the apartment the following morning. She banged on the door to no avail and again on the neighbour's, but lips were buttoned and shoulders shrugged. Despite the night's commotion not a whisper had been heard. Uncle Boyko arrived at Police Headquarters to be redirected to the courthouse. The Peoples Court was already underway and he found himself barred from entry. He waited outside in the crowded hall till learning Tatko was not included in the trials. Instead he had been sent to Belene Prison with no legal representation and an undetermined trial date.

When finished reading, Mama folded the letter. It was confirmed. We were on our own. The envelope of security she held close had been ripped from us and laid out in tatters but I failed to understand the enormity of his fate. There was no question in my mind that he would be back. It was unthinkable to consider otherwise. He would fix up the mess. My father; the problem solver. My father the one everyone came to, to be saved.

'We'll write to him and he'll know where we are,' I suggested.

She took my hand and squeezed it but the look on her face made me wonder how many times the world could cave in? She stood and walked to the bedroom and I sat in the kitchen. Moments passed before I followed her. She lay with her face buried in the last shirt Tatko had worn. The one thing of his she had held onto when they took us. When Raphael returned he found me sitting in the gloom staring at the ceiling paint that hung like torn handkerchiefs.

'Where's Mama?' he said as he buttoned down his coat.

'She's gone to bed.'

'Why?'

My eyes flicked to the letter. He pulled the chair out and sat down. 'What's this about?'

'News from Uncle Boyko.'

His hand slid across the table and straight away he read it. When he finished he put it down and his open hand tapped the table. 'He'll come back. I'm certain.'

'Me too,' I said.

There was no choice but to get on with things. Each of us dealt with Tatko's absence in our own way. Mama appeared to welcome exhaustion. Her solace came from long days in the factory rocking the sewing machine treadle and early bed. Our sibling goading was shelved and Uncle Boyko's last words saw Raphael take on responsibilities beyond any previously expected. He instilled hope that Tatko was not lost to us and that it was a matter of time before we would be back together. He went about his business quietly but as for me, disobedience festered. I made up my mind to study hard and scrape a life back till Tatko's return. But I would slyly disobey the authority that sanctioned the break in our family.

Anna and I kept to ourselves but we always found things to do. Whether it was scooping tadpoles out of the creek, sitting in a cardboard box sliding down the slopes or climbing up the hill to visit Otets Bogmil, the lonesome priest. But one day it all "came unstuck", when there was talk in the village about his death.

'What possessed him to ring the bell is beyond me,' declared

Mrs Stoeva to her friend as she wiped down the shop counter.

'He didn't mean to do it,' said the other woman.

'Then how did it happen?'

'An accident. They said his robe got caught in the rope. It lifted him off the ground and he fell heavily.'

The priest had been found a day after Easter with his head smashed on the belfry floor. Seven times the bell had rung and Anna and I knew who was responsible.

The little church above the village had long since held a congregation. There were still a few folk venturing up the hill to talk with God but mostly it stood empty. The exterior was crumbling but inside there were golden walls and colourful icons. It was a twenty-minute hike from the base to the top but the view was worth it. For Anna and me it was special, and weather permitting, on Saturday afternoons that was where we could be found. The church was many things to us. It was a place to look down on the world, and dream of something better.

At the rear of the building was a room where the old priest lived. According to Anna he once had a wife but she died four years ago and with his devalued status most of his time was spent in his garden. His beard was as long as a straw broom brush and his belly as big as a melon. Well that is what he said. He loved nothing more than to have a good joke with us.

'If you eat melon seeds you could grow a melon belly like mine,' he chuckled.

We knew he was joking but from then on I was careful to filter the fruit seeds for fear that maybe there was an element of truth to it. Plus Anna felt sure Andrey Hristov, the class bully, had mustard seeds growing in his ears.

Otets Bogmil was seventy-two but it was hard to imagine one could live that long. His garden patch was his pride and joy and he was generous with his pickings. We never returned home empty- handed. When it was cold and the wind was up we would marvel over the religious icons, and the church took on a whole new theme. It was our theatre, our Aladdin's cave. On occasion when the priest felt compelled, he read to us from what he called his 'God book'. But a man who died in order to rid the world of sin did not make much sense to me. I was more fascinated by the dint in the old man's head and the dome in the ceiling.

'Could we ring the bell?' asked Anna one day.

'No,' he said.

'Why?'

'They tell me it disturbs the peace.'

'Who?'

He shrugged.

'It's not a good idea to upset people.'

'What about one dong?' said Anna.

'No. And anyway it hasn't rung for years. It's probably rusted up.'

We looked at one another unconvinced.

'Why does the church have a bell?' I asked.

'To remind people of the presence of God. Every Sunday I'd ring that bell. And after Christmas and Easter services I hardly had energy to lift up a glass of breakfast Boza.'

'When's Easter?' she asked.

'Two weeks.'

It was getting late and we left him polishing his altar relics and headed down the hill.

'I'd love to ring that bell. Just once,' said Anna. 'It would be so much fun.'

'Why don't we?' I whispered, with a twinge of excitement. 'We could ring it at Easter. He's not allowed but nobody said we couldn't.'

'Yes let's do it. I'm sure he'd like it.'

It was agreed. We would rise early Easter Sunday. We figured three goes at the rope would be all it would take before the old priest was alerted. After which it would mean high-tailing it down the belfry steps and down the hill.

Sunday arrived and I woke to the jingle of goat bells. The herder was on his way to greener pastures and I watched blurry-eyed from the window. Anna and I agreed to meet on the track to Levisky's apiary. I quickly dressed and slipped out of the house. The golden dome on the bell tower was barely visible through the mist. We had to be up there before the priest woke so there was little time to spare.

We ran along the same narrow track and far enough behind the herder that he did not notice. There was little movement in the village below as was normal for Sunday. By the time Anna and I made it to the top the mist had subsided and the dome on the bell tower looked splendid. We climbed the stone stairs till we reached the small wooden ladder leading to the belfry. The rope hung straight from the bell ball with three gripping knots tied thick and dusty at the end. I took hold of the top knot and Anna the bottom.

'Ok. On the count of three we pull... One, two, three!'

At the bottom of the first yank the ball slammed into the bell louder than we had imagined. Our arms rose up almost out of their sockets and down again. Excitement took over and instead of the agreed three rings, four extra rang out across the valley. I let go of the rope and jumped back sending Anna's feet off the floor. Next we were clambering down the ladder and running down the steps. It wasn't until we arrived at the base of the hill that we collapsed in a fit of giggles. Debris on the bell had fallen into our eyes but it was well worth the discomfort.

'Everybody in the village would have heard that. It made me want to do it again,' I said.

'Me too,' said Anna.

The chatter that surrounded the death of the priest was almost unbearable and the struggle to remain silent agonising. We would never know what happened to our elderly friend other than being left with the feeling that our actions had somehow caused his death. From that day on we never looked to the top of the hill. Our friendship was no longer the only thing shared for we held a secret, a guilt and a shame. Several weeks later Anna appeared to cope better but my concentration faltered and weariness overtook me. Somehow we did not fit together as we had before. I was ok one day and not okay the next. Ok one month and not ok the next. Until eventually things fell into place though not in the place, that they should have been.

CHAPTER 4

THREE YEARS HAD PASSED since the death of the priest and four years passed with no news of Tatko. It was the year I was set to graduate, the year I grew five centimetres and the year I turned sixteen. My grades had slipped but there was no reason other than a lie to prevent me finishing my high school education with a certificate. I swept my hand across my side of the desk. Text books scattered, pencils fell and the class sat gob smacked. Within seconds the teacher was by my side with her hands on her hips.

'What's got into you, stop this behaviour this minute!'

I grabbed my coat. Anna whispered something but words failed me. I kicked over the chair and ran out. Before my outburst I had been summoned to the principal's office. I tapped on the partially opened door and a voice called out.

'Enter.'

When I walked in Comrade Avramov's head was down and he continued to write. I stood still on the other side of his desk waiting with my hands clasped tight. Through the rear window the light danced on the lattice of his thin hair, highlighting his pink scalp. Several minutes passed before he put his pen down. He placed his rimless glasses on the pad in front and pushed back into his leather seat. I froze as thoughtful disdain crossed his face.

'Lidia.'

'Yes, Comrade.'

'There have been complaints about your behaviour.'

'Pardon, Comrade?'

'Don't interrupt me,' he snapped.

'It has been brought to my attention that your behavior with some of the male students has been inappropriate. This is something the school will not tolerate. As a consequence you are to be expelled.'

I stood wide-eyed. 'But that's not true.'

'There's nothing more to be said. Return to class, return your textbooks and collect your bag.'

'It's a lie, Comrade! A lie!'

With that his podgy hand came down on the desk with a sharp tap. 'Pull yourself together girl. That is the decision. Now go!'

I stormed out and down the corridor to dump my education on the classroom floor. Before the teacher had time to take hold of me I was gone. I ran through the school gates with no thought as to which direction I was headed. From the school windows my teacher and students stared out. Anna was close on my heels holding tight to Captain Snowy. I ran as fast as I could. Not home but away from everything. Through the village square, past the beet fields and down the rise till I collapsed at the river's edge. I was bent over in a shamble of tears when Anna fell down next to me. Inside her pocket Captain Snowy lay still and flaccid. His longer than expected life had come to an end and we sat sobbing.

The next morning I trailed behind Raphael. Petar's dark eyes watched as I climbed up into the cart. Black curls flicked from under his cap and a worn collar hid a tanned neck. He was dressed in a grey shirt, haphazardly tucked in with a black leather belt holding tight to his patched trousers.

'Morning,' he said. 'There're boots over there. They'll serve you better than those.'

I took the boots and sat down next to Raphael, placing my shoes in the sack. The horse moved off along the stony road with its hindquarters rising and falling like greased pistons. In the half dawn five other farm workers climbed aboard. We passed through the village and arrived at the field were the smell of damp earth and root vegetables hung heavy in the air. Everyone spread out, but Raphael hung back with me.

'I'll show her what to do,' said Petar. 'Get a move on before the rain sets in.'

Half-heartedly Raphael slung the v-shaped hoe over his shoulder and walked off leaving Petar to size me up. He took hold of the wooden handle of the tool and with his cigarette bobbing at the corner of his mouth he gave me a quick lesson.

'This is what you do.'

In one swift action he raised the blade up and drove it back down with a thump to the earth.

'Ram this end into the ground next to the beet. Lever the weed up like this. Make sure you don't hit the root. Pull the weeds up along the row and when that's done move to the next.' He looked straight at me. 'Got the idea?'

I nodded and he handed me the tool but as I pulled away he maintained his grip.

'How come a good looker like you ends up working in a shit hole like this?'

His cockiness made me blush.

'You seem lost for words?' he said.

I shrugged. 'It makes no difference to me. It's just work.'

'I'm not so sure about that,' he said then grinned. 'Is it true what I hear about you?'

'What?'

'That you shake your tail feathers for the boys.'

I wrenched the hoe away. 'Keep your filthy mouth shut,' I spat back and stormed off across the paddock.

'Hey! Walk between the rows,' he called.

Raphael's hoe stopped mid-way above his head as he caught sight of me striding towards him.

'What's up?'

Petar's back was turned to us. He stood perched with one foot on the tractor tire and the other on the step. His head was hidden under the engine cover as he tried to inject life into the two-stroke engine.

'Him,' I said tossing my head sideways. 'I hope the bonnet falls on his oversized nut!'

Raphael put a hand on my shoulder. 'What happened?'

I looked back across the field. There were fifteen field hands, nine horses and a red Belarus tractor, which did not live up to the Russian manufacturer's claim of value and reliability.

'He's got a filthy mouth,' I said picking up the hoe.

'Don't let him get to you.'

'How can you say that?'

'Because we have no choice."

I looked up at him. 'If this is our life, then I'm not sure I want to participate.'

'You mustn't say that. You've got to believe it'll change.'

'I can't believe anymore. Tatko use to say you reap what you sow but if that's the case we've been given bad seed.'

I looked down at the black soil at my feet where an unwanted dandelion_ fresh and green_ pushed its way through the crumbly earth. I reached down, uprooted it and tossed it aside. Five hours later we sat eating lunch at the edge of the field. Petar kept his distance; he sat under the tractor canopy with his nose in a book and a thermos of coffee propped between his knees.

'What's with him?' I said pointing my chin in the direction of the tractor. 'I bet he couldn't even read a road sign.'

'He's not bad. He's a bit of a loner that's all,' replied Raphael hacking off another slice of bread.

'I wish he'd leave me alone. Arrogant idiot.'

'He told me he was sent to a labor camp,' said Raphael before taking another bite.

'Really? Do you know what he did?'

'He got caught drawing a moustache on Lenin's photo in his

folder. Got thrown out of university and sent to a camp.'

'That's a surprise.'

'What?'

'That he made it to university.'

'It's hard to work him out I know. But he's no idiot. And he's not the only one around here with a gripe.'

By mid-afternoon the rain reached the field and the mud was making the work doubly difficult. It took ten hours for the whistle to blow and bring an end to thinning and weeding. We climbed onto the cart for the return journey and dangled our legs off the edge of the tray. Night was rolling in covering up the remaining daylight on the hillside. Along the way workers were dropped off until we were the ones left alone with Petar. There was an awkward silence between the rear and the front of the cart, broken only by the sound of the horse's hooves on the ancient Roman road.

The next day Raphael stood in the middle of the field watching as Petar called me back. A brewing anger caused the blood to rush to my temples and I prepared myself for the next insult from his thick lips. I glared at him. His hand rubbed the back of his neck and he looked at me.

'Sorry about yesterday,' he said.

In the seconds it took for me to reply I glared at him. 'What did you say?'

'I said I'm sorry. I should never have spoken to you like that.'

I looked at him up and down, stretching the moment. 'Prove it,' I said and I strutted off with my chin high.

Over the month the tension between us relaxed but despite

Raphael engaging him in conversation, I preferred to keep my distance.

A heavy cloud rested on the mountains to the north. It was late September and a snap of cold air was causing our jaws to chatter. Even the rooster found fit to tuck his stiff beak under his warm wing. We stood at the gate hopping from one foot to the other. Through the blanket of moist whiteness the cart appeared but this time there was no sign of a rolled cigarette glow fading in and out.

'Where's Petar?' asked Raphael.

'Didn't he tell you?' replied the broad bellied man whose cap was firmly pulled over his ears.

'No.'

'Word is he's trading the tractor for a Volga.'

'How's that?' I asked.

'The Mayor has snapped him up. Going to be his driver.'

We looked at one another and the man continued.

'He's certainly got the cream of the work,' he said, shifting a little on the hard plank of the seat. 'But they say scum floats to the top.'

Any further enquiry was met with a disinterested shrug and we were left none the wiser. Petar was not seen in the village for six months. His lack of interaction with others meant he flew under the village radar. He was untouched by local curiosity and I assumed he had been sent away for some sort of training.

Soon, a busy harvest was underway, with the field labor more than tripled. A distinctive smell of sugar wafted over the land as the first consignment of beets tumbled through the factory crusher. The crop was piled in heaps at the edge of the field creating a steady supply for the short processing period. My job was to top the beets. It was summer and loaded trucks roared through the valley on their way to the processing plant five kilometres south.

I sat on a crate alongside Rosa, trimming and tossing beets into a clean pile. I liked her. She made a mundane job easier with her irreverent sense of humour

'The livestock loves this stuff,' she said. 'But it's best to keep your distance when they have a belly full. God knows why they don't use these leafy tops in the military. It could gas all those Yankees with one truckload.'

In the distance the Mayor's car passed the line of trees and came into view. Another beet hit the pile and together we looked up.

'Now what brings the Mayor out to these parts?' she said.

We watched as the car coasted to a stop ten metres away, and to my surprise Petar climbed out. A river of unease flowed through me. We watched him saunter towards us. His hand combed through his hair and he stood directly in front of me with his legs astride.

'I see you're working hard, Lidia.'

'Yes,' I said. 'Not like you.'

Rosa chuckled and my comment appeared to take him off guard.

'You're right. Life has taken a turn for the better.'

'What brings you out here? It can't be the smell of sugar,' I said.

'No. Something sweet, but not sugar.'

'What then?'

'You.'

I felt a sudden rise of color up my throat and Rosa raised an eyebrow. She looked away as if disinterested but I knew her ears were tuned in.

'Come, I need to have a word with you,' he said nodding over his shoulder towards the car.

I placed the knife on the ground and stood up with my arms folded and my chin out.

'No need to look at me like that. I have a proposal for you,' he said.

He took me by the elbow but I pulled my arm away and we walked to the car. On reaching it, he lent his body against the hot door panel.

'I want to help you,' he said.

'And why would you do anything for me?' I replied with my eyes narrowing.

He smiled back and continued. 'One time we spoke you challenged me to prove to you I was sorry, so I want to do just that.'

I listened with curiosity.

'I now work for the Mayor and he needs an extra person to help out in the office. So he asked me if I knew of anyone who would be suitable and I thought of you.'

I dropped my hands to my sides. 'What's the catch?'

'No catch,' he said.

'Is this some sought of trick? If it is, I don't find it funny.'

'The job is there. If you want it you can start tomorrow at 8:00am. Otherwise it will be offered to someone else. Anyway,' he said. 'I've got to get going.'

He turned his back and climbed into the driver's seat. I stepped away from the car. The engine rumbled into life and he drove off, leaving me standing dumbfounded at the edge of the road.

I walked over to Rosa and sat down on the crate.

'What did he want?'

'He says there's a job for me at the Mayor's office if I want it. Starting tomorrow.'

'Well now, I'd jump at that one. It sure beats the beets.'

Rosa was right, and it occupied my mind for the rest of the afternoon. There was no possibility of discussing it with Raphael because at the start of the harvest he had been sent to the processing plant. It was not until I returned home that I was able to tell my news.

'And what does this boy want from you?' remarked Mama.

'He's ok,' said Raphael. 'He keeps to himself but he spent time in a camp. Maybe he can relate to us. It's a good opportunity.'

'Just pay attention. Nothing comes for nothing,' she added.

The town hall was a pink building with a flat roof and Balkan stone foundations. It appeared out of place on the edge of the square, for it was the only modern building in the village. To the left was the flagpole and to the right a life-sized statue of

Stalin with his chin raised and his hand pointing to the centre. The statue was erected in 1952 and not long after we arrived in the village a pair of dirty underpants was slung over Stalin's finger. The sign placed around his neck read, "THIS PLACE STINKS."

According to Anna there was a lot of speculation in the bar about the perpetrator, with suspicion directed at the new arrivals but the culprit was never identified.

I arrived early and was shown into the office by a middle-aged woman. 'So you're Lidia?'

'Yes, Comrade.'

'I'm Lilliana. I run the office. I'm not sure why the Mayor needs extra help. What were you before?'

'Field worker,' I replied.

'I can see you're going to be a lot of use to me,' she said snidely. 'Wait here.'

She turned abruptly and left me standing in the centre of the large office looking about and careful not to disturb anything. My eyes shifted from left to right. There was nothing particularly special, save for three tall metal-framed windows and a large glass- topped desk positioned next to the wall radiator. By the door was a smaller desk with a typewriter where a woman's cardigan was slung over the back of the chair. The interior of the room was as austere as its concrete exterior.

Minutes later the Mayor entered. 'Good morning, comrade,' he said and he placed his hat on the hat stand.

His pants were hitched high by braces and buttoned to his waistband giving him the appearance of a trussed goose. He crossed the room, patting his baby fluff hair down from a lick on his palm then held out his hand.

'Pleased to meet you,' he said. 'Petar tells me you're a smart girl so let's hope you don't let him down.'

'I'll do my best, Comrade,' I replied.

'Good. Let's get started. Can you type?'

'No, Comrade.'

'Then the next two weeks you can familiarise yourself with the typewriter. That should be time enough.' He walked to the door and stuck his head out. 'Liliana, show Lidia how to use the typewriter.'

She jumped up immediately. 'Yes Comrade.'

He turned back to me. 'Good. Hurry on out now. Lilianna will look after you.'

I could see Petar through the window. He ran the yellow chamois over the glossy panels of the black Volga parked outside. Now wax polish replaced the soil under his fingernails and he appeared to relish the change. It seemed working for the Mayor he got to enjoy the party perks, a flash vehicle and 'carte blanche' to drive to any location without question.

Liliana walked towards me and I quickly turned my head back. Her mouth was as tight as the bun on her head. Whether it was her profound lisp that was the cause of her unhappiness or having to share office duties with another woman, I could not tell.

'You can sit here,' she said dusting off the small table next to the window. Her fingers ran across the keys. 'It's old but certainly good enough for you.'

She placed a manual headed "A USERS GUIDE" beside the typewriter and gave the cover a little tap. 'I'll be working on correspondence this morning. In the afternoon I'll give you a lesson.'

She turned sharply and with short, purposeful steps walked back into the Mayor's office. What followed was a furious tap, tap, tapping interrupted by the bell from the carriage return. The thought of an afternoon under her instruction and watchful eye was intimidating. I flicked through the manual and opened the beginner's tutorial. My hands hovered above the second row of keys and after an hour's practice I lifted my fingers off. I clenched them several times and looked out the window. Across the way, on the seat outside the store, Rahseed's vacant eyes steered towards Petar. The boy's daily appearance in rain and shine secured him a place in the village environment. He was an odd human fixture and as much a part of the square as Stalin's finger-pointing statue.

The Mayor's car was speck free and shiny. Petar wiped a final stroke across the bonnet with the soft cloth. He seemed satisfied and stood back eyeing his handiwork. He turned, looked at Rasheed and flicked his cigarette butt in his direction. I was left wondering if it was his frustration with life in the village that made him react the way he did towards others. I was grateful he left me to get on with my work and after two weeks Liliana had me typing addresses on envelopes and making trips to the store to post the mail.

I settled quickly into the job and gradually the initial wariness I had towards Petar diminished. He was rough around the edges and his cockiness could trip him up at times, but he knew how to work the system and lived off his wits. He was striking, eight years older than me and had a casual confidence. He could be funny and at other times brandish an unexpected charm. There was restlessness to him too, as if the next moment was of more interest than the present. He dreamt big, bigger than I could ever imagine and it wasn't long before we were sharing our stories. I learnt more about him in the following month than I had in the four years we had lived in the village. It became a playful tug of war as to who could outwit the other. The more I saw of him the more I grew to like him. I started at eight thirty so there was time enough to chat. The Mayor kept a later schedule and Liliana capitalised on this by arriving five minutes short of nine.

'Lidia is a very noble name,' said Petar nodding to himself and propping his thigh on the corner of my desk. 'I think you and I are very similar.' He watched me hang my coat and walk over to my desk.

'What makes you think that?'

'Because girls called Lidia make their own decisions, are independent and crave freedom.'

I held my feelings close but it was as if he saw through me. Somehow he was attuned to the goings on of my heart.

'Oh really?' I said.

'Yes really... Plus girls called Lidia have other desirable attributes,' he said and he raised his eyebrows a number of times.

I rolled new paper onto the typewriter and cleared my throat. 'Don't think I'm going to fall for that. I bet you say things like that to lots of girls in the village.'

He leaned across and his eyes drilled into me. 'No I don't actually. Anyway I'm not interested in the girls around here.'

'Why not?'

He shrugged. 'I like smart girls.'

'I'd have thought you would have the pick of the girls in this place.'

'Not so,' he replied.

I smiled up at him. 'I must admit your initial approach didn't endear you to me. Maybe that's your problem?'

'No, it's deeper.'

'How's that?'

'My family used to own half the countryside. We were the largest landowner in the district until our land was seized and made into the collective farm.' He let out a sigh. 'We were considered landed gentry, so folks around here think we got what was coming to us.'

'Do you come from a large family?' I asked.

'No, I'm the only son.' He glanced at his watch. 'I better get going I've got some errands to run.'

He took the car keys from the hook and left.

CHAPTER 5

'GET UP?' I said and I nudged the man's leg with my toe.

His disheveled body lay at the top of the steps, lifeless save for a heavy wheezing out and a grappling breath in. The worn leather soles of his boots faced out and it appeared his clothes had never been washed. I prodded him again, this time harder.

'Wake up!'

He jolted and his lids flicked back revealing eyes sunken deep. It was a struggle for him to sit upright and he stared at me with a gnarled hand extended.

'I'm not touching you. Find somewhere else to sleep,' I hollered.

For a short moment he seemed speechless and his jaw trembled.

'Get up. This is not your house.'

'Lidia,' he said, with a voice hoarse and feeble.

I reeled backwards as if hit by a lightning bolt. 'Get away from me! You filthy man.'

He lurched forward to grab me but I darted aside and stumbled backwards nearly toppling off the porch.

'It's me… Tatko,' he said. 'Lidia look at me.'

When I straightened I could barely look at the man disgracing my father's image.

'Tatko has black hair. Get away! You're not my father,' I screamed.

He looked from me to the fields beyond and the tremors in his hands took hold. He hugged his knees tight to his chest and I sat three metres away staring at him. Slowly he pushed his sleeve up his forearm and he spoke low. His eyes were firmly fixed on me.

'Look,' he said pointing at the mole on his arm. 'You used to say it was the heart I wore on my sleeve.'

My seventeen years came to a halt in that very moment. As if a switch had shut off every thought, every breath, every sense. Perhaps a second, perhaps two. Everything held in limbo until my scrambled thoughts pulled back into line and joy, horror, and disbelief collided.

I rushed forward. The musty fabric of his coat swallowed me up. He rocked me close and I cried into his wheezing chest. He was fifty-two kilos of skin over bone, with white scruffy hair glued to a sweaty scar at the base of his skull. It was hot and the surrounding fields parched but no heat could dry the muck that hung thick in his lungs.

'Tatko! What happened to you? I thought you were never coming back. I thought you were gone forever.'

'I'm here now,' he said and he held me tight. 'Look at you. You're all grown up.'

'I'm so sorry. I didn't know.'

'It's no matter,' he said and he stroked my head. 'I know I don't look like your father anymore but I am and I love you.'

His appearance was as far removed from the memories I held, and even the tone of his voice had changed. Having a front tooth missing probably did not help.

He looked about. 'Where's Mama and Raph?'

I pulled up but I could barely get my words out. 'They're working. They won't be here for an hour.'

'We'd best go inside and wait then,' he said, and the smile stolen from him for years, returned but not as wide as it once was.

I got to my feet and held his hand. All the fat had vanished from his body but he was a tall man with big bones and I struggled to help him to his feet. When he was upright he teetered for a moment and I clung to him tightly as he gathered himself together. First the left foot then the right, then the first foot and so it went. We shuffled into the house, each painful step causing him to wince and suck his breath in sharply. It was hard to imagine how he had made the journey to us in his broken-down state. I helped him remove his coat. I undid his laces and placed his large shoes side by side in the corner of the room. He sat with his mouth partially open and his eyes watched me bathe his face with a cold wet cloth.

'I'll make you a drink.'

'Water will do,' he said, and his chin rested on his collarbone.

I placed the glass in his calloused hands. The liquid rocked about but he managed not to spill. He raised the glass to his lips and his jaw slipped to the side like a misaligned castanet.

I stroked his cheek. 'What happened?'

'Broken,' he said. 'I don't know what your mother will say. I've not looked in a mirror. I must look hideous.'

'Mama will be so happy,' I said.

I propped the pillow behind him and he lay back with his eyes shut and I watched him fall into an exhausted sleep. His appearance was so unfamiliar; I tried to envisage the remnants of what he once was and what he could be again. Maybe in a few weeks the purple under his eyes and the grey in his fallen cheeks would be replaced with new health. I pulled the cover around his shoulders and for a moment I thought he had woken.

'Are you all right?' I asked.

But he seemed far from the world. The only sign that death had not staked its claim was his rattling rib cage. An hour passed. The gate squeaked and I jumped to my feet. Mama stopped in her tracks on seeing me fling open the door and hurtle down the steps.

'Tatko! Tatko!' I yelled.

A look of foreboding washed over her face and immediately her hands shot to her heart.

'Oh God,' she wailed and her palm pounded her forehead.

'No, he's here!'

She grabbed my shoulders and shook me hard. 'Where?'

'Inside.'

I'm not sure whether he sensed her or it was the commotion outside that caused him to wake. She broke from me and by the time she entered the room he was standing as straight as he could manage. She flew at him with outstretched arms and despite the welts that oozed under the fabric of his shirt he did not flinch.

'Aleksi! Aleksi,' she cried.

'Malina,' he said and he rested his cheek on the top of her head and she cried uncontrollably. In that very moment it felt as though they were the only two people in the room. I watched on until they released.

She raised her chin up. 'Oh dear God look at you. What have they done?' She stepped back to take him in. 'Come sit down.'

Together we held his forearms and eased him on to the edge of the bed. Looking at him was heart breaking.

'How did you get out? Do they know you're here?' she asked.

He shook his head. 'Don't know but don't worry.'

She covered her mouth and her eyes darted back and forth. 'We must be careful. We must keep this quiet. Everybody knows everything in this place. Did anyone see you come?'

He patted her hand. 'It's all right,' he said. 'I was free to go.'

'How come?'

'They closed the prison.'

'Why would they do that?'

'Not sure,' he said and he let go a long breath. 'I was one of the lucky ones. Most got transferred to Lovech.'

'Thank God. Thank God you're safe,' she said fussing around him. 'But look at you. There's nothing of you.'

I sat at the foot of the bed. 'So they won't take you away again?' I asked.

'No my darling girl. I'm no use. They don't need me.'

'Well we need you,' said Mama, running her hand across his forehead. 'You are everything to us. You will get well. We will make sure of that. This is a miracle. You're going to be ok.'

But looking at him something was gone forever behind his soft brown eyes. I felt helpless and at a loss to know what to do.

'How did you ever find us?' asked Mama.

'I called the old apartment. A stranger answered. Said you no longer lived there. Then I rang Boyko?'

'So Boyko and Iva know you're here?'

'Yes. He wanted to collect me but I couldn't wait the two days. It was all so unexpected. I was fearful I wouldn't make it back to you. I just had to get out.'

Mama puffed the pillow. 'Come,' she said. 'Lie back down. Lidia go heat the water for his bath.'

She unbuttoned his shirt and peeled the yellow fabric from his back then lovingly brushed her hand across his chest. 'When this is all washed off you'll feel much better.'

I poured pot after pot of heated water into the bath and when it was ready I left them. I sat in the kitchen behind the closed door and waited. When it was over he emerged clean and pale skinned, with his wet hair slicked to his head. He wore Raphael's trousers, which finished mid-calf, and on his back the shirt Mama had clung to on leaving Sofia. When Raphael returned from work he poked his head into the room and stopped dead as if his spine had been fused.

'Hello son,' said Tatko and his arms stretched out. But on his deep breath the air got caught in his throat and he could say no more.

Raphael dropped his bag to the floor. 'Tatko!'

It was not the time for handshakes and back pats. It took

moments for them to release, as though holding tight gave them the strength not to weep.

'Let me look at you,' said Tatko. 'Where's my skinny son?'

Raphael stepped back with wet eyes. 'I want to kill them for what they've done,' he said.

Tatko cut him short. 'Don't talk like that, son. It's over. It'll do no good.'

CHAPTER 6

I ARRIVED at the bus stop where women gathered for the five-kilometre trip to the garment factory.

'My mother is ill today,' I said. 'She won't be coming to work. She has a stomach virus and she asked me to tell you.'

Her absence was accepted without question and I walked across the square to the Town Hall and waited. Tatko's return had sharpened my memories of life before it took a turn for the worst, and I sat on the step in front of the main door deep in thought. It was 7:30a.m. and there was a half hour's wait before Petar appeared. He had the responsibility of opening the office and the general tidy up before the Mayor and Lilianna arrived. He walked across the square and soon his shadow was over me.

'You're early. What's up? Something the matter? Looks serious.'

I was not sure what to say and instead I shrugged.

'Sure you don't want to tell a friend? Maybe I can help.'

'Is that what I am to you?'

'What?' he said as he unlocked the door.

'A friend?'

He smiled and his eyebrows jumped up and down. 'I like to think so,' he replied and with that he swung the door open and I followed him through.

I walked to the window and pulled the wooden venetian blind high enough to let the sun onto my desk. He picked up the waste paper basket and tipped the contents into his sack, but his eyes hardly strayed from me.

'You might not consider me your friend,' he said. 'But who knows, I might be able to help.'

I had never mentioned the subject of Tatko's absence and he had never asked. I wondered whether to tell him now. But then again he had the ability to wrangle what he wanted and maybe he could do that for me.

'My father came home last night,' I said.

He immediately straightened and his chin receded. 'I assumed he was dead.'

'Pretty much,' I said. 'I hardly recognised him, he's so ill.'

'Where's he been?'

'Belene concentration camp,'

He looked at me for some time as if mulling over what to say. 'Not many of us got out of that place alive,' he said.

'What do you mean? Sounds like you know about it.'

'You could say that.' He hesitated for a moment and then he said. 'I was there.'

'You never told me.'

'You never asked.' He pulled tobacco from his pouch and arranged it on a small white paper. Then he licked the long edge, rolled it and stuck it in his mouth. I waited for him to continue. It was obvious he was struggling to speak and needed a moment to compose himself.

'It's not something I like talking about,' he said.

'How long for?'

'Long enough not to want to remember. How did he manage to get here?'

'He sold his gold tooth for two bus tickets.'

'Christ. How is he?'

'Bad. I'm not sure what's going to happen.'

'Did he escape?'

'No, they closed Belene and let him go.'

'That's downright incredible.'

'But he's got this terrible cough,' I said.

'Don't worry. He'll come right now he's out of that hell hole.'

He plunked himself on the corner of my desk and leant towards me. 'If there is anything I can do, just ask.'

'Thanks. He needs medicine.'

'That's hard to get but leave it with me. I'll see what I can do.'

He walked out leaving me with a feeling of hope. True to his word, as I left the town hall that afternoon he stepped out to meet me. He pulled his handkerchief from his pocket, unknotted it and placed five tablets in my hand.

'Here, take this,' he said. 'I didn't want to take too many so as not to raise suspicion.'

'What are they?'

'I think they're painkillers but whatever they are it's better than nothing. I couldn't get hold of antibiotics. That's all Liliana's handbag could offer.'

'Won't she know?'

'I doubt it. See how they go. If they help I'll get a few more.'

I quickly stuffed them in my pocket and hurried home.

That night I lay in the darkness mulling over the recent change of events. It was too much to ask that Tatko would be the father I remembered. His wonderful free spirit had taken flight and he was left empty. Lying on the couch was comfortable enough for me with a few fist punches to the cushions but sleep was elusive.

The nights that followed we each went to bed with a pit full of fear. At around midnight his nightmares became ours. On waking his anxiety seemed to trap him for a good half hour. It was only Mama's tight hold that seemed to bring him back from the edge. Not only was he lost to us but he seemed lost to himself. He spoke little of what had happened but when he slept his mutterings could turn to violent lashings out, which on waking could pin him to the bed. It was not that it happened every night but wakeful hours were spent not knowing what the night had in store. Three weeks later Petar handed me new tablets and Tatko slept.

'Don't ask where I got them,' he said.

As the months rolled by I treasured the time I had with
Tatko. It was a privilege to start work later and for an hour in
the morning I shared his company. His wounds healed but the
rattle in his chest and his laboured breath sapped the dregs of
his energy. He ate less and smoked more. It was the one thing
that seemed to calm his jitters. My endeavours to find out what
happened to him were met with silence. Occasionally a wincing
smile froze his cheeks but I doubted it was due to my attempt
to entertain. Most days he spent seated by the stove. But as the
weather had taken a turn for the better I dragged the old chair
out on to the landing thinking the sun would do him good. His
tall frame hobbled next to mine as I clung to his arm and eased
him into the seat. I upturned the small wooden crate that Raphael
used for his work boots and sat down next to him.

'This is like old times,' I said.

'How's that?'

'Don't you remember how I'd sit at your feet?'

'Yes,' he recalled. 'Always full of questions.'

'Yes but you used to answer me then.'

His brow rose and he let go a short sigh.

'All right, ask me something.'

Suddenly all the things I craved to know left me tongue-tied.

'What are you thinking?' he asked.

'I don't know. Sometimes I feel like a mouse on a wheel. No
matter how fast I run it's the same rotten route to nowhere.'

He began to cough. I waited till it settled.

'You're doing all right,' he said. 'You've a good job.'

'But no education,' I replied.

'Education counts for little nowdays,' he said.

I looked down at our hands locked together and I held to the shaking in his.

'Freud was right,' he said. '"If your lips are silent you chatter with your fingertips."'

He squeezed my hand. 'What do you need to know? '

'Why they took you away.'

'My idea of freedom tripped me up.'

'What do you mean?'

He let out a long sigh. 'I was foolish.'

'But you did nothing wrong.'

I put my arm around him and I rested my head on his shoulder. I could smell the decaying acetone of his breath and he raised a hand up and stroked my cheek.

'I did. I ruined this family.'

'Don't think that way. You always did the best for us.'

'Sometimes ones best is not always right.'

He stopped talking and I waited a moment, then he moved up in the chair and paused to catch his breath.

'It's ok ,' I said. 'Tell me some other time.'

'I'm all right,' he said and continued. 'I knew I was in trouble when they took me but no idea how much. I thought I would be sent home after a good stripping down. Even six months later when I went to trial I still believed I'd be going home.' He looked down at his splayed hand. 'I bargained my wedding ring to get a message out to your mother but it was pointless. They took it anyway, and never sent it.'

'How could it be a trial without a defence?'

'I did have. They gave me a young law graduate, Todor Rakladjiev. I was his first case. Too clever for his own good. If it weren't for him I'd have got a death sentence.'

His voice faltered and I watched him closely. I handed him the cup of water and it was a challenge for him to swallow. He turned away and with a distant gaze stretching far beyond the mountains he fell silent.

'Do you think things will change?' I asked.

He shrugged. 'Don't know. But remember this, you can walk on a daisy but tomorrow it will stand up.'

The following afternoon was unnerving. He was unaware I sat beside him and he babbled about things I found difficult to comprehend.

'Dead men,' he said. 'That's not vegetables in the crates. Get the pigs away,' he yelled. 'Get them away!'

I rubbed his back and slowly bought him back but he remained agitated and there was an urgent tone in his voice. I felt uneasy that perhaps he sensed time was running out.

Thirty-one days later as the leaves dried and loosened their grip, so did he lose his hold on life. That morning I had leant across him and he dragged his fleshless arms from beneath the cover. I kissed him and rested my cheek on his neck. Suddenly he seemed small. I stroked his head where his short feathered hair had lost direction.

'Lidia,' he said.

'What?'

His long arm propped up and his hand took hold of mine. 'I'm not going to be around much longer.'

A hooting gooey cough interrupted him and his eyes closed. 'Don't say that.'

'You must be strong,' he said. 'Be careful. If there's an opportunity to make a better life, take it.'

I held him gently. His chest rose and fell rapidly and I could hear short gasping. I lifted my head and looked at him. It was the first time I had seen him cry. At that moment I wanted to say, I want to go where you're going. I want to go with you. Instead I stroked his hair, soft and grey, and kissed his forehead.

'I love you, Tatko,' I said.

He offered a faint smile and shut his eyes. Death was but a few steps away.

When I found him he was seated as I had left him. A blanket wrapped around his shoulders and his large hands clasped in his lap. In the days leading up to his death he had fallen into trances and a soothing tap would bring him back. Now he sat as if some deep thought had suddenly ended but his empty shell held on to his inherent dignity.

At first I gently rocked his shoulder, but the present unbroken moment saw not a flicker of recognition return. His blue skin had turned to cold marble.

'Wake up, wake up, please wake up,' I pleaded.

His body shifted to one side and still he stared. I wailed 'NO!' To the heavens and 'NO!' to hell but the desolation was relentless.

Quiet and still. The tail end of innocence left me rattled and empty. A good man's life interrupted too soon.

I sat at his feet gasping as if I had run a marathon. The glue was gone and with feelings so profound there were no words.

We buried him in a small corner in the old cemetery and Mama planted sunflower seedlings in the shape of a cross. In the centre where the shape intersected, I placed my treasure, my "Freedom" butterfly trapped in a brass lid jar. At the edge of spring, small shoots weaved their way out of the earth to snake towards the sky. By summer their dusty green stalks, bent at the top, were holding their defiant yellow heads high. And when the sun slid past the poplar trees, they turned to face the West.

At night I heard my mother weep. She muffled it, but her short little breaths out followed by small sucking sounds in were amplified in the stillness. We managed as best we could and much as we had before, but there was a finality to hope with each day eating up the next. The loss of Tatko was always with me. Some days I'd catch myself searching for hidden messages, be it a bird perched on the windowsill, a shape in a cloud or the long shadow that followed me home. One day I woke early, certain he stood in the doorway but grief plays with the mind. Seconds later grief slapped me hard and I lay still in my bed.

CHAPTER 7

'HE'S NO GOOD that boy,' declared Liliana dumping the Mayor's dictated notes on my desk.

I swiveled around. 'I've finished the filing,' I said sitting up quickly

She glanced out the window again and shook her head.

'You'd do good to steer clear of the likes of him.'

'What should I do next?' I asked.

Her eyes flicked around the room. 'Dust the bookcase and tidy your desk. I don't know how you can find anything. A little organisation wouldn't go amiss around here.'

In the six months following the death of Tatko, my friendship with Petar grew. His own experience in the labor camp drew me to him more than ever and he gained my respect. He was resilient, courageous, and had a hidden defiance of authority. Not that the Mayor noticed as Petar's outwardly eager-to-please attitude had stood him in good stead. It was astonishing to hear about his life in the camp. I concluded his youth had been the overriding factor to his survival. His revelations filled in the gaps my father was unable to.

'I can't imagine how bad it must have been,' I said. 'Tatko would never say. Every time I asked him he changed the subject or went quiet.'

'It was hell,' said Petar. 'My closest friend ended up in the same cell. We made a promise that whoever survived would send their letter to the other's family.'

'What happened to him?'

'He came to Belene five months after me. He was unrecognizable. I couldn't believe it was him. He was like an old man.'

'Where's he now?'

'Dead.'

He took a long drag on his cigarette, stopped talking and then raised his eyes as if in deep thought.

'One night in the middle of winter they dragged him away. They stripped and roped him to a stake by the river. He was dead by morning.'

He shook his head and stubbed out his cigarette then momentarily looked away. 'No one's going to control my destiny,' he said. 'I'll find a way to get out of this fucking hole. And one day I'll be the one in control.'

I looked at him, and for a moment it seemed he had forgotten I was there.

Behind the town hall stood the garage and the workshop.

Half his time was spent in there and the other half driving the Mayor.

'Why don't you have lunch with me instead of sitting in here? Get away from that old buzzard of a boss of yours,' he said one morning.

So at 12:20pm I ducked around the back of the town hall and into the garage. He lay flat on his back with his legs sticking out from beneath the car.

'You're early,' he said.

'Yes,' I replied and I crouched next to him.

He slid out on his little trolley and his hand poked out from under the car.

'Hand me that wrench, will you?'

I reached down into his toolbox and passed it over. He tightened the bolt and slid out from underneath. 'So what are we going to talk about?' he asked as he wiped the grease from his hands.

'Tell me about the camp. Did you ever think of escaping?'

'All the time, but the moment I was put in the back of a truck my hands were cuffed to an iron bar that ran the length of the cabin. The driver had his fun watching ten of us lurch forward and back all the way to Belene. The only way off the island was to survive your sentence or die.'

At home I never discussed what he told me. I figured it would do no good. Instead the injustices festered in my thoughts. A week later with a mind far from office duties, I looked over the typewriter. He stood in the doorway smiling.

'I'll swap this orange for your thoughts,' he said and he stretched out his hand.

I rolled the sheet of white paper onto the typewriter carriage. 'My thoughts are worth more than that.'

'You're right. A smart girl like you must have many thoughts.' He peeled the orange segment-by-segment placing each piece slowly in his mouth and I found it hard to concentrate.

'What do you want?' I asked.

'America. I want to go to America.'

I laughed. 'That will make a border guard happy when he gets rewarded for putting a bullet through your crazy dream.'

'Yes it's not for the faint hearted. You need to be brave,' he ignored my eye roll and continued. 'You don't believe me,' he said playfully leaning over me.

'One day I'll send you a postcard from Hollywood.'

I was the only one privy to his dreams and although it was inconceivable, there was no doubt in my mind that he intended to achieve it.

'And you? What do you dream of?'

'I've stopped dreaming.'

'That's a pity. Life without the freedom to dream is not a life? Don't you agree?'

'The only freedom I can see is a box in the earth.'

'Perhaps that can be arranged.'

I shot a look straight back and my mouth fell open.

'No, freedom, silly. I mean real freedom.'

The door swung open and Liliana entered. 'Hadn't you better attend to your work comrade? The Mayor's leaving in fifteen minutes.'

'Yes,' he replied. 'I wasn't sure what time his meeting was. Just checking.'

She turned to me. 'As for you Lidia, concentrate on your typing.'

He tossed the handful of orange peel in the waste basket and left.

I did not see him after that for several days but one afternoon I spotted him through the window. The car was parked outside the office with the bonnet propped open. He had not long returned and was busy topping up the radiator with water. I watched him. His sleeves rolled up over his strong arms, a shadow of dampness down the centre of his shirt and the V-shape of his back as he leaned over the engine. Right on four-thirty I packed up my things and said goodbye to Liliana. I walked out through the entrance doors eager to continue our conversation. Down one step, down the next and a tumble on the third. He dropped the can and rushed over.

'Are you ok?'

'Yes, I'm fine. Silly me,' I said with a flush of embarrassment to my cheeks.

'You're not the first person to take a tumble,' he said and he picked up my bag and handed it to me.

'Where've you been?' I asked.

'I had to pick up a few things in Ruse for the Mayor but when the stuff wasn't ready I hung around for a few days.' He looked at me questioningly. 'Why? Did you miss me, Miss Lidia?'

'No.'

'Then why have your cheeks changed color?'

I clutched my bag tight to my chest. 'I thought you must have run off to America.'

'I wish,' he said. 'But sadly I'm still here so you'll have to put up with me a little longer.' Then he qualified it adding, 'But not for long.'

'What do you mean by that?'

There was no one within earshot and he spread his arms out wide. 'You and me,' he said. 'We are more than this.'

'Meaning?'

'That's all.'

'No, that's not all. There's more to what you're saying.'

He tightened the radiator cap and turned to look at me. 'You're a smart girl. Too smart for this place. Before you know it twenty years down the track you'll be bored out of your wits and complaining about your husband.'

There was an element of truth to what he said but I wasn't going to let him believe that he knew the sum of my future.

'I don't think so,' I said standing tall.

He moved closer and his hand went under my chin. 'See there?' he said pointing upwards.

'What?'

'That should be your limit.'

'What?'

'The sky.'

We looked at one another and from that moment we knew our paths were intertwined. His face was close and his dark eyes mesmerizing.

'Looking at you makes me want to be the very best.' His

hand went down my cheek softly. 'If you were my girl, I'd make sure you had it all.'

I took a backward step. 'I'm not your girl so you can get that out of your head,' I said.

But deep within me small jabs of excitement pulsed and his smile made the heat inside bubble higher. He had the ability to instantly drag me out of the doldrums and rekindled remnants of my dreams.

'Are you blushing?'

'Stop it, you're embarrassing me,' I said pushing him away.

'Good, maybe you like me a little more than I thought?' He tipped his head sideways.

'It would be nice to go someplace without Liliana staring out the window.' Then he looked back at me. 'Can you keep a secret?'

'What do you mean by that?'

He placed his hand on my arm. 'Meet me by the bridge tomorrow afternoon at 5:00pm. I've got something to tell you, but keep it to yourself.'

The smell of smoke wafted between village chimney tops and drifted towards the black hill where a shot of pink sky struggled to stay lit. With work over, I briskly walked across the square. Once through the village I raced along the narrow track, my hair loosely floating behind. It was a fifteen-minute walk from the town hall to the stone bridge dividing the northern fields. There was no sign of him, but as I approached he stood.

'I can't stay long. If my mother and Raph are back before me they'll be worried.'

'That's ok... I'm pleased you came,' he said and his hand combed through his dark hair. 'I wasn't sure whether you would.' He took my hand. 'Come. Let's sit under the arch.'

I hesitated and looked about. There was not a soul to be seen.

'Relax. You're safe with me,' he said and he tugged my hand.

I followed and we moved into the shaded side. I felt nervous but excited all at the same time.

'This is better? We can talk without Lilliana's ears flapping.'

'I nearly didn't come,' I said pulling back a little.

'Why?'

'The thought crossed my mind that perhaps I wasn't the only girl you've bought down here.'

He took a backward step. 'There's not one girl in the village I'd give a second look. And I think you know it.' With that he stepped closer and took both my hands.

'I'm crazy about you. I see you every day and all I want to do is pick you up and take you someplace else.'

He took a few steps back and sat down.'Come sit,' he said patting the grass.

I tucked my dress under and joined him but maintained my distance. 'What's the secret?'I asked.

'If I tell you, you must promise to keep it to yourself.'

'I promise.'

'When I spoke about America it wasn't a joke. I'm dead serious.'

'That's impossible.'

'Most people would agree but I'm not most people. I've been planning this for years.'

'Planning what?'

'Escape.'

I pulled my chin in. He made it sound as if he was planning a holiday. Not making a life-threatening decision.

'I know it's dangerous but freedom as opposed to a mind-numbing future leaves me with no other choice. And I know it sound's impossible, but it's no hair-brained scheme. It took me a year and a half to get an opportunity to be the Mayor's driver and now I'm ready for the next part of the plan.'

I hugged my knees in and my stare was firmly fixed on him.

'Anyone who has access to an official vehicle can travel wherever they like unrestricted. My plan is to take the Mayor's car and drive as far south as possible. Dump it and continue on foot to the Turkish border.'

His words left me speechless.

'I'm serious,' he said on seeing my mouth drop open.

Suddenly he stopped talking. The sound of approaching hooves kept us silent until the cart had crossed the bridge.

'I can't believe what you're telling me,' I said.

'Well that's what I intend to do. I'm leaving before the harvest. Any later and the fields will have less coverage, which makes concealment difficult. There's also a lot more activity at that time on the roads,' he hesitiated. 'So what do you reckon?'

'Downright dangerous,' I replied, and a rising nervousness settled in my gut. I trembled as if touched by a shiver from some grave and in the distance the countryside seemed to take on a menacing hue.

'Why tell me this? How do you know I won't report you?'

He placed his hand on my shoulder. 'Because of your father. Because deep down I know you crave a better life just as much as I do.' He paused. 'Have the courage to change things. I'm offering you a chance to get out of this place. Come with me.'

I looked across the fields and in the impending night it seemed as though the whole world was tuned into our conversation. He gently turned my head back and placed both his hands on the side of my face. He kissed my cheek softly then pulled back.

'Meet me again tomorrow.'

My head was scrambled, and I ran home as fast as I could. When Mama and Raphael returned it was all I could do to maintain an expression of normality. At one point, Mama looked at me from across the table and I could have sworn somehow she knew, but nothing was said. From that night on Petar took up all my thoughts.

He was not there when I arrived at the Town Hall and it wasn't until mid-morning I saw him. He passed the window and winked at me, subsequently each time I caught a glimpse of him I lost concentration. At the end of the day he came into the office and hung the car key on the hook.

'The bridge,' he whispered and walked out.

I felt a rush of heat. All too quickly I was locked into his plan and a longing had been unleashed. Once again I followed the path to the bridge where he waited. He grabbed me straight off and whirled me around in his arms then lay me down. At that moment I wanted to bury myself in him as far as I could, to hide, to be safe, to have him take control. We did not discuss how we would run away but rather spoke of the riches and excitement that would be ours on making it to America. I felt dizzy with the dream and reality did not hit home until the following day.

I stood by the post as Raphael marched across the yard with the other end of the wire. It was Sunday morning and we were fixing our make-shift clothesline. He climbed to the first sturdy branch and pulled the wire tight then wound it several times around the branch and tucked it under the flat head of the nail.

'That should fix it,' he called.

I looked up then sat on the grass. It was not the straightest of lines but one end was good for socks and the other was good for sheets. He seemed proud of his achievement and he climbed down and walked back.

'You seem preoccupied. Is there anything the matter?'

'No,' I said but he was undeterred and he looked straight at me.

'Are you sure? It seems to me there is?'

'I don't know what you're talking about.' I answered and I got to my feet with every intention of walking away. But what he said made me stop still.

'You're lying.'

'I am not?'

'I know you didn't have to work late.'

'How do you know that?'

'Because you were spotted yesterday, not walking home but headed in the direction of the bridge.'

'Who said?'

'That's irrelevant. The point is you're lying?'

'I'm not.'

He took hold of my arm.

'Look at me. Tell me to my face.'

He knew that would bring me unstuck. It had always been the family joke that I could never tell a fib without a rapid eye blink, and that was exactly what was happening. 'I can't say.'

He gave my arm a tug. 'Who's messing with you Lidia?'

'No one.'

'Then tell me what it's about. I'm not going to let it rest. You either tell me or I'll find out myself.'

'I can't say. I've promised.'

'So that's how it is. You lie to Mama and stand by a promise to someone outside the family. You're a disappointment.'

'Leave me alone!' I yelled.

I wrenched away and took off up the side of the house. He called after me but I kept on running. Half a kilometre along the road I crumpled to the ground. My head hung between my knees and I cried. It was entirely my fault and no amount of running could escape the wretched feeling of my deceit. I sat there for thirty minutes until a farm truck passed, kicking up stony pellets. I pulled myself together and walked back not knowing what to say. Fortunately, Mama's afternoon nap meant she had no inkling of the discussion but Raphael was waiting on the front steps.

'We have to talk,' he said.

I nodded.

'All right but don't tell Mama.'

'Ok.'

The frown on his forehead turned to a look of disbelief on hearing the plan. 'Are you crazy?'

'It beats living here for the rest of my life.'

'You can't be serious. It would kill Mama.'

He stormed into the house and I screamed back. 'Who said I agreed to it anyway!'

The anger with which Petar responded took me by surprise. We met again on Monday afternoon as arranged. This time I was particularly cautious not to attract attention making my way to the bridge. He stood up in the long grass. His smile was wide and so too his arms but I did not walk towards him with the same eagerness as the previous time.

He flung his arms around me. 'I've been waiting for this moment,' he said. He took hold of my hand and led me under the arch. 'I hope you have good news.'

I shifted from one foot to the other.

'What's the matter?'

I looked at him but it was hard to find the words.

'What's the problem?'

All at once I blurted it out. 'I told Raphael.'

His eyes grew wide and he let go of me. 'You what?'

'I couldn't lie. Someone saw me walking here yesterday. They told Raph. He... he kept pestering me. He said he would find out for himself if I didn't tell him. I didn't know what to do.'

He grabbed my forearm tight. 'What did I say to you?'

'Not to tell anyone.'

'Exactly! You've jeopardised everything!'

I could not bear to look him in the eye and I pushed his arm away. He walked a short distance with his hands clasped behind his head. The silence between us was agonising until he turned and walked back.

He pinched the bridge of his nose. 'Stop crying, it's not going to improve the situation. You'll go home with puffy eyes.'

'I'm so sorry.'

'I'm sorry, too. It's been in the planning for so long. You're the only one I've ever told.' He took me in his arms and my body loosened. 'I told you because I wanted you with me,' he whispered, stroking my hair.

My shoulders heaved. 'I had to tell him. There was no choice. I don't know what to do. I can't leave them.'

'We'll think of a solution,' he said pulling me close.

I buried my face in his jacket. 'I know Raphael would never break my trust. He promised.'

He placed his hand under my chin. 'What if I say he can come? Would that change things?'

'Could my mother come too?'

'I'd like to tell you yes but it's not possible.'

In my gut I knew he was right. Any doubts I had ever held about who and what he was melted away. I understood then that this man who held me close believed and cared for me whole-heartedly.

'It's going to be Ok,' he said. 'I'll make sure of that.'

My knees buckled as he lay me down on the grass. His

mouth was wet and he smelt good. His hand ran up the front of my coat and his fingers slipped in and unbuttoned my cardigan, then my blouse. One hand cupped my breast then the other and his cheek brushed over me like fine sandpaper. A warm wet mouth sucked my nipple. I felt dizzy as if I had spun a hundred times, and I surrendered. At that moment I was his. He would lead me and I would follow. With one hand on my back and the other between my legs he held himself up on one elbow and looked straight at me.

'You're my girl,' he said and at that moment the wickedness of the world fell away.

I kissed him back. A rhythmical sensation rippled through me and nothing could turn the moment around. He fumbled to unbutton his trousers. I never saw him fully but I felt him ram into me. A short pain and it was over. It was brief but explosive. He lay back and I curled beside him. We were at one.

'I want you to be with me,' he said.

'Things are moving so fast. I need time.'

'Don't leave it too long.'

My head rested on his chest and his arm lay across my body. There we stayed. Dusk settled in and black birds floated high above. Time went quickly and it was later than I anticipated. I knew by now both Mama and Raphael would be home.

'We better get a move on,' he said and he stood up and tucked his shirt into his trousers.

'Bring Raphael here tomorrow night and I'll talk with him.'

My fingers picked and combed the grass from my hair and I hurriedly brushed myself down.

CHAPTER 8

'WHERE'VE YOU BEEN?' said Mama the second I opened
the door. Raphael's steely stare was fixed on me as I shamefully
conjured an excuse. I turned away and removed my coat.

'I had to work back,' I said.

She sat at the table with her hands on her hips and a tilt to her
head. 'I've been out of my wits with worry.'

'You've got to stop worrying. Everything's fine,' I said as I hung
my coat up.

I joined them at the table but my lie did not rest well on my
tongue. She stopped questioning but as I flicked my eyes over to
Raphael his glare drilled into me. We ate quietly and on finishing
she pushed her chair back and cleared her plate. She untied
her apron and pulled the pins from her hair. A lock of grey fell
forward as she bent down to kiss me goodnight. Raphael said
nothing until she had left the room.

'She knows you're lying. You can't keep up this charade.'

'I'm not going to.'

'Good. What did he say when you told him you're not in on his stupid scheme?'

'He wants to talk with you.'

'Tell him I'm not interested,' he said with his voice low. 'Tell him to stay out of our family.'

'Raph, please.'

'No, that's the end of it.'

'It's not. You could at least hear him out.'

'And what's that? That his hair-brained plan involves my sister. That he has a total disregard for her life and her family.'

'Stop it. That's not true.'

He rolled his eyes and shook his head. 'I can't believe you're sucked in by him.'

'I'm not. You automatically assume I agreed to it.'

'The fact that you didn't say no tells me otherwise. For God sake come to your senses.'

'I promise I will. But please come with me tomorrow night to talk to him. Just hear him out.'

'On one condition,' he said.

'What's that?'

'You tell Mama..

'No.'

I looked past him and she stood at the door. Her face was pale and she looked at me questionably. 'What do I need to know?'she asked.

'It's nothing,' I said.

She sat at the narrow end of the table.

'It doesn't sound like nothing to me.'

Raphael glared at me and I stared back willing him not to speak.

'She's got something to tell you.'

'What?'

'It's nothing,' I stammered. 'I just said that Petar jokingly told me he was going to escape to America. Now Raph accuses me of wanting to do the same.'

'And do you?'

'Of course not.'

'Look at me,' she said.

All my thoughts of running away left me. The shame I felt was almost unbearable. My words were muddled and stuck on my tongue as her eyes were fixed on me.

'Don't worry,' said Raphael. 'I'm going with her tomorrow to talk to Petar. Lidia has no intention of running away and__'

She raised her hand stopping him mid-sentence and she looked across at me.

'You have your father's headstrong ways and it worries me. I fear I'll lose you and that terrifies me. But running away of your own free will is preferable to having you ripped away by someone else's. This is not the life we imagined, nor the future. There's no certainty anymore. Your father's wish was for you both to be happy. He wanted you to have the freedom to make choices.'

'I won't leave,' I blurted.

'Just listen,' she said.

She looked first to me, then Raphael, pausing as if questioning her right to protest. But she never did. She looked to the darkness framed by the window and the kitchen light cast a harsh shadow beneath her eyes. The thought of leaving her made my heart sink to the floor. Gone were the days when she chattered for no reason other than to fill up the space. Little did we know that since the death of Tatko she had developed an inner resolve, an inner strength. Larger matters had overtaken the smaller ones.

'Whatever decisions you make in life I won't stand in your way. The thing I ask is that you carefully consider what it is you want. If that means you go further afield, don't tell me when that day comes.We'll speak no more of this.'

She took a deep breath stood up and kissed us. 'Goodnight.'

Petar held out his hand and Raphael gave it a hard shake.

'So what do you think of my plan?'

'It sounds ludicrous,' said Raphael and he shoved his hands back in his pockets.

Petar raised his chin a little higher and smiled. His eyes flicked over him before he replied. 'For a man who knows nothing you seem pretty sure of yourself.'

'Fair enough. Enlighten me.'

'All right then,' he said eyeing Raphael up and down. 'This must be kept a very close secret. There'll be dire consequences if it gets out, and the same goes for any others you may tell… Understood?'

We nodded.

'I aim to leave the night before May Day. The holiday gives

me a day's grace and a few months to prepare physically because part of the journey will be made on foot.'

'Have you a vehicle?' asked Raphael, pulling on his ear.

'I do.'

'Whose?'

'The Mayor's.'

'Are you kidding?'

'No, that's one thing I don't do.'

Raphael swallowed hard and Petar continued.

'Unfortunately for the Mayor, the car is going to have some major mechanical issue the day before May Day. I'm taking it that night. I figure it will take a day before they realise something's up but by then I'll have passed through Haskovo and into the southern zone.'

Raphael closed his eyes, raised his eyebrows and pinched the bridge of his nose. His hand dropped to his side and he shook his head.

'You're crazy. The countryside will be crawling with police.'

'True, but I'll travel at night and once I dump the car I'll hide out during the day.'

'Every dog's going to be on your scent. You're nuts!'

Petar leaned towards him and Raphael took a backward step.

'Don't mock me. If it wasn't for your sister I wouldn't be telling you. But now I have, you're equally implicated. So my advice to you is to listen and keep your mouth shut.'

The sudden realisation that we were equally implicated was enough to keep us hanging on his every word.

He reached into his coat pocket and pulled out a map. 'I've

plotted a route.'

'Where did you get the map?' I asked.

He smiled. 'Ask no questions. I'll tell you no lies.'

We huddled together under the bridge in the dusk. There was sufficient detail of the Haskovo region but the squiggly red lines indicating the smaller hiking tracks were barely visible.

'See here? We follow the river south, re-connect with the main road but steer clear of Dobroselets. From there we go south east to the Sakar, dump the car and rest up during the day.'

'Where?' I asked.

'On the southern side of Sakar Mountain. There's plenty of spots to hide. From there on it's only twenty kilometres or so to the border.'

'That's a lot of ground to cover in a short time,' said Raphael.

'Yes, but we've three months to get fit.'

'And the river? How do we get across that?' I asked.

'My grandfather lives fifteen kilometres south of Radovets. I haven't been there for six years but nothing changes. He keeps a small dinghy upstream. I know the area like the back of my hand. I used to spend time catching eels there.'

He took another drag on his cigarette and continued. 'A fence runs along the border. It's anchored across the tributary to stop anyone from crossing. My fishing lines use to get caught in it. That's how I discovered the weak point. Two of the fence anchors have worn. I reckon with enough force we could prise it up and slip the boat through.'

He stopped talking and watched Raphael carefully. 'Remember, anyone who knows of this plan is now implicated.'

He folded the map and stuffed it into his back pocket. 'That's it. Are you in?'

We started training with a run up the hill to the church and a scramble back down. By the second month our time had halved. Raphael and I tried to out-run Petar but he was always fifty metres in front. He had an athlete's natural ability. His agility and quick reflexes gave him the edge. Then one day he disappeared from view. A large stand of mature trees stood on the slope at the bottom of the hill. The pine needles on the ground muffled the sound of footsteps. We slowed down having missed sight of him.

'Where do you think he went?'

'I don't know,' said Raph. 'Maybe he's gone for a piss.'

Raphael walked to the creek which feed into a larger pool. It was a place where locals came to soak their arthritic joints in the spring water. He bent down and splashed his face. I followed suit, scooping up handfuls of water and gulping it down. When I looked up, suddenly Petar was there. He had his hand on the back of Raph's head forcing him under the water. Raphael struggled but was unable to pull away. Shocked, I jumped on Petar's back.

'Get off him!' I screamed and thumped him on the side of his head.

He let go and red faced Raphael fell backwards coughing.

'What the fuck did you do that for!' Raphael screamed. 'Are you crazy or what?'

'Just testing,' Petar replied cooly.

'You idiot!'

I was horrified that without provocation he had attacked Raphael. 'You could have killed him!' I yelled slapping him hard on his shoulder.

'I don't think so,' he said with a dismissive wave. 'It was for your own good. Just teaching you both a lesson. Don't ever take your surroundings for granted. I hope you learnt it. This is not a game. You're going need your wits for what we're about to do.'

From then on that's what we did, and although it seemed a hard lesson, it was something that stayed in our minds.

CHAPTER 9

LIGHTS WENT OUT. We descended the front steps and as our feet crossed the yard crickets fell silent. Spring had arrived and red and white dolls dangled from tree branches throughout the village. Folk-law said that if the owner of a Martenitsa doll saw a nesting stork they would be blessed with luck and good fortune. I made sure mine hung high. Under the old pine I scrambled onto Raphael's shoulders and found a sturdy branch. When I climbed down I looked up and the doll swung ominously in the darkness. Behind, all was still in the house. We had not told Mama of our intention to leave that night but I had the feeling she watched from the window.

We arrived at the town hall puffing. I could just make out Petar's silhouette with his foot propped against the stone wall. We followed him to the rear of the garage.

'Mind where you walk,' he whispered.

With a twist the padlock snapped open and we stepped through the side entrance. He took hold of my arm. 'Did you bring a dress?'

'Yes.'

'Good. Get changed. When we get going you'll sit up front with me.'

He turned to Raphael. 'You'll have to ride it out in the boot. If we get pulled over, having you in the car will only complicate things. Lidia's different. As far as they're concerned I will tell them she's had too much to drink and I'm taking her back from an official's party.' He looked to me. 'And on the off chance we do get stopped let me do the talking.'

He opened the driver's door. 'Let's get this thing out,' he said and he tapped the side of the car.

Raphael stood his ground. 'You never said I'd be travelling half way across the country in the boot. I could suffocate.'

'Don't worry, there's plenty of air in there. Anyway what were you expecting, a first class ticket to freedom?'

I slipped the dress on and stuffed my trousers and shirt in my rucksack.

'I'll steer, you push on the bumper,' said Petar.

The car coasted out and once clear he yanked on the hand break. I sat in the passenger seat as he lowered the roller door and locked up. Raphael hunched his shoulders and climbed in the boot. The tail gate came down with a thud and Petar jumped into the driver's side.

'What's the matter?' he said.

'Nothing,' I replied.

He touched my cheek. 'One day this night will be in our memory.' He nodded towards the back of the car. 'Does he know?'

'What?'

'About us.'

'No, why?'

'I just wondered, that's all,' he said and he shunted the gear stick into first.

'I don't think he needs to know right now,' I replied.

'Yeah brothers can be a pain in the arse when it comes to looking out for their sisters.'

'What do you mean by that?'

'Nothing. Only joking.'

'Not funny,' I said.

I slipped down below the windows and we drove away from the village in silence. When we were clear I sat up and stared out the window with his comment about Raphael irking me.

'Anything the matter?' he asked, glancing over.

'What are we going to do when we get to the West?'

'How would I know?'

'You plan everything,' I said. 'I thought you would've planned that too.'

He smirked and wound the window down as if hoping to cool the overheated atmosphere. 'You're still angry with me, aren't you?'

I could not look at him. We had already started out on a shaky path and things were not boding well. I was crazy in love with him but sometimes he could be infuriating. So often he left me wondering what he was thinking, crying out for an explaination. I trusted him with everything. I knew in time we would figure things out in our relationship but the time had been short and we still had a long way to understand one another.

'What if they send us back?' I snapped.

'That's not going to happen.'

'How do you know?'

'We'll be important. Once they find out we're legit they'll treat us like heroes. They love it when people defect.'

One black field followed another. We drove along the narrow two-lane road, turning onto the main highway south. With every approaching headlight my eyes were left stuck and staring. By the time we reached the Haskovo checkpoint, Porgovo was a good hundred and fifty kilometres behind. There was little movement on the road, and as the distance stretched away my nerves calmed.

We followed the bend till suddenly in the blackness a bright light waved up a head.

'Shit,' he said.

He reached across and hit the button on the glove box. Inside a half bottle of vodka was jammed up against a small hard leather case.

'Take a swig.'

I grabbed it and unscrewed the top. One gulp sent a burning shot down my throat. I screwed the lid on and shoved it back. We pulled in next to the checkpoint. With not a flinch of nerves, he wound down the driver's side window.

'Evening comrade,' he said.

The policeman bent down and leaned in. 'Which way are

you headed?'

'Elhovo.'

'There's been an accident up ahead,' he said. 'You'll have to take the route via Polski Gradets.'

His fleshy face leaned closer scrutinising me. Then he looked to the back seat and back again to me. 'She's a looker,' he said with an approving wink.

'Yes,' said Petar. 'It's amazing what a little vodka can do to a woman's complexion.'

'Good party?'

'Yes, she'll suffer tomorrow,' said Petar.

The policeman slapped the side of the car. 'Ok, get going.'

We moved off the highway and a surge of cool air whistled through the driver's window. I leant forward and opened the glove box and Petar glanced across.

'What are you doing?'

'What's in the case?' I asked.

'I didn't want you to see that,' he said sighing. 'But seeing you asked, it's a pistol.'

'What for?'

'Protection. You don't think we're going to escape without a backup? I didn't tell you because I thought it would scare you.'

'You're right, it does.'

He smiled and winked at me. 'I've never fired one in my life but I'll sure as hell use it if push comes to shove.'

'Where did you get it?'

'It's the Mayor's. That little Malokov was his pride and joy. He always kept it in the glove box. He loved to mouth off that it was the best gun in the Soviet Union and home-grown design. Don't worry, we'll be fine,' he said. 'Now where's that smile of yours?'

A smile was far from my lips and I closed the glove box. Not long after his eyes shifted to the petrol gauge and he slapped the steering wheel hard.

'What's the matter?'

'We're running out of fuel.'

'Can we get some at Polski Gradets?'

'Not likely. Nothing open and too risky.'

'How far before it cuts out?'

'Pretty soon. You better get changed.'

I wriggled back into my trousers and shirt. The last dribble of petrol passed through the carburetor and we came to an abrupt stop. The moment the boot opened Raphael sprung out.

'Thank God, I need to pee,' he said and he took off towards the bushes. Minutes later he returned more relaxed. 'I could think of better places to take a nap,' he said hitting the boot. 'My hip and shoulder have been pummeled in the back of this thing.'

'Well you don't have to worry about that now,' replied Petar.

'Great, does that mean I can sit in the back like a normal person?' said Raphael, stretching left to right.

'No,' said Petar. 'That means we've run out of petrol.'hael immediately straightened and his hands went behind his head. 'What are we going to do?'

'Leg it,' said Petar and he pulled a compass from his shirt pocket.

'Hadn't we better push this off the road?'

'No, we're ditching it here.'

'Why?'

'It doesn't matter.'

'Yes it does. They'll know we're not far,' said Raphael.

Petar swung round. 'I'm trying to think of a fucking solution so shut up. They'll know it anyway. They'll soon find out we diverted at the checkpoint.'

He climbed into the back seat and spread the map across his knees. We stood nervously at the rear and waited.

Minutes later he emerged. 'Come on. From now on we'll need to keep off the road as much as possible. Smear this on,' he said bending down and grabbing a fist full of damp earth.

We plastered the mossy mix into our cheeks like cream. We ran from the road across fields, over fences and down steep inclines towards creeks where logs and tangled vines straddled the path. The time gained in the initial leg was quickly whittled away. Endless kilometres followed with short stops for direction.

Petar squatted down. 'Here take this,' he said and handed the torch to Raphael.

'Where are we?'

'Not sure.' He unfolded the map and stretched it out. 'Shine the light here.' he said tapping his finger towards the lower section. 'That's better.'

He studied it carefully and his finger slipped over. 'It looks like we're here. Now listen up, we won't be able to talk until we are well out of earshot... Understand?

He looked up at us and we nodded willingly and he continued. 'We'll scout east avoiding Dobroselets, then head for the mountains this way,' he said.

'How long will that take?' I asked.

'Probably three hours but we're going to have to keep up the pace.'

The night-life scattered up ahead as we ran through a karst landscape which rose up blacker than the night sky. By four in the morning we reached the base of Sakar Mountain. The adrenalin that had propelled us thirty-five kilometres was all but gone, and the rain on the limestone track made it difficult to find a footing. I could feel the broken blisters ooze into my socks with every step. Limestone boulders sat on the mountain slope like the dismantled limbs of a giant, and we wound our way in cheerless silence_ my head foggy and my gut queasy. A hundred metres further up a fist-sized rock moved. My left foot crumpled beneath me and gravel ripped across my palms. Raphael lunged forward but my hand slipped away.

'Lidia!' he yelled.

Petar swung around. 'Keep your voice down.'

'She's hurt,' snapped Raphael.

'Telling it to the world is not going to help,' replied Petar. He dropped his back pack and climbed down. By the time they reached me I was staggering to my feet.

'Sit down for a moment,' said Petar. 'It's not far now.'

'I'll be Ok,' I said but I knew full well it was not exhaustion making me gag.

It had been six weeks and the light spotting of the previous month held a shocking truth. I was pregnant.

At a careful pace we arrived at the opening to a cave no wider than a double door. It was an eerie resting place concealed in the hillside, quite dark and chilly. Slow drips echoed around the limestone walls like the sound from a torturer's tool, and a faint howling wind channeled through the underground network. Far off a sound like water under pressure was rising from the lower slopes, and shortly after a colony of squealing bats surged into the cave. We covered our heads but their waste glued to our hair and sleeves. Armies of gnats and ground beetles scattered across the floor feasting on the shower.

When they settled we lay back exhausted. I thought about Mama waking to an empty house. I thought about the grip in my belly. And I thought about how my condition would fit into Petar's plan. I passed my sleeve across my nose and looked up at Raphael. He seemed to sense my anxiety but little did he know how much my life was set to change in the months ahead.

'Come outside,' he said. 'The rain will wash this stuff off.'

Petar squatted at the entrance smoking and looking out across the valley. I sat down next to him and he put his arm around me.

'Looks like this weather has set in,' he said. 'How are you feeling?'

'Better.'

'One good thing about this, they won't be able to trace our path too easily,' he said.

'I wonder what will happen to us if we make it?' said Raphael.

Petar glanced across. 'There's no "if's" about it. We'll make it.'

'And then?'

'Freedom,' he replied, and white smoke floated from his

sighing lips.

Raphael sat tracing his finger in never ending circles in the dirt. 'Then what do we do?' he said. 'Don't speak the language. Don't have money. Don't know anyone. We could be in deeper shit than we are now.'

'You're good at throwing up questions and dishing out the negative,' replied Petar. 'But so far you haven't come up with a solution. It's all very well whining about stuff. Why don't you back off with the negativity and give me a break.'

He took a long drag on his cigarette then stubbed it hard against the entrance wall. 'If it makes you feel better I've thought about it. I wouldn't be surprised if they roll out the capitalist red carpet and give us jobs,' he said.

Raphael walked back into the cave and lay down. As for me I had nothing to say. Months down the track my ability to work would be severely hampered, and what difference did it make if I ended up pulling weeds on one side of the border as opposed to the other.

By mid-morning the drizzle turned torrential and rivers were fast flowing down the goat tracks to the plain below.

It was pitch black when Petar nudged my foot. I looked up and he handed me the bottle of water. 'How are you feeling?'

'Not good, I must have sprained my ankle.'

'We have to go. It'll be all right once you get moving,' he said and he helped me to my feet.

I hobbled towards the entrance as a funnel of bats flew out. Under an eerie moon Petar led the way. Raphael struggled to help me but once on the plain a strong determination to keep up caused the pain to ease. Every now and then trucks laden with wheat roared through the night on their way to the mill, causing us to dive into the muddy roadside strip. The rain was making it almost impossible to see, and our shoes bogged.

Suddenly, a bark followed by a deep growl stopped us in our tracks. Petar turned slowly. The whites of his eyes were wide. He gestured for us to back off, but a man called out and the barking stopped. We were one kilometre from the border with two hours left to cross the river in darkness. A watchtower stood in the distance with a Kalaznikov cocked to send out a sling of bullets.

'Listen up,' said Petar. 'It's about a hundred metres to the trees. Not far but we can't run it. We're going to crawl. I'll go first. When I'm across you follow, then Raphael. Don't hurry. Nice and slow. Understand? Go straight, otherwise we could lose sight of one another.'

He looked at me. 'Give me your bag.'

We watched him slip out of the shadows and dip down low on his hands and knees. Slowly he made his way across the open grasslands like a stray goat. Soon he was out of sight.

I hugged Raphael. 'We're going to make it.'

'Sure we will,' he said.

I looked about suddenly terrified. It took ten minutes to cross but it felt like eternity. My knees slid one behind the other and my hands squelched into the wet ground. When I reached the woods Petar was squatting down waiting.

'Good girl,' he said.

I sat on a carpet of pine needles and strained my eyes to see

Raphael. No sooner had he made it, when metres away we heard the sound of breaking branches. A shadow moved closer through the woods. We dived head first into the undergrowth and my heart slammed against my stiff ribs. Petar poked his head up and fell back into the bushes. For a split second I believed he had been hit by ten millimetres of cold lead.

'Holy shit. It's a deer,' he said and he slapped his sides.

We did not laugh but rose out of the bush ghostly white. It was hard to comprehend how he had the ability to see the funny side but because of it our fears eased.

'I thought we were done for,' said Raphael.

'No not yet,' replied Petar.

'How much further?' I asked.

He scratched the back of his head. 'I reckon a kilometre and we'll be at the river. But we can't stuff around.' He brushed himself down and spat into the bushes. 'Let's go and keep up.'

I placed my weight on my foot and winced. The bone of my ankle was covered by a cushion of throbbing fluid and the thought of one more kilometre seemed as daunting as one hundred. 'I can't.'

Petar took hold of my elbow and gave it a forceful tug. 'You have to.'

'Back off,' said Raphael.

He stepped between us and shunted Petar with an open hand to the shoulder. Petar swung round and returned the gesture but with more force. Raphael toppled backwards and we both ended up hitting the ground. He stood over us with his thumbs tucked into his belt.

'Keep your hands off me. If you two can't pick yourselves up you're done for. And don't think I've come all this way to stop now.'

'Neither did I,' I spat back. 'Look at my ankle. I'm just saying I can't go any faster.'

'Christ!' he said. 'Keep your voice down.'

'Then don't bully me.'

He ran his hand through his hair and held out his hand to pull me up. 'I'm sorry. Let's forget what happened. We're tired. Apologies all round.'

Raphael stepped up and unhooked his arms from his rucksack . 'I'll take her. You take this,' he said and he handed Petar his bag.

I slung my arms around Raph's neck and we moved off through the woods. The downpour had stopped but the flood waters of the Tundzha could be heard rushing past a hundred metres up ahead.

After a time I slid off his back, placed my heel gingerly to the ground. Pain shot up my leg but together we hobbled hip to hip and arm in arm. We followed close behind until confronted by a four-metre-high fence woven into the landscape with skin ripping barbs. I stared up at its impossible height but we kept on.

Away from the river, was a small tributary and a short distance on an old dinghy was partially concealed under the lip of the bank. On seeing it I threw my arms around Petar's neck and planted three rapid kisses on his cheek. It took Raphael by surprise but my show of gratitude saw him hand out a friendly slap to Petar's back.

'See,' said Petar. 'Have faith.'

We heaved the two-and-a-half-metre hull along the mossy edges and away from its muddy resting place. We were three black silhouettes, slipping and sliding in the early-morning dark. There were no more questions, only the dragging sound of the small craft heaved forward by a collective will power.

The fence spanned the creek and attached to its base hung a heavy mesh chain anchoring it to the creek bed. The boat sat lopsided on the bank with Raphael and me at the stern. Petar let go and walked to the left of the bough. He bent down and removed his boots and socks then tossed them into the boat. He entered the creek parting the reeds with his hands and groping for the submerged chain.

'I've got the edge of it, Raph. Help me pull it back. Lidia, keep a hold.'

Raphael flung his boots into the hull and plunged in, grabbing Petar's waist. With the added weight and forceful side- to- side rocking it lifted from its base. It slowly peeled back but a sudden release sent them tumbling in. They stood, gasping for breath and dripping in greenery like creatures from the underworld. Raphael took hold of the mesh again and Petar clambered across and took the stern.

'Ok push,' he said.

He slid under the fence, pulling on the rope shackled to the front of the dingy. I pushed with every reserve of strength left. With blood rushing to our temples and teeth gritted the dinghy slipped into the gap. But the increasing width of the timber beam soon wedged it between the bank and the steel. On cue the sound of a water bird ruffled and warbled. Petar let go and scooted through the gap. He dived under the water but no amount of rocking and twisting could release the adjoining anchor.

'If Lidia comes over on my side and rocks it some more the bolt will free up,' said Raphael.

'No, it's not going to budge. She can help me tip the boat to one side. You keep your weight back on the chain.'

'But_'

'No. Just do it.'

I thought the small veins behind my eyes were about to burst and my breath held stiff in my chest. We pushed as hard as we could and a sudden release saw the bow slip through. We dragged it a few extra metres until the little vessel was set to launch into the ten-knot current.

'Get in,' said Petar.

I climbed in and sat on the seat plank at the stern. The boat dipped down under my weight but Raphael held it firm and the water sloshed around his feet. Suddenly Petar raised his finger to his lips and terror froze us to the spot.

'Stay,' he said. 'Don't move.'

He crab crawled his way up the bank, turned and nodded indicating we were not alone. I heard nothing. The only movement had been an oversized water rat zig-zagging its way across the creek. Its long bristly nose poked between the debris and it sniffed the air for rotting morsels caught in the vegetation.

Our ears and eyes strained to pick up any sight or sound of imminent danger. Everything was frozen in a petrifying numbness. One moment Raphael stood beside the boat and next a bullet peeled back the soft tissue of his cheek and burst the globe of his right eye. His heels remained stuck in the mud but his body reeled backwards spread eagled. I rose up roaring with the pieces of my brother splattered and glued to my cheeks. The boat tipped and I hit the water screaming as if taken over by an unknown force.

Down under, twisting and turning with lungs about to rip from my chest, then a greedy grab for air. Under again… then swimming… then under… Pummeled and heaved in the angry flood dividing our two opposing nations and carried within the deluge of last summer's waste. A hollowed out log with half a straw nest stuffed in one end slammed against my rib cage, knocking the remnants of my breath from me. Instinctively my arms clamped around it and I was sucked into a whirlpool and carried diagonally downstream a hundred metres, until the straw tip of the log hit the first boulder, pivoted, smacked into the next and sandwiched the remainder between rocks.

I landed in the mud, rejected by death and rewarded with bitter freedom. My fighting spirit lay on the other side of the river and the world turned black.

CHAPTER 10

What The Solider Saw

MY NAME IS Gabir Yilmaz. I remember that time. I remember her sitting in the mud. She was the saddest soul I had ever seen.

We heard the crack of a gun as we came over the rise. It reverberated throughout the valley and it was hard to determine in which direction it had come. My friend Josef shot a look at me then slammed on the brakes.

'Where the hell did that come from?' he said.

'Not sure, but swing it around. I think it was in that direction.'

He shunted the gear stick into reverse then back into first. The wheels spun furiously, and at a speed more suitable for a sealed highway we took off in the opposite direction. Our shoulders jostled against the seat as we drove through ditches filled with ankle deep water. The river was eating up embankments and carving out new ones as it raced along the border. The season would be remembered as one of the wettest on record.

'Ok this'll do,' I said.

'Don't you think it was a bit further?' said Josef, waving his arm back through the open window.

'Maybe, but we'll try our luck here.'

We stopped twenty metres from the river. The searchlight above the cabin washed the area in a fierce white light. I pressed the lip of the binoculars to my eyes but saw nothing, only long shadows stretching out from silver tree branches. We set out to comb the area in heavy mid-calf boots and guns slung across our chest.

'I don't think it came from our side,' said Josef.

'Me neither.'

'Poor bastard. If he's fallen in there he'll sure as hell be on a fast ride to Greece,' he said.

For twenty minutes we searched, but with no luck. It was zero-five-twenty and the sun was set to rise in thirty minutes.

'Let's go have breakfast then resume the search,' I said.

The army post was a mud brick hut formally used as a shepherd's shelter. We came to a rolling stop at the front entrance. I unstrapped my helmet and walked in. Josef followed close on my heels, dipping his head at the entrance. We had been on patrol since the evening changeover and most of the night was taken up discussing the upcoming wrestle match. The next day we had free and we were keen to put in some solid training. Josef towered over me and although I was of medium height, pound-for-pound I liked to think I was equally strong. We had been friends since my family settled in Edrine and despite my higher military rank it made no difference to our relationship.

'Maybe the seven-thirty shift will have more luck,' he said and he reached for the long handled pot and filled it with water.

I loosened my boots. 'Possibly, but if we do find someone it's more likely to be a body.'

On a normal night there was little to report so a gunshot across the river was cause for speculation. Goat's cheese and flat bread occupied the gaps between our talk until daylight crossed the threshold. We rinsed our tin cups and re-kitted, eager to resume the search before returning to barracks for a well-earned sleep. I pulled the rusty-hinged door shut behind.

'Which way?' asked Josef, turning the key in the ignition.

'I think we should head three hundred metres downstream then double back on foot.'

The fog hung low over the river but was rapidly disappearing as morning moved down the valley in small patches of blue.

'This'll do,' I said. 'Stop here.'

We parked under a Turkish oak where cicadas rubbed new wings together like the short strokes on a violin string. Despite the tiredness that accompanied the end of night patrol we sprang out. Not long after I heard her. We both stopped still.

'Hear that?'

'Yeah, it came from over there,' said Josef pointing and

straining his neck forward.

The sound was different to the cries of nature coming from the countryside. I walked to the scrub at the edge of the bank and there covered in the mud below sat a wretched soul. She hugged her slimy knees and rhythmically rocked back and forth as if to a desolate tune. I tore back the branches and leaped down the metre drop. Josef followed. She appeared not to notice. When we reached her I squatted down. Her fingers tore at her cheeks, her face and her hair. I pulled her flaying arms down and wrapped mine around her.

'Are you ok?' I said. But looking at her it was hard to imagine that was the case.

Suddenly she was silent. She stared beyond and across the river as if seeing some unimaginable horror. Long muddy hair strands crossed her cheeks like black tentacles and I scanned her for any injury.

'Is she shot?'

'Doesn't look like it,' I said. 'Pass me the water bottle.'

'Sure.'

He fumbled to release it from the slot in his webbed belt and handed it over.

'Here, drink this.'

The water dribbled to one side of her mouth but I tilted her head and instinctively she swallowed.

'She's a mess,' said Josef.

I nodded. 'I don't think she'll be able to walk back. Best you go get the jeep and I'll sit with her.'

He scaled the bank and took off along the track. Her satchel

was strapped to her back and her boney knee poked through the
rip in her trousers. I stood and walked over to her brown shoe
caught in the debris. I rinsed it off at the water's edge then walked
back and eased it onto her left foot. She had the appearance of
a battered doll with vacant eyes, as if her soul had up and left. I
slid her arms out of the straps and looked inside the bag. At the
bottom and beneath a soaking red dress I found a tin cigarette
case. In it was a letter and a ring. I read it and looked down
at her. It seemed to me it was the only thing left in her world
and knowing it would be confiscated I slipped the case and its
contents into my pocket and buckled up her bag. And on that
steamy morning I sat with her, under the ledge of the riverbank
as tears ran in an endless trickle down her filthy cheeks. The jeep
careered towards the river and Josef lumbered towards us. I stood
and slung her satchel over my shoulder.

'You take one side, I'll take the other.'

'She needs a feed that's for sure. She'd be lucky to weigh fifty
kilos,' said Josef.

We hooked our arms under her armpits and carried her to
the jeep.

'What do you think they'll do with her?'

'Write a report,' I said. 'And transfer her to Istanbul I guess.'

He opened the rear door and pushed our gear onto the floor.
I propped her against my hip and gently laid her down on the
back seat then tucked her legs up. Her face was buried deep in the
gap where the worn leather seat met the back support. I climbed
into the front and looked back.

'Beats me how she survived,' said Josef with one hand on the wheel and an elbow out the window. 'Even to get through the border fence. Makes me wonder if she had help? Do you think there are others?'

'Could be.'

I struggled to get her upright then carried her into the hut. On siting her down a closer check revealed there was no bullet wound but her trousers held a deep stain.

'She's bleeding,' I said.

'I noticed. Do you think it's woman's stuff?'

'Maybe. I guess they'll check her out when we get her back to camp. I'll clean her up. You make tea.'

I grabbed the towel off the hook next to the sink and poured a litre of water into the aluminum pot. She was slumped over with her elbows on her knees. The back of her long pale neck was curtained by muddy hair. I brushed a lock aside and with the wet towel wiped her face. Another rinse flushed the grime from her nose, her mouth and her eyes. Again and again, like tarnish from silver I wiped. Two pools of black despair looked back at me and as I knelt before her laced shoes on her blistered feet something unforeseen touched my heart. I decided then not to disclose the cigarette tin and its contents. I would find a way to give it back to her.

With military precision the replacement patrol arrived. We lifted her into the rear cabin and she sat limp between us. It was hot yet she trembled. There was a distinct smell of male sweat and the dank humidity made me open the canvas flap and secure it to the metal frame.

We rolled through the countryside towards Kirlareli military base, sixty kilometres east of Edirne. An hour later the truck drove through the archway of the main compound where the flag hung limp overhead. We coasted around the parade ground and passed the rows of single-story barracks until grinding to a halt outside the administration block. Joseph jumped down and we carried her up the stone steps and into the office. The desk clerk looked up. He was seated with the blunt end of his pencil busy digging out a fortnight's supply of buttery wax from his ears.

'Where did you drag her up from?'

'The river.'

'God, you're a filthy bastard, Moustaf,' said Josef. 'Can't you pick your ears someplace else?'

'You can talk,' scoffed the clerk pointing one finger. 'Where did you get your girlfriend? From the septic tank?'

'I need to fill out a report and put a call through to security. Tell them we have a defector,' I said.

He slid a clipboard with a pad of blue forms across the desk in my direction and picked up the phone.

'Private Malas speaking, I have a female detainee awaiting processing. Corporal Yilmaz has bought her in, sir. Yes, sir.'

He put down the phone and minutes later an officer entered. The folds of his shirt sleeves were pressed razor sharp and a woman accompanied him.

'At ease,' he said and he looked from me to the girl.

'So where did you find her, Corporal?'

'On the banks of the Tundzha, Sir.'

'Do you think she was alone?'

'It does appear that way, though she's having difficulty

walking. She could have been left behind.'

The woman walked out and returned with a walking stick. She tapped the girl's shoulder and helped her to stand.

'Come,' she said, and walked her through the doors leading to the infirmary.

'We heard one gunshot an hour before we found her. We believe it was discharged on the other side of the river.'

'I see,' said the officer. 'Is this her bag?'

'Yes sir. I went through it but there was only a water bottle and a dress.'

'Very well, Corporal. That's all. You're dismissed.'

The following morning Josef and I were busy packing our duffle bags for our weekend release. A lift back to Edirne had been arranged for nine o'clock and we were eager to get going.

'I reckon Yusuf will win the competition again,' I said.

'Yes, getting a leg over him would be like trying to jump Mt Ararat. That bastard's huge,' said Josef struggling to fix the jammed zipper on his bag.

Suddenly the dormitory door opened. We looked up half expecting our lift had arrived early but instead a young p rivate entered.

'Corporal Yilmaz.'

'Yes.'

'Your weekend's leave has been postponed. The captain needs

you. Report to D block in ten minutes.'

He turned about, leaving me open mouthed.

'Damn. Couldn't he have waited till Monday?' I said throwing my bag back on the bed with a thump.

'You unlucky bastard,' said Josef shaking his head. 'Bad timing. I wonder what it's about?'

'God knows. But he could have picked a better weekend'.

Josef gathered up his bag and walked to the door. He left me pulling on my khaki's and buckling up my belt. I folded my civilian clothes and placed them back in my locker then strode across the parade ground and up the steps to D block. The thick rubber of my polished boots squeaked along the linoleum. I tapped on the captain's office door and entered.

'Sir,' I said, raising my right hand to my forehead.

'At ease, Corporal,' he said.

I stood with my hands at my sides.

'The girl you bought in yesterday doesn't speak Turkish. I want you to interpret. She's in a shaky state of mind and I thought seeing you found her and you speak Bulgarian, you may be of benefit to the investigation.'

'Yes, sir.'

'All right, come with me,' he said and he grabbed his pen and pad.

I followed him to the small ward in the infirmary. We walked in and he crossed to the window and jerked the ring of the blind. Instantly it shot upwards with a sucking sound and coiled around itself, concealed behind the pelmet until evening. A shard of orange sunlight streamed through the blue smoke that wheezed out through his jowly jaws.

'Good morning,' he bellowed.

She rolled to the edge of the bed and dangled her thin legs to the floor. Her cheeks were red raw. It was unsettling and I wondered if it were her nails that had gouged her pale skin. He took five heavy steps across the floor and stared at her intensely then looked at me.

'Pull up a chair, Corporal.'

I lifted the chair tucked under the bed opposite and carried it back.

'Ok, ask her name, her nationality and why she's in Turkey.'

I shifted in my seat and leaned in.

'What's your name?'

'Lidia Ivanova,' she said.

The captain watched her closely, until the hot embers of his cigarette stub caused him to reach for the tin ashtray on the windowsill. He turned his back and she looked at me.

'What's your nationality?'

'Bulgarian.'

'Why are you in Turkey?'

She began to weep and from then on said nothing. I raised my hand from my lap to comfort her but thought better of it. Instead I rubbed my temple. The captain walked to the towel dispenser and ripped off a course sheet of paper.

'Here take this,' he said, dropping it in her lap. 'Repeat the question.'

I asked again but the little breakthrough we had was short lived.

The captain rubbed his chin. 'Go to the canteen, bring her

back something to eat and keep an eye on her till I return.'

'Yes, sir.'

'As for you young lady, let's hope you can talk with a full belly.'

We left her in the sparse room, amongst her miserable thoughts. The captain walked out into the sunshine, across the gravel yard to the officer's quarters and I headed to the kitchen. Breakfast was over and the noisy sound of lunch was underway in the mess hall. I joined the lineup of plate holders passing the bain-maries. Scoops of army slop was ladled out by two cooks struggling to keep up with demand. It was always the same unabated routine of filling plates three times a day.

'Nice try, Yilmaz... Already coming back for a second serve before he's eaten the first,' came a voice in the queue three heads back. 'It's not for that skinny wreck you bought in yesterday is it? Better make sure she doesn't bite your hand off when you give it to her. Those Bulgarians are a bunch of "desparates".'

'Hey, I didn't know Yimaz was going to give it to her?' said another, which caused a chain of laughter down the line.

I turned my back and moved a few steps forward. The plates were loaded with cabbage dolmas, scoops of eggplant yogurt and flat bread. I carried the tray out of the mess hall and along the corridor where a private from my division was bent over on cleaning duties.

'What are you doing here?' he asked. 'I thought you were gone for the weekend.'

'Me too. I have to help with the questioning of the girl we bought in.'

'Bad luck,' he said.

'I guess that's the way it is around here. Anyway, I've got to keep moving,' I said negotiating my way past the bucket and mop.

I had missed a day's competition training but now my mind was far removed from the championship. I opened the door to the room and walked in to find her with her face obscured by a tightly held pillow. I bent down and placed the tray of food on the metal cabinet next to the bed, then coughed. She rolled over and slowly eased herself up.

'Here, eat some of this. You'll feel better,' I said offering up a spoonful.

Her lips sluggishly parted and the tart yogurt slipped down her ready throat. When the plate was empty she lay back looking up at the ceiling and I sat back encouraged. I moved my chair closer. I knew our time alone was limited so I slid my hand into my trouser pocket.

'I have something for you. If I get caught I'll be in serious trouble so I have to be careful.' I pulled out the cigarette tin and a look of confusion crossed her face. 'I don't know whether you remember,' I said lowering my voice. 'When my friend went to get the jeep I searched your bag for identification and found this.'

She stared down at the tin and I continued in a whisper. 'I felt it was personal and that it would probably be confiscated. So I kept it.'

I took the tea glass from her hand and placed it on the side table. I opened it and slid the ring on her middle finger then handed her the letter.

'Read it, and when you're finished give it back. I'll keep it safe.'

The parade ground sergeant with vocals in full throttle and the rumblings of the supply truck passing the window, all went mute and the room was quiet. Suddenly there were footsteps in the corridor. I snatched the letter and cigarette tin back and shoved them into my trouser pocket. I picked up the glass, put it in her hand, the door flew open and the captain walked in.

I sprang up. 'Sir.'

He shot a glance at me and then across to her. 'At ease,' he said. 'It looks like food has done everyone a bit of good. I've made some phone calls and I want you to tell her what's planned.'

'Yes, sir.'

'She's to be transferred tomorrow morning to Istanbul. You're to accompany her.'

I hesitated, surprised by his decision to send me. I told her of his plan and could not help noticing she had swiveled the ring around her middle finger. The red stones were nestled inside her clenched palm and went unnoticed.

The next morning shimmers of heat were rising from the sealed driveway passing the infirmary. We sat quietly on the white bench waiting for our transportation south. Her ankle was strapped with a tight crêpe bandage and her body appeared lost beneath army surplus trousers and shirt shoulders that slipped half way to her elbows. In her bag a laundered red dress, a change of underwear and some basic toiletries. In mine was the captain's report.

Directly opposite on the parade ground the last of B Division marched out to receive their patrol orders from the short sergeant with generous lungs. Two military trucks were parked next to the supplies store ready to transport eighteen soldiers to their border posts. Josef was last in line and it was clear the weekend's wrestle had taken its toll. I shook my head and smiled to myself. I missed seeing him that morning and was eager to know how his training had gone. I watched him fall into line as the sergeant checked irregularities in the dress code and strutted passed puffy-chested. I mouthed the words "how did you go?"

His face screwed up then he grinned proudly.

'CELIK!' screamed the sergeant.

'Yes sir!'

The sergeant's chin clacked back and forth like a ventriloquist dummy and his ten toes did their best to gain another ten centimetres to eyeball Josef.

'When I say attention, wipe that smile off your face!'

With a sharp about turn, he marched back to the front and continued to belt out more morning instructions. Josef winked, I smiled, and a black Mercedes passed the entry gates to the army barracks. It coasted down the driveway and stopped outside the infirmary. I sprang to my feet and the driver walked around the bonnet of the car and saluted.

'Is this the detainee?'

'Yes,' I said. 'I'll sit in the back.'

I opened the rear door. She moved forward, bowed her head and slid across the leather seat, closely followed by me. The driver removed his cap and jumped into the front. She stared through the gap in the open window with her head against the door frame. Her arms held tight around her waist as if she was bothered by a pain or a cramp. The car hurtled along secondary roads avoiding the traffic delays on the highway. Soon, a good breeze was whistling through the back window. I slid my hand into my pocket and removed the letter. I tapped her hand.

'Give it back before we reach the outskirts of the city,' I whispered.

She took the letter and I thought it strange she never read it. Three hours on, the Istanbul haze appeared in the distance and fleecy clouds hung low over the Sea of Marmara. The letter returned to my pocket.

It was midday when we pulled to a stop. Long shadows laid their temporary claim across the street in front of the stone building. Its imposing entrance was flanked by substantial granite pillars and above the lobby in large lettering read the words National Intelligence Headquarters. Our country was the buffer between the West and the Soviets and a hot bed for intelligence gathering. Here was a place where close attention was paid to any hint of a covert operation. The building gave the impression of having had a grand history and although it retained its fancy facade, the atmosphere inside was far from frivolous. Once through the hallway we were taken to a small office.

'Tell her to remove her shoes and stand over there,' said our escort. She shuffled to the white wall and lined up next to the measuring stick.

'1.7 metres,' announced the man jotting it down.

He took her by the shoulders and turned her sideways then walked back to the camera for another shot. One flash sideways, a second flash forward.

'Done,' he said. 'Come with me.'

She slipped her feet into her shoes and we trailed along the hall to a landing that led to the lower basement. It was a stark contrast to the opulence of the floor above. A short walk along the corridor and we arrived at a dingy room three metres by four. It was furnished with a metal-legged chair, a small laminated desk and behind two brown leather chairs on wheels. A large mirror took up most of the space on the left wall, leaving me with an anxious feeling. She sat down on the metal seat.

'The girl stays here. Corporal, follow me.'

I turned to look back, then walked out and he locked the door. In the adjoining room, behind the two-way mirror a shiny headed man in a double-breasted suit stood close by observing the goings on in the room. He looked at me, his smile appearing out of place on his otherwise serious face.

'So you're Gabir Yilmaz?'

'Yes, sir.'

'There's no need to salute here, Yilmaz. Call me Husni. I'm not big on formalities. A handshake will do.'

I held out my hand and his shake was more than firm.

'We're going to play a little game,' he said with a nod to the mirror.

'A cat and mouse game of extracting the truth. I'm the cat, she's the mouse and you're the chunk of cheese that I hope will prove her weak spot'.

'I'm not sure I understand.'

'You don't need to. I've thirty years' experience under my belt and a good record of extracting the truth. All you have to do is be nice. She may tell you things that she'd prefer not to tell me.'

The idea I was the pawn in his game unnerved me. Now the little trust I had fostered could be misconstrued? Through the glass she sat under a yellow ceiling and buzzing fluorescent tube. Her crying streamed through the speakers next to the mirror. I was struck by an overwhelming desire to rip the wires from the bawling boxes and tear her away.

Next to him was a woman in her early forties, dressed in a tailored navy blue suit.

'This is Sahlia, she will be doing the psychological assessment.'

I gave her a nod.

'Do you have the Edirne report?'

'Yes sir,' I said and I opened my briefcase and handed it over.

His eyes quickly scanned it.

'That's not very enlightening. Never mind. The Greek report was sent through this morning,' he said and he flicked it open.

The mention of another report was confusing but the Greek border was ten kilometres away and I assumed other escapees might have been picked up downstream. Husni flicked open the report, read for a moment then drummed his fingers on the table.

'You never know with those heedless Greeks. A spy could turn up amongst the grapevines wearing a thick moustache, a false set of tits and a blonde wig and they'd still think he was legit. Best we do our own little investigation,' he said and he closed the report and looked to me. 'For the moment you'll stay here. I best get started then.'

Sahlia sat stern-faced at one end of the desk and I at the other. Both of us had keen eyes on the two-way mirror. It was an hour after midday when we watched Husni walk into the small cell. He moved behind the desk. She was face down with her arms shielding the back of her head and he flicked his tie over his shoulder and sat down. He leant across with his outwardly stretched hands clasped together on the tabletop. His voice was low and close but conveyed a menacing message that he was not a person to be messed with.

'You are here because we need to establish why you're in Turkey.'

She slowly lifted her head and her eyes looked back under swollen lids.

He shifted in his seat and leaned a little closer. 'Do you speak Turkish?'

A silence hovered between them and he clacked his tongue in his pallet.

'Hmm... It appears not,' he said leaning back and rhythmically rocking the high back of the chair.

His hands were clenched together and his thumbs twirled across his stretched belly. He opened the file in front, and with the fluency of a native spoke to her in the language she understood.

'You're here in order for us to verify the details of your story. It says your name is Lidia Ivanova. Is that correct?'

She nodded.

'It states here, you're eighteen and you escaped with two accomplices.'

She nodded again.

'What were their names?'

'Raphael Ivanov and Petar Borev.'

His mouth drooped and he shook his head doubtfully. 'Here's the problem,' he said. 'How did you pass the border undetected? You see there's a flaw in your story?'

She squirmed in her seat. 'Through a gap in the fence,' she answered. 'Say that again, I didn't hear you.'

'A gap in the fence?'

He leaned back. 'A security fence with holes. That's rather convenient, wouldn't you say?'

He pushed his chair away, stood up and hitched his pants. Then he took four paces around the table and bent over her. 'I suppose you are going to tell me there was a boat on the riverbank too.'

She nodded.

He readjusted himself once more and returned to his seat. 'Maybe escape is not the right word' he said and with a hardened expression he paused a moment to watch.

'You're a long way from home. Surely you would like to go back to your family?'

There was no reply and he scratched the dermatitis at the base of his earlobe and his left cheek bunched in a smirk. His eyes were fixed on her and he slowly stood. Sahlia's fingers tapped the typewriter keys with vigor, recording everything in detail.

'Maybe there's another side to this story. You see, it's hard to believe you and your friends managed to avoid the Bulgarian border patrol with such ease. I'm suggesting you were assisted.'

He turned his back and took a few steps away, as if counting the seconds. The back pleat of his suit jacket puckered under his clasped hands. Unexpectedly he swung around and walked back. He propped his meaty thigh on the corner of the table and leaned in. 'Beggar's belief!'

His sudden open hand slammed down onto the file in front of her and her head jilted.

'I'm suggesting you crossed the river with an ulterior motive. I believe things didn't go according to plan and that you and your friend accidently parted ways. I also believe you and he staged the shooting of the other fictitious character in order to add credence to your story.'

Her head jerked back and she rose from her chair with a roar. 'NO!...They killed him.'

He placed his hand forcefully on her shoulder and she sat down hard. 'Who was killed!'

'My brother!'

Husni rubbed his chin for a moment then got up and poured a glass of bottled water. Behind the glass I looked over to Sahlia and she glanced sideways at me.

'His bark is worse than his bite,' she said.

'Could have fooled me. How long do you think they'll keep her here?'

'Don't know. He'll sniff out the truth quick enough.'

She looked back down to her notes and the conversation ended. Husni slid the glass over.

'Drink this,' he said and he picked up the file and walked out.

When he re-entered the room he looked straight at Sahlia. 'So what do you think? A bit of theatre or genuine?'

She stroked her forehead then adjusted her glasses. 'Possibly genuine. She appears to have suffered some sort of shock.'

With that he strolled over to the window and watched. 'Yes there's something crazy about her,' he said. 'She keeps brushing herself down like she's got something stuck to her.'

He flashed a looked at me.

'What do you reckon, Corporal? Give us a layman's opinion.'

'I'm not sure what you mean Sir.'

'You know what I mean. Do you think the girl is a bit on the "loopy" side?'

I stammered to give a reply. 'No Sir.'

He smirked. 'I always think it's best to ask the questions then listen to what's not said. Do you agree Sahlia?'

She stopped flicking the pen between her fingers but appeared to ignore his comment. 'Can her story be verified?' she said.

He flicked open the Greek dossier and scratched his neck. His chin puckered and his mouth turned down. 'Possibly. Then again, maybe they had a hand from the "Commos"?'

He stopped talking seemingly giving it some thought. For a fat man the bulge in his belly was doing a fine job pivoting him back and forth as he rocked on his heels. He stood with his nose a centimetre from the glass.

'Her brother's death explains the trauma,' said Sahlia.

He stretched and let out a sigh and his steamy breath left a saucer-sized fog on the mirror. Then he shifted his sleeve cuff up his wrist and looked at his watch.

'Sahlia bring me a coffee and something to chomp on, will you?'

'Sure,' she said uncrossing her legs and standing up as if hampered by a sudden rush of pins and needles.

He stood for some time with one hand cupping his chin and the other hooked in his belt. But when she returned, the smell of coffee and the glaze pastry interrupted his thoughts. He raised the tiny Turkish cup to his lips but on the third slurp lost concentration. A muddy slush filled the gaps in his front teeth like mortar and clogged his stiff moustache.

'Damn it!' he said checking the front of his stained white shirt.

With half a glass of water he took a good swig and spat it back into the empty coffee cup, vigorously blotting his shirt with his handkerchief. He screwed up the pastry wrapper, shoveled the contents into his mouth and hitched up his trousers. He looked over to me as if sizing me up. A grin tugged at the corners of his mouth and I was not sure what was happening next.

'She's quite a beauty, isn't she boy?' he said.

'Yes Sir.'

'Do you fancy her?'

'No sir.'

'Come on. A young buck like yourself, I bet you do. I think you fancy her a lot.' He chuckled to himself. 'We'll give her some time to pull herself together. Meantime Sahlia, can you put together your thoughts in writing. I'll make a few external calls and Yilmaz go get her a coffee and sit with her.'

After he told me this, I was certain I was now the chunk of cheese being offered to the mouse as the cat stood behind the wall ready to pounce.

I entered the room with the coffee and closed the door. Moving past the mirror left me with a feeling of disquiet. I placed the coffee on the desk. It was hard to know what to do. I was the one familiar face albeit the time had been short. I leant down and tucked a strand of hair behind her small ears. Her nose appeared clogged and her eyes hardly opened.

'This must be hard but if you tell me what happened I'm sure it will help your situation,' I said.

There was no reaction and the rubber on the chair legs juddered as I shifted in my seat.

'All right, I'll tell you about me and then maybe you can tell me about you.'

She did not look up but I began anyway.

'I'm from Bulgaria too. My parents were Turks. I left in fifty-one,' I said keeping my eyes on her. 'How about you?'

She didn't budge and, undeterred I continued.

'There weren't a lot of choices for me other than to work the land or join the military so I chose the army.' I stopped and looked over to the mirror. 'Sometimes I wonder whether army life was the right choice,' I said.

She sat picking at the quick of her thumbnail.

'Where's your family from?' I asked. To my surprise she answered.

'Sofia.'

'I've never been. Are they still there?'

'No.'

Her head remained bowed and it was difficult to pick her reaction.

'Where are they now?'

Slowly she raised her head and in a flat tone replied. 'My father's dead. I don't know what they will do to my Ma...' Her words petered out and she stopped a moment then said. 'They shot my brother.'

'Who?'

'The border guards.'

I placed my hand on her shoulder. 'I'm sorry for you.'

A moment passed.

'What about your friend?' I asked.

'I didn't see. They shot him too I guess.'

I took a sip of cold coffee. Nothing more was said. I wondered whether it pleased Husni that his hunch to use me was paying a dividend. I hoped like hell that his interrogators gut feeling was satisfied. I felt certain it was nothing more than a grab for freedom. She laid her head on the table. A half hour later the door opened and a short woman with a tray of food entered. She was wearing a white smock and white shoes.

'I'm Fatima. I've been sent to attend to her.'

I stepped away and she placed the tray on the desk. She bent down and tapped Lidia's arm. 'Eat,' she said.

The woman slid the chair back against the wall and sat down. I had the impression that a job was a job and no extra care was available. She pulled her magazine out from under her arm and began flicking through the pages. It probably suited her that I cared enough to do the encouraging. I slid the tray closer, hoping the waft of steamy vegetables and meat would rouse her appetite.

She sat for a time with her fork shuffling between the grey meat and grey vegetables and the meal soon cooled.

Fatima stood and stretched. 'You haven't eaten much,' she said and she walked over and picked up the tray.

'I'll be back shortly. When I return she'll come with me and the boss would like to see you next door.'

'Where is she going from here?'

'To the shower then to bed.'

'Is she ok, nurse?'

'I'm sure she will bounce back.'

'What's wrong?'

'She lost her baby.'

Husni closed the report and pushed it to one side. He looked up at me with a flat expression. I dreaded to think of what he had concluded.

'You'll no doubt be happy to hear this. She's off the hook. We've arranged a lift for you back to your barracks. A car will be brought around the front in ten minutes. So wait out there. Thanks for your help.'

'Where will she go from here sir?'

'The Marmaris Hotel.'

I left relieved, though confused as to why they would be sending her to a hotel.

CHAPTER 11

GREEN SOAP and a nail brush did nothing to take the feeling of Raphael's flesh on my cheek but the more the brush ripped across my face the better it felt. On the shower floor I bled like never before. I was dizzy. I slid down the tiles and woke in another place, shaken to the core.

On the walls scrambled messages and names of previous others laid claim to the room's history. Tiles the colour of burnt butter scaled half way up and in the back corner the bunk took up half the room. I lay back on the mattress. Above a light bulb hung like a teardrop on a dirty cord. Muffled voices and dragging feet slipped past the door until I fell asleep.

On top of the hill Mama stood waving. The sun shone behind and with a quickening step I ran towards her. Laughter echoed all about. Then a sudden thunderclap. Rain and hail pelted me. But the rain was red and the hail soft and thick. It clung as if I was the centre of attention. I strained to see her but the crest of the hill was bare and the charcoal sky glistened over the mess.

I woke screaming.

It was hard to tell if it was morning. No light reached the basement. I felt a firm nudge to my shoulder. It was the same woman from the previous night and she gestured for me to dress. I pushed myself up and rubbed my eyes. My ankle was tender but the pain overshadowed by the gripe in my belly. I dressed and she led me down the corridor, into a room where the interrogator waited.

'Good morning,' he said. 'Be seated.'

His approach was different but the smell from his liberal dose of cologne almost made me gag.

'Are you feeling better?'

I nodded.

'You've been given a temporary permit to stay in Turkey until the UNHCR can find you a host country. The process takes around six months. During this time you're in the hands of the Ministry of the Interior and you're also registered with the police. We'll be sending you to a "guest house" here in Istanbul for the duration of your stay.' He looked over at me. 'Any questions?'

He read at such speed he had hardly taken a breath. I nodded though nothing was clear. He marked a cross under the lines I was to sign and pushed three papers across the desk. My finger was dipped in blue ink and pressed onto a paper sheet. When the documentation was finalised I was taken up stairs to a waiting car. I climbed in clutching my bag. By mid-morning we arrived outside a two-storey boarding house. The sign above the parapet read Marmaris Hotel but the paying guests had long departed, along with the maintenance. It was a place where uneventful days turned to months and "guests" waited for acceptance to a foreign land. At reception a middle-aged woman stopped typing. She stood and with a pasted smile she walked to the counter. The driver signed my papers and left. I stood in the lobby as though no longer a part of that which was going on.

'Karşılama,' Lidia,' she said.

Her bored eyes looked me over and she picked a small key off one of the many hooks above the filing cabinet. She flipped up the counter top and walked through.

'Beni takip,' she said.

We went out the side door and into the courtyard where a pathway ran round the perimeter. It was a warm day and most of the occupants were milling about. Some hung over the three levels of balcony smoking while others sat in the courtyard sunbaking. I was taken to the section where the women and children were housed. The building had room for a hundred but poor sanitation and frequent disputes kept two edgy policemen on constant call. The chatter stopped as I walked into a room where four bunk beds lined each side. I was given the top bunk in the corner and a key to the corridor lockers. Three women sat at a small metal-legged table by the window. They acknowledged me with a nod and resumed their conversation.

A hawkish looking woman, stooped with oversized eyes and a bob of bleached curls sat apart. She watched me closely.

'I'm Irinushka,' she said. 'And you?'

'Lidia.'

'Bulgarian?' She asked with her chin jutting out.

I nodded.

'You're on tonight's roster,' she said with a heavy Russian accent sounding like sand paper across concrete. 'You'll be working with me.'

Then a knowing smirk crossed her lips. 'Welcome to this cosmopolitan dump, where ninety percent of the population is illiterate and the other ten have a hard job counting to three.'

Looking at the other women it was clear to see by their body language that Irinushka did not endear herself to a single one. Their chatter resumed and I lay down. At five o'clock I went with her to the kitchen and we ate before the dining room filled. She rolled up her sleeves and plunged blue rubber gloves into the steamy water. As soon as the dirty dishes returned to the kitchen clean ones were restacked on the serving table. I stood by the sink as she took her frustrations out on the crockery. Soapy dishes shot out and clinked against the mounting pile draining on the bench and it was hard to keep pace.

'Don't worry, you'll get used to this. I've been here for four months. So much for the American dream,' she said shaking her head. 'How long does it take? All they have to do is sign a few papers and I'm out of this hole. Four months!'

She placed another glass onto the stack and gave me a nudge

in the ribs with her elbow. 'What's your story?'

I grabbed the glass beaker but it slipped through my hand and smashed in thick chunks onto the floor. 'Sorry.'

She rolled her eyes. 'The world is full of dim wits,' she muttered and pointed behind. 'The broom and dustpan are over there.'

I placed the tea towel on the bench and grabbed the small blue brush and pan inside the cupboard. Piece by piece I shoveled it up. One large shard remained next to the skirting board. I picked it up and placed it in my apron pocket. I tipped the remainder into the bin and kept drying. When the last of the dishes were stacked I returned to the women's quarters to bide my time. The bathroom was crowded with mothers getting children ready for bed, but I was in no hurry. I waited until the chaos died down and the lights had been out for an hour. The chatter in the dark room turned to quiet mutterings then gentle snores and I made my move. I slipped from the bed and tip-toed barefoot out of the room. The bathroom was close by. I pushed the door open on the second toilet cubicle and latched the door behind. My eyes adjusted quickly to the dark and I sat on the floor with my body pressed against the dividing wall.

I took the chard from my pocket. Now the shiny piece of glass had a new purpose. I would make sure it cut deep enough to bleed the life out of me. With my jaw and hand clenched, I held the thickest edge then lined the raiser-sharp side above my left wrist. In the darkness it was as if the pulse under my thin skin was guiding my fingers to the precise point of contact.

The damage inflicted was swift. The edge sliced through like butter. My left wrist quickly seeped a warm gore. There was no gush, but it left the glass wet and slippery. I pinched it between my nightdress and my fingers. It gave a better grip and I dragged it across my right wrist. Warm, wet and deadly still. I felt as if I lay on the floor of the ocean. There was no reason to care, and no care to reason. I lay there in a blanketing comfort until the light filtered through and foggy shadows circled. I felt a brush to my skin. A heavy thump to my chest again and again and again. I was taken up, whirled this way and that in a maddening current. Then a prick to my arm and blackness came rushing in.

I came to listening to muffled voices but unable to understand until Irinushka took over the conversation.

'All that blood. You're lucky I saw your foot sticking out from under that cubicle. The doctor said it was a good thing you didn't know what you were doing. If you'd of slashed up your arm it would have been a different story.'

CHAPTER 12

I WATCHED the trail of ants carry the fly carcass past the rusty leg of the bench seat. Past my shoe, and down into the dark void between two slabs of broken paving. It had been a two-minute struggle of mammoth proportions and a collective willpower. They stopped, started, regrouped and pulled until the fly was no longer visible. If I had not been a witness no one would ever have known the fly once existed. I stared at the nest entrance as if I had watched the closing scene of a Greek tragedy. I was half expecting to see the fly and the cast of black foot soldiers return to enthusiastic applause, when an interruption from the nasal tones of the administrator crackled through the courtyard speakers.

'Lidia Ivanova. Come to the office... Lidia Ivanova. Call to the office.'

'Hey Dreamer, that's you,' yelled Irinushka.

I looked back. Three weeks in the boarding house had taught

me to steer clear of her. Her argumentative nature and constant rants about finding a pegging position on the overcrowded washing-line caused others to do the same. The last time she had spoken to me was after the incident when I had been carried back to the dormitory. 'Toughen up,' she said. 'You're not the only one here with a problem.'

I flicked my plait to one side, rose to my feet and made my way across the yard. I climbed the steps to the office and pulled the door open. As if to catch my breath, my hand went straight to my mouth. There in the foyer the soldier stood. I froze on the spot in my faded printed dress with my bony knees and my toes turned in.

He smiled and held out a warm hand. We shook.

'Good to see you, you're looking a little better,' he said.

'Why are you here?'

'I came to see if you're ok. Thought you might like a visitor.'

'How did you find me?'

'Husni told me. He said you were staying in this place. Though looking around it doesn't look much like a hotel.'

He looked at the receptionist.

'I need to talk with her for a while. Is there some place we could go?'

She raised one eyebrow and gave a permissive wave causing a multitude of gold bangles to jangle. 'The courtyard,' she said.

I led him through the side door and out into the sunshine. Sly discussion and curious glances were directed our way. It was unusual to have a visit from an outsider. We walked across the white stone and passed the washing racks steaming under the

July sun.

He reached into his shirt pocket as we sat down. 'I brought your letter. I didn't want to send it so I decided to deliver it myself.'

'Thank you,' I said and I raised my hand to shade my eyes from the sun.

His eyes flicked to my bandaged wrists. I lowered my arm and clasped my hands in my lap.

'It looks like a good place to dry clothes,' he said.

He gave me the letter and looked about. A small group of children rolled colourful marbles along the path leading to the kitchen. Mothers sat on the steps to the women's dormitory and men smoked and argued in a multitude of languages.

'Are they treating you well?'

I nodded but as I held my mother's letter in my lap a hard lump formed in my throat. I felt sure if I were to open it was bound to pull me apart. 'Thank you,' I said.

'That's ok. I'm pleased to get it off my hands.'

'You took a risk.'

'What do you mean?'

'Keeping it for me.'

'Yes, but I'm glad I did. It was just one of those spur of the moment things I guess.'

We sat a metre apart. The conversation was stilted, the words not forthcoming. The future was uncertain and the past best left unsaid.

When the hour was over he stood up and smiled. 'My mother used to say the medicine for a sad soul is to sing. I'll be back in a few more weeks. Be strong.'

True to his word, on the first Sunday of each month he came. As time wore on he became skillful at filling in the gaps in the conversation, and when he left I marked the days till his return. He did the talking and I the listening. It did not seem to bother him that I said little. He told me his family had lived in Bulgaria outside of Svilengrad and had been in the village for three generations.

'Back then I was called Gabir Yilmazov. My father had added the −ov at the end of our name long before the Government enforced it. I never thought I was different until one day a teacher said: you've got a few brains for a Turk.'

'I'd never known any Turks,' I said.

'Probably not. Most of us lived in the south until it became too restrictive. Finally my father said enough was enough. We turned our back on the land and left with our suitcases and the government welcomed our departure. At the time, the last thing I wanted to do was to kiss Turkish soil but it was the best thing to happen. My parents had known nothing else but tobacco farming and my sister and I would have surely gone down that path.'

Over the six months the visits amounted to six hours of time spent together. It was the lifeline I needed to keep me looking forward. Many times I asked if he had heard news of Raphael and Petar's bodies having washed up on Turkish soil but there was none. The thought of them slain on the riverbank was at times almost impossible to bear.

There was a definite change in the weather and despite the chill in the air I pulled the dress from my locker and lay it on the bed. My hand slipped across the soft red velvet remembering another time. Back then, I had sat up in the half-light of the old house and across the room the dress hung on the door handle. That morning I threw the bed-cover off and tip-toed across the floor. As I lifted it up my spirits lifted too. Mama had turned the red curtain into a full skirt, and a scooped neckline. I slipped it over my shoulders in no time and in that short moment, I was special. In the evening I had stood in front of the speckled mirror and Mama knelt next to me with the measuring stick marking the spot from which to hem. There was nowhere to wear such a dress but the fact that it hung in the wardrobe evoked dreams for both of us.

Now I slipped it over my shoulders with my fingers fumbling for the cold tab of the zipper. I pushed my arms into the sleeves of my coat and crossed the courtyard to the office. On reaching the door I took a deep breath and entered. He stood by the window with his eyes firmly fixed on the door. In a brief moment his gaze held me still. His brows lifted and he appeared to take a backward step.

He cleared his throat. 'Red suits you,' he said.

I drew in my shoulders and clasped my hands in front suddenly feeling clumsy. The receptionist jutted her jaw forward, puffed out her bosom and looked on.

'I'd like to take her to tea,' he said. 'Is that ok?'

She glanced down at her nails and shrugged. 'I suppose an hour would be all right.'

I hastily buttoned my coat.

'Come on,' he said.

A trickle of apprehension ran through me. He took my hand and we walked out through the main entrance of the hostel. For the first time in months the cultural melting pot that was my home peeled back. Across the street an old man roasted chestnuts in an iron barrel, while a shopkeeper further down scooped up chewy ice cream. There was so much to take in. I could never have imagined a street packed with so much food and colour.

'We'll try this teahouse. It looks good,' he said.

My hand was tight in his. We slipped through the white haze where old men sat smoking apple tobacco through flexible hoses. It felt good to sit alone. He lifted the tea to his lips then placed the glass back down on the brass tray.

'What are you thinking?' he asked.

'Why you bothered with me?'

'You're my excuse to practice Bulgarian'.

'That's no answer.'

He tilted his head. 'I know what it felt like to be dispossessed. Now you tell me something for a change.'

'I don't know what to say.'

'Tell me about growing up in Sofia. About the things you loved. The things that made you.'

It was hard to know where to start. I began with my father but I caught myself saying my father was this, my father did that and then the words got lost.

'You'll find your place… I want you to know, wherever they send you I'll keep in contact. I promise. You are not alone and you are not to worry... ok?'

I nodded and we sat still in the little courtyard garden and time slipped away. When we arrived at the door to the hostel he gave my hand a reassuring squeeze and said goodbye. I watched him from the window. He walked down the street whistling and his head turned twice to see if I was there.

December saw an end to our meetings. A week later, I was summoned to the supervisor's office. When I entered a man in a suit pushed aside his coffee cup and slid the folder to the centre of the desk. He removed his glasses and looked up. I stood in front of him fidgeting.

'Don't look so worried. I have good news. Please sit.' He gestured with his hand to the chair. 'Sit.'

My eyes were glued to my name on the folder. He took the document and read it out but I struggled to take it in. It wasn't until he walked to the shelf by the window and spun the plastic globe of the world that the significance of what he had said dawned. The globe slowed and his index finger landed on Australia.

'Australian Immigration shall be taking over your case. You will be resettled there.'

He walked back and sat down placing his glasses on his nose to read the fine print.

'You'll be leaving Turkey this coming Wednesday. The

Australian Consulate officials will be visiting you tomorrow afternoon to organise your departure. You'll fly to Athens where you'll continue the journey to Australia by ship. Do you have any questions?'

I could not think of one. Six months in the "guest house" had not been ideal but it had provided familiar faces and the comfort of a routine. There was a sense of community. Our loss of identity had given us a common bond.

'There are three papers I need you to sign, and that's it, all over,' he said with a smile. 'Why such a poker face? You're a very lucky girl.'

CHAPTER 13

ON THE 14TH DECEMBER 1960 a drawn-out horn resonated across Port Piraeus. Hordes of people laden with luggage formed into a messy queue that stretched along the wharf and moved up the gangway in a steady stream. Above black diesel smoke billowed from the ship's chimney and streamers zig-zagged down from the hull where the connection to families below was soon to be severed. There was a good deal of excitement. But the blood orange sunset did nothing to warm my heart.

Gangways rattled back and two tugboats pulled hard severing our ties to the dock. The shouts from the wharf faded and I stood in the cool air and watched for an hour as Athens receded. I wondered about Gabir and whether he knew that I had been shipped out. He was the only one I had, and I was going to miss him.

Next day we were guided into Port Said and by evening the

ship was loaded with supplies. In the early hours of the morning we joined the southern convoy through the Suez Canal. Ahead lay a four-week journey across the Indian Ocean, with rough seas causing the desertion of the dining room and queasy sprints to the bathroom. I attended the mid-morning English classes, though it was directed more towards the Greek majority. I learnt little other than to sing "Waltzing Matilda" and those with sufficient English also struggled to understand what billabongs, jumbucks and swagmen meant. Nevertheless, the song had the capacity to lift spirits.

On a hot Melbourne night I stepped onto Station Pier, along with hordes of others eager to stand on dry land. An empty train slid onto the dock sending my thoughts back to another place, another time. Two hours later I stared through the carriage window as paling fences from outer suburban backyards flashed by. Further on intermittent lights from sheep stations and country towns struggled to illuminate the dark. I stayed awake listening to the rhythmical clacking of the wheels on the track. It was near midnight when we arrived at Bonegilla Migrant camp where brown grass and concrete paths webbed a way around iron corrugated iron huts, a recreational hall, a kitchen, a dining hall and an ablution block.

A sombre mood had replaced the excited cries on the wharf. With a few paces forward, a stop and a further two paces we shuffled to the front desk where Alien Registration Certificates were given out. I looked up the queue, and a middle-aged man stood three metres ahead. He was taller than most and his action of removing his felt hat suddenly cemented me to the floorboards.

He took his certificate, replaced his hat and moved towards the next line waiting for X-rays and medical examinations. He looked nothing like my father when he turned but for a moment in time, his long neck, wide ears and frame had a derailing effect.

'Come on, missy, move up,' said the official with skin like a crocodile.

I picked up my suitcase and stepped forward. With the formalities over I was handed a knife, a fork, a spoon and a black blanket. The line snaked through reception and into the dining hall where lamb stew steamed from large aluminum pots and five counter staff waited with ladles in hand.

'Come on, let's get these "wogs" fed,' called the head cook.

I woke early to the sound of our expanding iron hut on a hot day rising. I climbed from my stretcher bed and tip-toed across the wooden floor. Outside, a dusty landscape, an endless sky and white birds with yellow crests jigged and squawked along white tree boughs. My forehead rested against the warm windowpane and I stared into the distance where kangaroos grazed. In the next bed a woman with a complexion of undercooked strudel lay asleep but shortly after her own manufactured snort caused her to wake with a start. She rubbed her eyes and squinted towards the window then fumbled for her glasses on the bedside table.

'What's happening?' she asked as she scuffed her feet into her slippers.

'It's the birds,' I said.

It had been years since I had heard German and I was grateful to have her company despite her stale breath.

'Huh! No wonder they give us an Alien Certificate. This is a very alien place,' she said and we laughed.

'What's your name?' she asked.

'Lidia. What's yours?'

'Hilda Gruber. What number did they give you?'

'Eighty-nine.'

'I'm ninety-four. We'll probably be in the same group for the meal sitting. I came with my husband but they've put him in the men's quarters.'

At mid-morning I joined Hilda and a group of twelve others. We sat under the gum trees taking an English lesson in the scorching heat. Each of us was handed a booklet titled "English for the Migrant" and it came in handy, swatting away dozens of black flies hell-bent on sucking the moisture from our lips. The rest of the day was spent strolling about with Hilda and her husband, familiarising ourselves with the camp layout.

'Günter's off to find work in Melbourne next week,' said Hilda tightening her hold. They walked arm and arm and she looked up at him, down at the mouth.

'So we girls will have to stick together.' She giggled.

'Do you have any idea of what you want to do, Lidia?' asked Günter.

'I don't know,' I said and we walked on.

By late evening it was quiet in the hut. Inside, the atmosphere was close to claustrophic yet outside was a vast landscape, appearing to stretch to infinity. The sticky heat was exhausting but at the same time it robbed me of sleep. Three metres away was the front door and I sat up thinking I would do better to take in fresh air than stale. I kicked my sheet to the foot of the bed and made my way across the floor. As I opened the door it gave a slow creak causing me to cringe on closing it behind me. There was not a whisper of a breeze but the welcome scent of the eucalyptus freshened the air. I breathed in deeply and sat down on the cool step. A block away a dark figure briskly walked toward the ablution block.

Under the blackest sky embracing a multitude of stars I thought about my past and my future. A number of events may have been the catalyst for all that had gone wrong but I had come to the conclusion long before, that blame stopped at my feet. Time and again bad thoughts could shiver to the surface. And I was haunted by a bright-eyed child standing at the front of the classroom telling tales of balloons floating high in eastern skies. I hoped against hope my mother's resolve would give her the strength to believe one day we would be re-united. She had no way of knowing what had happened. But any attempt to communicate meant exposing her to undue attention. I looked up wondering if she, too, was looking at the same sky. One day I would return, but until then there was no other option but to get on with things.

A week later all the new arrivals appeared to have settled into a routine, and in a field not too far away, down a gentle slope, the waters of Lake Hume gave a welcome relief from the heat.

I walked across the cracked earth. Sharp grass stood motionless as if every living thing was crying out for the afternoon breeze to kick in. Shouts of joy could be heard at the water's edge as children splashed and cavorted, most unable to

swim and fearful of the deep. If any strayed too far it was cause
for a mother to rise to her feet and beckon them closer. White
strips of sunlight flickered and danced across the lake and to the
west smoke from a bush fire streaked its way across the sky like
a charcoal smudge. Controlled burning is what they told us but
within fifteen minutes it covered the western skyline. Shade was
fleeting and there was not enough time given for roots and leaves
to relax before the heat closed off any portholes of moisture. There
was something about the day that felt edgy but then maybe it was
just difficult to understand how fire was controlled with fire. The
warmth on my shoulders was soothing and I chose to ignore the
inexplicable feeling of unease taking hold.

With two other women we spread the sheet out and slipped
off our shoes. I lay on my stomach with my skin turning pink.
From one hundred metres Hilda Gruber sent out a welcoming
wave. She hitched her paisley cotton dress into her knickers and
her chunky legs carried her across the field. Within three days our
little group of four women had formed a friendship while their
husbands were off seeking work. The others were Serbian and
although our languages crossed over, if we didn't understand one
another, gestures, smiles, and broken English filled in the gaps.
On reaching us Hilda plunked herself down, and let out a sigh.

'I don't want to see another dish. Look at the state of my
hands. It's a wonder my fingernails haven't floated off,' she said
wiping her brow.

Having said that she pulled off the lid of the biscuit tin and
fanned herself. Rivulets of moisture ran down the back of her
neck. I watched the children play, heartened by their enthusiasm,

until a sharp nip to my ankle caused me to sit up quickly and slap a bull ant. Not far away two men sat out of earshot. As I glanced across one smiled. He looked straight at me, nodding to his friend but I got the feeling he was not really listening but rather sizing me up. I looked away quickly and lay back down. I'd seen him before, the one with the fish, a big man, not so much in girth but a build that was not to be messed with. He was taller than most, though I guess that was not hard as the majority of the migrants were from southern Europe.

I smiled to myself remembering what Tatko use to say. "The closer you lived to the equator the shorter you were." He said, "You need to shrink from the sun a little. Where as the people from the north need to stretch to get some heat". I lay down wondering if there would ever be a time when the memories of those I loved would feel like a nudge to the heart rather than a jab.

'That's Milankovich,' said Lena nudging my toes. 'He's got an eye for you, Lidia.'

I lifted my head but lay back down. I remember seeing him the day he had bought fish to the camp. Any reason not to have mutton was a blessing and the reward for his efforts was a few cold beers. But the manner in which it was caught was alarming. He arrived outside the camp kitchen with his legs apart, his hands on his hips and a bulging hessian sack at his feet.

'Fresh fish for the cooks,' he called.

His friend was at his side when they had devised a method of catching trout from the lake.

'One stick of dynamite stuns half the population,' he said. 'Then you just wade in and scoop them up.'

No one bothered to ask where the dynamite came from as everyone was happy to partake of a fish.

He grinned widely and slung his arm over his friend. 'You've got to give credit to "Pete the Greek", he's got some damn good ideas at times.'

I poked my head between the onlookers and our eyes met. He smiled and winked but his attention left me cold. Not so for Hilda who now sat marveling at his broad shoulders and tan.

'He's a fine looking specimen. Doesn't matter his nose is a little crooked. Real manly if you ask me.'

The other women giggled.

'We need to find a husband for Lidia,' said Hilda teasingly. 'It's our female duty.'

'What did you say his name was?'

'Drago Milankovich,' replied Dora.

'Hmm. Another Serb. Similar language to Bulgarian, Lidia,' said Hilda. 'But who needs language when he's built like that. Don't you agree, ladies?'

I lifted my head.

'I prefer brains.

They laughed.

'A woman needs a husband,' continued Hilda. 'And there's no shortage of suitors in this place.'

Through the crook of my elbow I spied him but there was little to inspire me. He held his cigarette between his thumb and forefinger as he sucked the last of it into his bunched cheek. Smoke exited through his lips and he muttered something to his friend causing them to chuckle. Whatever he had said I preferred not to know. Why the other women considered him a good catch was beyond me. He glanced over and smiled knowing he had gained our attention. He sat with his elbows on his knees; pants rolled half way up his calves and a white singlet with a few extra holes. He pushed his hand through his sandy coloured hair and under a brow that dominated his face, his eyes were set deep and lines of a joker ran down either cheek. Sweat glistened on his thick olive shoulders.

Not far away three boys carried a raft made up of three car tires bound together with rope. They launched it at the waters edge and were quickly surrounded by excited children eager to get on board. The three boys pushed off battling to master the action of the paddle. In the distance the white dam wall rose up over the lake appearing to quiver in the haze. Hilda continued to prattle on in the background as I watched. Soon they were a good twenty metres out. One boy stood up and the other followed suit. He proudly folded his arms across his skinny chest and the other was balanced with his feet spread and his arms angled up as if he was the king of the lake. The smallest of the three sat dangling his feet over the tire edge. It was unclear whether boyish bravado or a dare had caused them to jump but seconds later excitement turned to horror.

Suddenly Drago was pulling off his boots and singlet and sprinting ahead.

'Goodness me, Lidia, what have you done? Scared him off already,' jibed Hilda.

I jumped up.

'What's wrong?'

'The boys, they're in trouble.'

Drago ran into the water and children parted ways. Waist deep he spread his arms and dived in. He was swimming for dear life. Out on the lake the boy on the raft was screaming. If not for Drago's keen eye and ability to swim the tragedy would have been greater. A woman rose to her feet. Her hand covered her mouth. One by one people stood. I shaded my eyes and strained to see. Everyone appeared to hold a collective breath, all willing him to swim faster. But in less than a minute he was there. A boy flayed wildly, his head thrown back as he struggled to keep his face above water. On rescue he latched onto Drago and climbed him as if he were a ladder. The wrangle ended when Drago ducked under and came up grabbing him from the behind. Together they moved towards the raft and he left the boy gripping the ropes. He seemed to be talking to the younger boy who was pointing down to the water to his right. With a forceful kick he dipped under once more. The gasping boy scrambled aboard aided by a hand up from his friend. Seconds later Drago popped up on the other side. His head went left to right and right to left. The third boy was nowhere to be seen.

The tall blonde woman stood on the shore with her hands either side of her head as if shock was about to take her brains out. She screamed hysterically. Three more men dived in, one holding a life ring. Word was out and people were coming from all directions. I could see Drago's head bob up only to disappear again.

'There he is,' came one voice. 'What's that floating down river?' said another.

Everyone had an opinion as to where the boy may have been. But I saw nothing just leftover ripples from Drago's desperate dive under until he emerged holding the boy. Relief rippled through the crowd but all too soon came a crushing realisation. In the time it had taken to save one life, another young soul had slipped away. Breath no longer required. The boy's mother broke loose. She ran into the water, one arm raised, the other arm swishing from side to side. Her sodden dress dragged behind and her cry stretched out across the lake. In waist deep water she slapped the sides of her head as if to wake herself up from a nightmare.

With a firm hold, Drago swam purposefully back. He held the boy's limp body close, propelling himself forward with one arm and giving out a strong driving kick. Behind him two men paddled the raft with the boys sobbing uncontrollably. Drago staggered to shore holding the boy in his arms. He lay him down gently and as two medics took over, he pushed through the crowd clearly shaken and exhausted. He sat away with his head hung between his knees.

'Move back. Move back!' yelled the medic to the people surging forward.

They rolled the boy's body to one side and then onto his back. One man laid hands on his small chest and the other placed his ear next to his mouth. No breath came and so commenced a rhythmical action of pushing air in and forcing air out that lasted twenty minutes, to no avail.

A kookaburra sent a juddering call skywards but the joyful sound was more like a cadaverous cry, driving a painful wedge into the afternoon. The mother sobbed uncontrollably, her head was buried in another woman's shoulder. The boy lay with his legs spread and his skinny chest blue from the pummeling. Terror was set tight in his cheeks. His mouth was agape and his eyes were open like peeled lychees. His expression was unnerving.

Suddenly I had the need to run. I turned and pushed through the group, walking briskly away. The memory of Raphael was still raw. I walked along the shallows where mud oozed between my toes. Eventually I came to rest under the shade of a eucalypt. In front of me the land stretched out in every direction. Gritty plains with blackened tree trunks wedged into the earth like twisted arrows. I sat down thinking about Hilda's throw-away comment.

'He wouldn't have suffered,' she had said. 'They say it's the best way to die. Your whole life flashes in front of you like a movie.'

But I knew otherwise. It was nothing other than pure terror. Every cell in your body screaming while your lungs pounded your ribs to tear wide open. It was a day that changed lives, mine included. If not for that day I may never have considered the attentions of Drago. An hour must have passed before a shadow moved over me.

'Cigarette?' he said.

I looked up, surprised to see him. He had changed into a clean khaki shirt, faded across the shoulders. His hands were stuffed into his wide legged shorts and his hair was wet and slicked back off his forehead. He was smiling down at me but not a smile of happiness, rather one to break the distance I felt towards him.

'No thanks,' I said with a shake of my head.

'Mind if I sit?'

'If you want,' I replied.

He sat facing the river and pulled out his smoke pouch. His thick fingers piled a few pinches of tobacco threads onto the paper and with one hand he rolled then licked the paper to seal it. With a strike of a match on his boot he lit up. An uncomfortable silence settled between us.

After a moment he asked. 'Are you OK?'

'Yes,' I answered.

'Sad business about the boy,' he said.

I turned. 'Did you know him?'

'No, but I do now.' He paused and continued. 'They came in with the last arrivals. Dutch. Only in the camp twenty-four hours. Darn shame.'

He drove his heal into the earth. 'Look at this place. You couldn't stick a shovel in, it's so dry.'

He picked up a pebble and threw it in the lake. It skipped along the surface a couple of times and silently sank. 'So you're Bulgarian?'

'How do you know that?'

'Your friend the German told me. Come here by yourself did you?'

I was not sure whether that warranted a reply. I had the feeling Hilda had already filled in the details and was a little annoyed she had taken it upon herself to align me with a man which I had little interest.

'Me too,' he said. 'Don't know if it was such a good idea though.'

'You did a good thing today, saving that boy.'

'One boy too short. Could have done better,' he replied and

he held out his hand. 'Drago's the name. And yours?'

'Lidia,' I said, my fingers slightly touching.

'Pleased to meet you, Lidia. So what have they got you
doing here?'

'Working in the mess hall. And you?'

'Working in the wood yard. Hopefully not for much longer
I'm waiting to hear back about a job. Trying to get work on
the Snowy.'

My look prompted him to clarify.

'The Hydro Electric Scheme, they're building it not far from
here. Big money to be made up there in the mountains.'

'What are you going to do?' I asked.

'My best,' he said, appearing pleased his light-hearted remark
had at least got a smile out of me.

'I don't have any qualifications but I'm good with a
jackhammer and can lift cement bags.' Having said that, he
angled up his arm and proudly slapped his bicep.

'I guess you could say construction worker.'

He leant back on his elbows, stretched his legs and crossed his
sandaled feet.

'Bastard flies,' he said with a wave. 'More flies here than on a
herd of dead elephants.'

I could not help but notice he was one finger short. 'How
did you lose your finger?' I asked shielding my eyes from the
afternoon sun.

'Bullet. I can't boost a war injury. It was my own fault.'

He looked down at his hand and turned it over, palm up.
'Then again where I lived the countryside was scattered with left

over "amo". Don't even think about it. It was so long ago. Dumb kid accident. Found a bullet it in the woods. Got home and thought it a good idea to hit it with a hammer. And hey presto,' he said wiggling three full fingers. 'Never caused me any problem. The pinky finger is so over rated if you ask me.'

He rolled on his side and faced me, his eyes scanning.

'How about you? Got any thoughts about what you want to do?'

'Learn English,' I replied. 'Maybe I'll be a nurse.'

'Nurse? That would be a waste, he said. 'Can't think of anything worse. All bed pans and bandages,' he smiled then added. 'A good looker like you would do better finding a good husband,' he said raising his thick eyebrows and swatting another fly.

I flicked my plait off my shoulder and stood. 'Nice talking with you,' I said. 'I need to get back.'

He quickly sat upright, but sensing I preferred to be alone he held back. I walked away knowing he watched me. The afternoon was drawing to a close. The fire in the hills had not spread, and shimmer grass quivered under the feathery breeze crossing the paddocks. From a distance the huts appeared like slater bugs. Those gray insects that hide in dark damp places. But the corrugated roofs that rolled down either side held a scorching heat, and on first arrival it had taken a couple of days to distinguish one hut from another.

Hilda jumped to her feet and waved on seeing me walking towards her.

'What got into you? I looked around and you were gone. Took off like a rabbit.'

'Just felt like a walk,' I said.

She sat down, shuffled over and patted the step to the front door. 'Is everything ok?' she said with a frown.

I nodded, sat down and stretched my legs out. 'No problem.'

For a moment she observed me. 'I've good news,' she said.

I looked at her thinking perhaps they had revived the boy. Perhaps he was right now kicking a ball with his friends and the winner's hoot I could hear was his. But it was not so.

'Günter has found work,' she said.

'Where?'

'Melbourne. He got a job with the Water Board. We're so lucky. He'll be back next weekend. He's going to find a place for us and then I'll be joining him. I'm so excited.'

'That's great news,' I said.

'He called this morning but what with the accident it took a while for them to pass on the message.' She smiled. 'Just think I could be out of here in a couple of weeks. What do you think you'll do?' she asked with her head cocked to one side.

'I hear a few of the single women have been offered work in Benalla,' I said. 'But the club supervisor suggests I work in the office. Said I could help as an interpreter on occasion. It would mean staying here. I'm not sure I want to do that.'

'It sounds good,' she said unscrewing her little jar of Ponds cream and handing it to me. 'Here have some. Can't let that lovely skin of yours fry to a crisp. Looks like you got a bit of colour today. Hope it doesn't bubble into a blister tomorrow.'

I swiped a finger full around the rim and rubbed it into my shoulders. 'What happened with the boy?' I asked.

'There's been quite a lot of activity up at the office. They took him away a couple of hours ago. The priest and a social worker are with the family right now.' She shook her head and her tongue tut tutted behind her teeth. 'Such a tragedy. That poor woman, she has four other children but it doesn't make the loss any easier.'

'Where's her husband?

'He was looking for work. He's with her now.'

Not far away two girls hopped over a skipping rope, their ponytails swung from side to side and to the left boys kicked a ball.

'I say Drago did an amazing job to save the other boy. I was speaking to him later. Did he manage to find you?'

'Yes.'

'He's rather nice don't you think?' Her eyebrows danced up and down. 'Quite a catch. Wouldn't mind him saving me,' she said then instantly reprimanded herself. 'God forbid if Günter were to hear me say that.'

She had made it her mission to find me a suitor.A girl alone. You need to marry. Make a family around you,' she said.

But family was not something that stayed forever. And when it went missing, you too went missing. She chatted on, undeterred, offering advice on the matters of my own heart. I knew she had my best interests but I would have preferred to organise and gather my thoughts in my own time, my own way. I wondered why there was a need to fill in the spaces. As if a gap in a conversation or a gap in one's life had to be instantly filled and replaced with something else. As if that which went before was something to be pushed aside and forgotten in order to continue living.

The sound of the dinner bell rang out and I welcomed the interruption.

'Come on, number eighty-nine,' she said tapping me on the arm. 'Hopefully we won't get that mutton stew. Oh, how I long for some pickles and sauerkraut.'

Soon Drago was joining our evening walks around the camp and I was feeling a little less wary. He was not quick witted but he was light hearted in a time when a rising discontent was spreading throughout the community. It had started with the Italians protesting over the food and snowballed into unhappiness that jobs were not as fast coming as anticipated.

It also took a funeral and a couple of weeks for the murmurs over the drowning to die down. All the talk about the "what ifs" and the "whys". Drago was praised for his action and a ripple of respect went around the camp, which was something lacking prior to the event. He could come across a little too loud and a little too reckless for most, but it had been that recklessness that had saved a boy.

CHAPTER 14

'HERE,' SAID HILDA. 'Put some of this on your lips.'

Her arms stretched towards me, in her hand a small brown bottle.

'What is it?'

'Cochineal. I got it from the kitchen. We might be short on makeup but we women must be resourceful.'

She slid the clips from her hair and yellow pin curls sprung out around her thick cheeks.

'Günter should be back in an hour. Got to look the best for my man,' she said pushing up her breasts and pouting her stained lips. 'Move over Marilyn Monroe. Look out, Günter!' she said with a wink.

Despite all her efforts and her twenty something years, her five kilos extra made her look more matronly than Monroe. Her eyes skipped over me disapprovingly. 'What are you wearing?'

'This,' I replied stroking the cotton sides of my gingham dress.

With her hands on her hips she shook her head. 'You can't go in that. All faded on the back like you've spent a lifetime digging up potatos. Didn't I see a flash of something red in that case of yours?' She pushed my shoulder. 'Come on, girl. Let me weave my magic,' she said pointing a proud finger into her chest.

Reluctantly I got down on my hands and knees. My arm stretched under the bed and I pulled on the strap of my leather case. She stood over, eager and curious. I pulled it out, lifted it onto the bed and unbuckled it.

'I knew it, I knew it,' she said grabbing the dress. 'You're a dark horse, Lidia. Where on Earth did you get a frock like this?' Then she sneezed. 'A little pat down and it will be perfect,' she said fanning it out. 'This is a man magnet. I guarantee by the end of the evening you'll be able to pick and chose.'

She lay it back down on the bed and clapped her hands together. 'Quick, quick, go get your skinny waist into it. I want to see.'

As I raised my arms up, the dress slipped down over my shoulders. For a second I shivered up a breath. It took a second longer before slipping my arms through. With my hair held high she buttoned the back then stood away with her hands on her hips.

'I wouldn't be surprised by the end of this evening there'll be a marriage proposal. Now lets get rid of that plait.'

She undid the rubber band, and my hair hung loose half way down my back.

'I'm thinking maybe this was a bad idea,' she said shaking her head.

'What do you mean?'

'I'm scared when we walk into that hall you're going to upstage me.' She laughed. 'Now let's see. How about footwear?'

'This is it,' I said kicking my Roman sandals forward.

She gave a dismissive wave. 'I know just the thing to spruce those up.' She rummaged around in her makeup suitcase and pulled out a pink ribbon. A snip in two and she tied a neat bow over each buckle. 'There,' she said standing back. 'Not the ideal colour but much better. Let's get going.'

There was a steady flow of people headed to the hall. A possum scurried along the wire, as far from the rowdy crowd as was possible. It was five o'clock. Outside, sack races and lollie scrambles entertained the young while inside fruit punch and a cool keg of beer warmed adults' cheeks. Green and yellow bunting hung in loops all around the hall. At the far end two trestle tables were covered in white paper laden with chocolate coconut-dipped sponge, asparagus rolls and small mince pies. On the stage a skiffle band was set to get the dance floor stomping. One ukuele, a T-shaped instrument with beer bottle tops loosely nailed to the cross bar, and a makeshift double bass made from a tea chest. In the corner, a round-bellied man lifted the old piano lid on boney yellow keys.

Hilda's elbow angled into my ribs. 'Here he comes,' she whispered from the corner of her mouth.

I looked up thinking her husband had arrived. Instead, Drago walked across the floorboards, his shoulders wide and a on his face a ready smile.

'Good evening, ladies. You've scrubbed up well.'

'Yes,' said Hilda. 'Hope it was worth it.'

'Sure was. You make a man feel like he's a kid looking at a lolly shop,' he replied, all brille cream and confident. I felt uncomfortable under his stare.

'That's nice of you to say,' replied Hilda.

I looked away and a woman with a large tin of Arnotts biscuits and box of Macintosh toffees came zeroing in on us.

'Want to buy a ticket for the raffle?'

'How much,' said Drago.

'One shilling. But six for five. All for a good cause,' she added. 'Going to the Van Dijks. The family who lost their boy.'

Drago bought twelve tickets. I was not sure whether it was out of compassion or more a need to impress.

'So Hilda, where's you husband?' he asked.

'He'll be here soon,' she replied and her eyes flicked around the room. 'He's found work. I could be leaving in a couple of weeks.'

'We'll all be out of here soon enough,' he said turning back to me. 'Except for you Lidia?'

His comment struck a nerve and I turned my head away. In the glass window I glimpsed my reflection. It was not what I remembered.

'Hilda!' A voice yelled out from the hall entrance.

On seeing his wife, Günter stood with his hands splayed out from his sides as if the doors to his kingdom had sprung open. Delight flashed over her cochineal lips. Seconds later they collided in a hearty hug. They held each other as if everyone else in the room faded away.

'Those two have got it made,' commented Drago and his hand rested on my shoulder. He gave it a slight squeeze. 'You look like you're in need of a glass of "happy juice". Wait here I'll be back.'

The band struck up and it was not long before Hilda and Günter were threading a path from one corner of the dance floor to the next.

'Come on, you too. Loosen up,' she said. 'I insist you dance the next one.'

'I don't know how,' I replied.

'Then it's time you learnt.' She nodded towards Drago. 'Show this girl how it's done.'

He twiddled the thin gold chain around his thick neck and cocked his head.

'I'd be happy to. What do you reckon, Lidia? Can I have the next dance?'

'If you don't mind me stomping on your toes?' I replied.

'My toes would love it,' he said and his grin stretched his thick moustache further across his cheeks.

He pulled me onto the floor and we were followed closely by Hilda and Günter. He placed my left hand on his hip and held my other hand.

'Just follow. Let me do all the work. Easy,' he said and he raised his leading arm up and pumped the air, scooting me in and out, forward and back. It was more like he drove me than a graceful glide around the dance floor but the rigid distance I kept fell away. Soon enough he held me to his chest, taking the liberty to fob off any advances from other single men. His size making it clear there was no dispute.

'No my friend, the lady is with me,' he said before I had a chance to reply.

By the third glass of punch I was relax and loosening my opinion of him. I looked up to see Hilda and Günter exiting through the entrance doors.

'So tell me,' he said. 'What do you want out of life?'

'I could have told you that a few years ago. I don't know anymore,' I replied.

'You must have some idea,' he probed.

I shrugged, and so he took it upon himself to tell me what he wanted.

'I do,' he said. 'I'm going to make a go of it. I can promise you that.'

'What did you have in mind?'

He leant back, raising the front chair legs off the floor. 'I'm going to save enough cash to buy a house. Then go to Sydney. Join a friend of mine working as a bricklayer. He tells me there are a lot of jobs up there. But first I'll make my money in the mountains.'

He looked over waiting for a reply.

'The difference between us,' I said. 'Is that you came here by choice. You had a plan of what you wanted to achieve. I've none. My English is not good enough to get a good job. So first thing I want to do is to learn English.'

His mouth turned down. 'English or no English, I reckon anyone can make a go of it here. This country is ripe for the picking. I'm going to pick it dry.'

He took a large swig of beer, as if seeking fortification, then wiped his arm across his mouth. 'I find out tomorrow about the job. Then I'll be off. Last thing I'd want to do is to wait around here forever.'

He drew in a deep breath and paused for a moment as if lining up his sights on a shotgun. He leant forward. His eyes bulged and his cheeks were taught. His next statement blasted all sensibility from me.

'Here's a thought,' he said. 'Why don't you marry me?'

It took my breath right out, causing a coughing fit. He jumped up and slapped my back a little harder than was necessary. In an instant I stopped and he sat back down on the edge of his seat, waiting.

'Well?' he said reaching for my hand. 'I'm serious. Think about it, it would solve your problem. I get a wife. You get a husband, a house, maybe a family and a life.' He added with a wink. 'And you won't have to scrub floors for a living.'

'You can't be serious,' I said. 'I don't even know you.'

'So? What does that matter? We'll have time for that. I'm healthy, a good worker and one day I'll have money in my pocket. What more could you want?' he said and his arms opened out as if he was a platter full of goodness. 'I could possibly get a company house. It's village is only three kilometres from the construction site.'

He pushed back into his seat and took a breath. 'What do you reckon?'

'I think it's a crazy idea.'

'Come on, Lidia. Just think. You could be a housewife.'

He said it as if that was a prize not easily dismissed. He rose to his feet. 'Come we better get a move on. Even the band has packed up.'

We walked back to my hut in silence. Above, a crescent moon sliced through a gun metal sky and hundreds of flying foxes glided silently north toward the orchards. When we arrived he stood in front of me with his two hands clamped on mine. There was nothing soft about him. He was no intellectual but he knew exactly what he wanted and that included me.

'The paper-work comes through in a couple of days.' He hesitated. I'd be a good husband. I'm no doctor or lawyer but you won't want for anything,' he said grinning. 'You don't need brains to make it big in this country.'

In the hut a restless night lay ahead, not helped by the sound of blood-curdling calls of possums mating outside. I looked over to Hilda's bed, which remained untouched. No doubt she was in the arms of Günter, the thought of which was sending an empty ache to the pit of my belly. I felt I was stuck in some sort of holding pattern. I had no idea of who I was anymore. What was the point? Falling from one situation to another. Would it be like this till time carved its marks on me and I faded into obscurity?

When I closed my eyes Tatko, Mama and Raphael were all there. They would always be there. Waiting in the darkness to walk into my dreams. To take me back to where I once was. Maybe they were there that night to tell me to move forward. I thought about Petar and how inspiring he was. His fearlessness, his unbreakable spirit, and how the river would have washed clean all his hopes. Perhaps Hilda was right. Choices were few. There was no subtlety, no sensitivity, and no mystery to Drago. But he, too, had dreams. With a man by my side, perhaps it would be a good life or the best that it could be.

The following day Hilda was gone and Drago was suggesting we go to the milkbar, a short walk out of the camp. It was a place where singles mingled over vanilla milkshakes and burnt cheese sandwiches, and a place where furtive looks exchanged. He flashed his pound note about and ordered two milkshakes, two pies and two lamingtons.

With a loud slurp at the bottom of his milkshake he sucked up the last dribbles. A creamy froth covered his moustache half way to his nose. He swiped his screwed-up handkerchief across his mouth, gave a vigorous rub and returned it to his pocket. He pushed the aluminum container to one side and sat back for a moment looking on.

'What's your answer?'

I looked down at my ring finger. It was not how I imagined it would happen, if it were to happen at all. Under normal circumstances people meet with no pressure, to discover they had a shared intellect and an inexplicable attraction. But the rules had changed and we were strangers in a strange land.

CHAPTER 14

SIDE BY SIDE in the small Bonegilla chapel I said the words 'I do'. Ten days later we left. By then I had warmed to the idea of a shared life. Perhaps the change would bring us close.

Three days of heavy rain had broken the drought but the climb through the mountains was difficult and the jeep rocked and skidded. Along the freshly-ploughed track the country appeared lifeless. Blackened stands of trees stuck out at odd angles on the slopes. It was hard to imagine the summer's bush fire could reach the highest point in the land.

When Cabramurra came into view it appeared more as an isolated outpost than a township. On arrival I wondered who in their right mind would willingly choose to live there. Unpainted prefabricated houses sat on wooden stumps and barrack accommodation was scattered between the snow gums. But we could count ourselves lucky. We had a house, be it small and humble, and for the first time in a long while I felt a glimmer of optimism. I waited in the jeep while Drago went to the office and came back with the key. But when the front door slammed behind us he picked me up and carted me to the bed. His mouth sucked on my breast the way he slurped his milkshake. A thick hand clutched one breast, the other groped between my thighs. Within minutes my legs were spread and he was pushing into me. The whole process a matter of minutes and a couple of extra before he was asleep.

I sat up on the edge of the bed staring out of the bedroom window. The small of my back held a dull ache having been twisted this way and that. My only consoling thought was the next day he would be gone for six. Eventually I rolled back into bed, curled away, careful not to wake him. His loud breath never faltered. In the morning I waved him off and was pleased to see him go.

The rain kept coming, forcing me to stay inside. There was little to unpack, as we both owned one suitcase each. Most of the household necessities were provided. I was at a loss for things to do until I heard a knock at the front door. A short, stout woman stood buttoned to the collar wearing an oilskin parka, muddy gumboots and a kindly expression. Her no-nonsense haircut was flattened from her little plastic rain hat. She looked up at me through bright blue eyes, framed by Edith Piaf eyebrows that were her only sculptured asset. I had the impression she was a woman who enjoyed a good mopping up of the dinner plate.

'Good morning. I'm Martha Wilson,' she said shaking the water from her umbrella.

'Lidia,' I said tapping my chest.

'Pleased to meet you, Lidia. Bloody awful weather today. I hear it's only going to get worse tomorrow too. Mind if I come in?' she said already toe heeling her boots off at the front door.

'I thought I'd pop in and welcome you to Cabramurra. I'm from the Country Women's Association. Here take these,' she said handing me a plate of warm food wrapped in a blue and white tea towel.

She unbuttoned her coat and slung it over the crook of her arm. I closed the door behind us and she followed in her thick merino socks.

'Excuse my attire, but up here fashion goes by the wayside. That is unless there's a function.'

She looked about. 'It's not the Taj Mahal, is it? But you're lucky, Sid and Joan Thompson moved on and it came available. Most married couples up here live in separate accommodation.'

I gestured to the kitchen chair and she sat down and let out a sigh.

'I'm the secretary to the CWA and also the accommodation officer up here on the mountain.'

She looked at me. My confusion was obvious.

'Sorry dearie, you probably don't understand a word I'm saying,' she laughed.

From then on her speech slowed and she resorted to hand movements and mime. No doubt she was used to dealing with new migrants and had perfected how to get her message across. She swept her arm about. 'You're going to need a few extras in here.'

Then she crossed her arms and clutched her shoulders. 'As well as a kerosene heater. A couple of months and the weather will be freezing the sheets on the clotheslines.' She smiled. 'But don't worry just leave it up to me, Lidia. I'll get you sorted.'

'Sorry English not good,' I said.

'We'll sought that out too, Lidia.' She laughed.

'How about we have a cuppa and a few of those pikelets. Mind if I put some water on the boil?'

She turned the kitchen tap, filled the pot then placed it on the stove. In her string bag she had bought a pint of milk and a packet of Bushells tea.

'Nothing like a nice cup of tea to get the conversation going. Now if there's anything you would like me to do or something you need to know just ask?'

I opened and shut my hands and splayed them open again.

'Books? she said. 'Is that what you want?'

I nodded.

'No problem, but they'll all be in English. Best we get you started on English lessons down at the hall. It's also a good way of meeting the other wives.'

She stopped to catch her breath. 'I hear you're newly wed,' she said tapping her ring finger. 'Maybe there'll be the "pitter patter" of little feet soon.'

I looked at her, confused, and she rounded out her hand in semi-circle over her belly.

'Babies,' she said grinning.

I shook my head. 'No.'

'Yes, probably be a bit soon for that. But you never know when

190

you hit the jackpot.' Her expression changed. 'Unfortunately for Bill and I, it wasn't to be. But dare I say we have our fair share of nieces and nephews.'

'No children. One day nurse,' I said pointing to myself.

'Are you saying you want to be a nurse?' Her eyebrows raised and her chin pulled in.

'Yes,' I nodded.

'But you're a wife,' she added.

I shrugged.

'I learn English.'

'Yes, that you can. But in this country you can't be a nurse.' She pointed to her finger. 'Married,' she said, shaking her head. 'I hear it's a bit different from where you're from. But here, once a woman is married she becomes a homemaker. A very fine profession it is too.' She nodded. 'You'll get all your first aid qualifications looking after your family. Believe you me. My goodness, yes. Bandaging knees and taking temperatures.' She laughed. 'I might not have children but my Bill is always coming back from site with a cut and a bruise.'

I could only pick up part of her conversation but she made it clear becoming a nurse was out of the question. I was confused. As she sat opposite sipping tea the impact of what she said settled in. Marriage was far reaching. What if I never grew to love Drago? What if children were to be the shackles to bind me to him?

'Yes, there's not a day goes by when there's some incident up there,' she said.

She nattered on as if to try and cover up for the look of disappointment she may have caused. But her smile had slipped away. I had no idea what she was saying. Her speech was coming fast and furious.

'God rest their souls,' she said. 'I try not to think about the mishaps that go on in those tunnels they're building. But one can't help worry. Especially after hearing what happened last month.' She shook her head and made a tut tut sound. 'Those poor Italian boys. Heads blown clean off. Bill said the blast went wrong. A rock sheared off and hurtled over seven hundred feet back down the tunnel. They shut down Tumult for the rest of the day. Men came back crying. Awful it was.'

For a moment her thoughts seemed far away then she stopped and looked over. 'Oh my goodness gracious me. I shouldn't be telling you this. It was just an accident. Could have happened anywhere,' she said placing her cup on the saucer. 'Let's cheer up. Lets try one of these pickelets before they get stone cold.'

I peeled one off the little stack smeared with lashings of salty butter and took a bite. The feather-light pancake glided down my throat.

'I'll tell you what. All's not lost,' she said. 'I'll have a talk to the doctor here. I'm sure a little help wouldn't go astray.'

Martha proved a great help. Within a few days she had introduced me to the little band of women in the community and I had attended one English lesson. When I told her the only thing I knew about cooking was how to peel a vegetable she was right by my side, eager to impart her cooking skills.

'Don't be shy with the salt. That's it,' she said, close on my shoulder. 'When the meat changes to grey you know it's cooked. "Hubby" is going to be so impressed.

She nudged me in the ribs. 'He's a lucky man. This is a never- fail recipe. My Bill can eat the whole pot full but I never let him get away with it. It's good to keep a little aside for leftovers on toast.'

Half an hour before Drago arrived home she waved goodbye. I felt sure he would be happy with my efforts, though I held mixed feelings about his return. I caught myself speaking out loud, 'I just need to get use to him.'

But when he flung the door open and hollered. 'Where's my Balk?' I felt worse.

It was the sixth day around six o'clock and his voice ricocheted off the walls. His safety helmet was tucked under his arm, and a thick layer of rock dust covered his face. He hung his coat and headed straight to the bathroom. When he returned he was all smiles.

'Aren't you happy to see me?' he said taking hold of me.

'Of course I am,' I said returning the smile but I wondered how long my charade would turn to genuine desire. Was it just a matter of time? Was it that I needed to change the way I viewed love? The desire I had experienced with Petar came out of nowhere. At first no, but in a few months he took over my every thought until I was prepared to throw caution to the wind. I looked into Drago's eyes and saw nothing. Maybe that, too, would change. When he put me down he planted his thick lips hard on mine. I felt the kiss of a stranger. He let go and kicked his kit bag to the corner of the room and sniffed the air.

'Hmm, something smells good.'

He followed me into the kitchen but not without a little squeeze to my bottom as I leant over the stove.

'I can see you've been busy,' he said approvingly. 'I hope you've been behaving yourself.'

'I had a visit from Martha Wilson,' I said lifting the lid on the pot and giving it a stir. 'She's from the Country Women's Association.'

'Hmm,' he grunted.

'She was very helpful. She gave me this recipe.'

'I like Martha already,' he said dunking a tasting finger into the pot and raising it to his lips.

'She's been really helpful. She showed me the library, I got some English books and she introduced me to the doctor.'

'The doctor. What's the problem?'

'Nothing. But she suggested perhaps I could help out at the doctor's room.'

'And why would she suggest that?'

'I just happened to mention I'd like to be doing something. Save getting bored. Be useful.'

'Useful? Well you better make sure that doctor keeps his sticky hands off you,' he said with a chuckle. 'Or he could be choking on his stethoscope.'

'You don't need to worry,' I replied.

'Oh yes I do. A doctor could have a field day up here in the mountains when husbands are slugging their guts out underground.'

'The doctor's a woman,' I replied curtly. 'She's very nice. Her husband is also working up at Tumult.'

'What's he do?'

'He's the lead engineer.'

'Huh,' he shrugged. 'One of the shiny white helmet mob. The type who doesn't know which end to light a stick of dynamite.'

I opened the cupboard and laid two plates down on the bench.

'So what else has been happening around here?'

'Nothing,' I said with a rising resentment.

He laughed. 'Ah the life of a woman, you get to do nothing and your husband feeds you. Speaking about eating?'

He pulled the chair away and sat down rubbing his hands together gleefully. His knees spread wide and his chin rested in his hand as if he had been waiting to be fed for hours. I placed my carefully-mastered meal in front of him. The niceties of our short courtship were slipping away rapidly. I was learning all too quickly companionship was not what he needed but rather a hot meal and a woman in his bed.

He dragged his nose over the food in a circle and inhaled deeply, then looked up at me with a satisfied grin. His knife and fork upright in his large hands. As I watched him shovel the meal into his mouth my own appetite diminished. The smell of lamb chops filled our kitchen and I sat opposite with little desire to continue the conversation. Hunched over his plate he dragged the chops between his clamped teeth. Back and forth, back and forth, this way and that, his "barn yard" manners in full view. Sometimes he looked up at me, the whites of his eyes showing underneath. As the bone exited his mouth with a suck and a slurp, his greasy fingers piled the remains in a shambled mess at the side of his plate. All too quickly his accumulating wisecracks blackened my mood.

Months on blizzards battered the houses, water froze in pipes and mountain men struggled with jackhammers and granite. But despite the conditions, my life was finding order. I came to treasure the days Drago was away on site. An introduction to Dr Ann Foster was a blessing. She was a tall, slim woman, fair skinned with round hazel eyes and calm manner. Calm, a necessary requirement in a place with little support and a great deal of demand. She sat me down next to the narrow bed with a crisp white cover.

'Martha tells me you're interested in helping out around here.'

'Yes. I learn English quick. My father doctor,' I added eagerly.

'I see. Well I won't be giving you much to do in that line of work but I would appreciate you keeping this room clean, and keeping an eye on what supplies we need.'

When I was not working with her, I set about to learning thirty English words a week. I figured by the time we left Cabramurra I would have raised my level of competency. However, it seemed the more I studied the more Drago mocked. Somehow he derived great pleasure from it. I tried to ignore him until one day I could no longer "hold my tongue".

It was Sunday night and we walked back from the community hall. His large arm swung around squeezing any affection from me. We entered the house. He undid his belt and sprawled himself out on the bed. I sat down at the table and proceeded to jot down a few words hoping my interest in the dictionary could delay the inevitable. But his head rose up on his tight neck and he slapped the side of the bed.

'Put the book down. You don't need that stuff. Come here and be a wife.'

I looked up from the table. 'I want to speak English,' I replied.

'Huh,' he scoffed. 'That's a waste of time. You're a woman. If you cut out the tongue of a woman she'd still gossip.'

I slammed the book shut. 'I'm not like you,' I snapped.

'What do you mean by that?'

'I'm not happy with a few words to get by. You don't want to know anything other than to know how to beat the other men at poker or how many beers you can throw down your throat!'

It was the first time I had challenged him. He jumped from the bed and with his finger pointed straight at me he poked the air close to my face.

'Remember who puts the food on your plate and a roof over your head. You and your education. Where did it get you… nowhere! Little Miss Fancy-pants.' He scoffed. 'You think because your father was a doctor and mine was a plumber that you're better than me. Well doctors and plumbers are no different they still have to clean up others' shit!'

He flung the door open and kicked it shut behind. Numbness

took me over and I sat unmoving at the table. I hoped he would be drunk enough not to bother me when he returned. The last thing I needed was a sweaty entanglement with a husband who saw me as little more than his chattel.

It took a few days before we were back on track. Or rather we gave the appearance we were. He seemed to be resigned to his unresponsive wife and me to his wise cracks. We communicated, but deep down it was obvious neither of us cared.

CHAPTER 15

FOR THREE DAYS a blizzard raged. Sleet blotted out the township and no amount of clothing could keep teeth from chattering or fingers and toes numbing. In the midst of the storm a baby was set to arrive. The Martinos had not taken heed of the doctor's advice.

'The baby's breech,' said Dr Foster. 'At thirty-five weeks it may turn but just to be on the safe side I suggest you spend a month in Cooma. That way you'll be close to the hospital if there's a problem.'

Maria's mouth turned down. 'Lorenzo needs to work another fortnight. He won't be happy Dr Ann. There's a big bonus coming if he stays a couple of weeks.'

'Well Maria, there is also a big baby coming. Would you like me to have a word to Lorenzo?'

'No, No Dr Ann. I'll wait. We'll go in two weeks.'

But things did not always go to plan and on a night where the wind gusts were a 100km per hour, Martha Wilson's solid frame struggled to cover the hundred metres between the doctors room and our house. Soon enough she was at the door banging her fist.

'Lidia! Lidia! Come quickly, Maria's waters have broken. The doctor needs us.'

We hurried back with our arms tightly locked together and our boots stomping a deep path through the snow. Despite the roar of the wind it did nothing to muffle Maria's screams. For a small woman her voice had the capacity to raise the roof and beyond. My heart pounded. I had never witnessed a birth and had no idea what the doctor had in mind for me. When we entered the room, Maria lay on the bed, her forearm covering her face, her knees up and in front a belly the size of a basketball.

'Martha, shave and clean Maria's privates. I'll prepare the birth kit,' said Doctor Foster lathering soap up to her elbows.

Martha's eyes bulged at the thought but as for Maria she was too far-gone to entertain an element of embarrassment. The doctor looked across to me.

'Don't look so terrified. If Maria catches a glimpse of your "roo in the headlights" stare she'll scream even harder," she said from the corner of her mouth. 'And right now if that baby of hers is listening to this commotion, I'm sure it's having second thoughts about coming out into the world.' She smiled. 'First time you've seen this?'

I stood in the doorway to the surgery with my head nodding at a rapid rate.

'Welcome to nursing, Lidia. Now listen,' she said, shaking her hands and drying herself off. 'The pipes are frozen up so go grab a large pot and fill it with snow. Let it melt on the stove and when it's boiled, pour it into the tub. Then repeat. We're going to need as much water as possible.'

By the time the tub was half full the baby's head was emerging.

'Good girl, Maria, I can see the head,' said Martha leaning over to take a peek.

Maria 's hand went down to feel but another contraction sent her bloody hand gripping the bed sheets. More yelling insued.

'Come on, Maria, a few more pushes and this will be over,' said Martha wiping her brow.

But the doctor knew otherwise. The head and neck presented but the shoulders failed to deliver.

'Dytocia, Turtle sign,' muttered Dr Foster grimly.

Maria was none the wiser, neither were Martha and I, but when the doctor muttered, 'We have less than four minutes to get this baby out,' the gravity of the moment hit.

'Pull your knees up, Maria. Hold them hard against your body. Martha call the time out every thirty seconds. Starting now. Lidia listen. We're going to turn the baby. I want you to push down firmly. Like this. Not too hard. Not too soft,' she said applying two hands just above Maira's pubic bone. 'Understand?'

I came around the other side of the bed and pushed down on Maria. The baby's face was in full view but I could not bring myself to watch, instead I looked away. Martha's eyes never strayed from her time-keeping, and Maria hugged her knees hard enough to turn her knuckles white.

At four minutes Martha's counting faulted. She cast an anxious glance at Dr Foster.

'Keep counting,' she said.

'One, two, three, four, five, six, seven...' Martha continued.

On the count of fifteen a slippery boy delivered into the hands of the doctor.

'You did it Maria. A baby boy!'

Dr Foster held the baby up by its ankles. It dangled lifeless. Not a sound. She rubbed its back vigorously. Still silence.

'Martha get the scissors. Cut the cord. Clamp it.'

She carried him to the table and placed him on the towel. His head was turned sideways and his arms splayed away. Death hovered close. She went about clearing his airways.

'Is he all right Doctor?' cried Maria, lifting her head up off the pillow. 'Doctor is he all right?'

'Yes,' she answered.

But we all sensed it was not the case. I lay my arm over Maria's shoulders and an agonising wait insued. The doctor's hands wrapped around the baby's torso and she pumped his tiny chest with her thumbs. His lifeless body rocked up and down. A minute later there was a faint twitch of the unbilical cord and a rosy colour flushed through his limbs. She dangled him high by the ankles and delivered a slap to his bottom causing his little face to skew. Never had a cry been more welcome.

'Whahoo!' hooted Martha clapping her hands enthusiastically.

'Mother Mary, Mother of God,' said the doctor. 'That was a close call. But your little man has come through unscathed,

Maria. You can be proud.'

She wiped him down, wrapped him in a clean towel and passed him over. Maria held him close and let out a choking sob.

'Thank you, Doctor Ann.'

'Well if it hadn't been for my helpers, I'm sure this wouldn't have gone so well.'

She smiled at Martha and I and my heart swelled with joy. Working alongside the doctor was giving meaning to my life. In that moment in the early hours when a howling gale bought down tree bows and froze over wombat burrows, new life had arrived and a new beginning for me too.

'Jack's off sick so I get to head up the team,' said Drago. 'We've formed up the west section. Tomorrow we'll be pouring the concrete. There'll be a big bonus if we can get it done quickly,' he said rubbing his forefinger and thumb together. 'Once it's set as stiff as a dead man's dick, we'll form up the next.'

He dragged on his working boots at the front door and slung his bag over his shoulder. As he turned his back to leave, a sense of relief went through me. He would be gone for another ten days.

By mid-morning the sky was clear. The sun was taking the rigidity out of the day as icicles dripped off the trees. Two months had passed and spring was softening the landscape. Far off came the sound of the delivery truck winding its way up the mountain, bringing supplies from Cooma. Two houses down a line of towelling nappies were pegged up and steaming off as the air warmed.

Initially Maria had struggled to cope after the birth and The Country Womens's Association had formed a roster to help. There were ten of us but we all pitched in. Twice a week we met in the little community hall. It was mostly a social gathering, with cups of tea and knitting needles clicking in the background. My English was improving rapidly though sometimes a few of Martha's colloquialisms slipped into my conversation causing the three Australian women in the group to laugh.

'Looks like there's trouble,' said Martha looking out the window.

All heads turned.

'Why?'

'The doctor has just been picked up.'

Knitting needles stopped and the lightheartedness went out of the conversation.

Accidents were common at the site but this was big. Just before midday five men were buried alive in a shaft. Shivers of dread settled throughout the town. There was nothing to be done other than to wait, and soon enough the disasterous news was spreading like a grass fire. Men returned to Cabramurra shaken and drawn. Pete stood at my door, hat in hand. Drago was dead. I knew that by the look on his face.

'Mrs Milankovich, I've bad news,' said his friend.

'Come in,' I said.

He sat down in our kitchen and spoke in short sentences.

'We were set to pour the concrete,' he said. 'Drago was checking the flow. He'd done it a hundred times ... Nine tons of concrete was backed up...' He shook his head. 'The rock loosened. There was no stopping the flow. No one's fault. We did everything we could. I'm so sorry, Mrs Milankovich, so sorry.'

I did not cry, just listened and when he finished he, too, fell silent. What was there to say? My heart was never Drago's to break. Nevertheless it was a loss and the sadness that had befallen the township was dark and palpable.

'The company will make sure you'll be ok, Mrs Milankovich. Anything you need. You just have to ask,' said Pete as we to the front door.

He bowed his head then left, passing Martha walking towards the house. She comforted me and I cried into her shoulder, but if the truth were known it was not for the loss of Drago. It was more the loss of direction.

'I've no idea what to do,' I cried.

'Don't worry dear,' she said. 'We'll think of a solution. I'm going to have a talk with the doctor. I'm sure she'll think of something.'

'What do you mean?'

'Maybe you can become that nurse. Maybe she can put in a good word for you.'

I ticked single in the box under marital status on the nursing application and signed off. On December 3rd I was accepted at St Vincent's Hospital, Darlinghurst, for preliminary training. In the New Year I stood on the platform at Cooma railway station and looked up. *"Beware of snakes, spiders and venereal disease"* read the sign. No mention of falling rocks.

CHAPTER 16

I SETTLED into my new living quarters well. It did not bother me the Matron kept a strict routine and regularly took it upon herself to inspect our rooms. I was not sure why she would want to check the wardrobes though. Perhaps she thought one of the nurses might take it into her head to invite a male back for a little romance. The majority of enrolled students found the evening lock-down and restricted night outs a nuisance, but for me life had changed dramatically. I had found freedom.

The accommodation consisted of two single beds with blue covers, a free-standing wardrobe and a west-facing window. My roommate, Louise, laid claim to most of the wall space with Ricky Nelson posters and family photos, highlighting the bareness of the wall above my bed.

She was a country girl who had taken to city life with an endless supply of enthusiasm. Any excuse to swap her farm boots for sling-back high heels on a night out was welcome. Her chatter was proof that life on the family sheep station had been a sheltered one. She was my ideal roommate and sensitive enough not to pursue questions about my past.

It was a Thursday afternoon and the night roster had seen us rise at midday. She lay on the bed with a head full of hair rollers, skimming the *Woman's Weekly* magazine. I sat cross-legged on the floor browsing the discarded newspaper. Suddenly I caught my breath and sat bolt upright.

'What's the matter?' she said. 'You look like you've seen a ghost.'

'See this man,' I said holding the newspaper up. 'I know him.'

'How's that?'

'He was my uncle's closest friend. He's famous back home. I can't believe it.'

The write-up in the *Sydney Morning Herald* gave Milan much fanfare. I stared at the photo then read the article with my head spinning.

VISITING VIRTUOSO VIOLINIST

The recent cultural exchanges between the East and West have seen an increase of Soviet companies coming to Sydney. The Bolshoi Ballet, The Berioska Dance Company and the Moscow Circus to name a few have seen record audience attendances. Now the extraordinarily talented violinist Milan Karavelov will be performing in Sydney on August 13th and 14th at the State Theatre. Following performances will include Melbourne 15th and 16th, Adelaide 18th and 19th.

Originally from Bulgaria, Karavelov was identified

as a child prodigy and at the age of sixteen was offered a
scholarship to the Moscow Conservatory. Although little
has been known of this talented musician here, in his home
country he has hero status. For classical musical fans, get set
to be dazzled. Tickets will go on sale on August 1ˢᵗ.

I dropped the paper in my lap and looked straight back. 'I
can't believe it, he's coming to Sydney.'

'Then we must go see him,' said Louise jumping off the bed
and sitting next to me. 'Does he know you?'

'Yes.'

'Does he know you live here?'

'No. Nobody does.'

'Why?'

'I can't write home. The mail's censored.'

'Maybe you can get to see him somehow?'

'No chance. He'll have minders. He can't mix with
Westerners. The only reason they allow artists to leave the country
is to show how superior the Communists are and to make money
for the government.'

Louise took the paper from my lap. She looked at the photo
with her brow creased. It was obvious she was not going to have a
bar of what I had said.

'Nonsense, I don't agree. There must be a way of getting him
to notice you. And if you could, he would be able to tell your
family he's seen you. There's got to be a way.'

She looked across to me and with an afterthought added.
'This is so exciting. It's like something out of a James Bond movie.'

I wanted to tell her that it couldn't be further from the truth. Her enthusiasm for an adventure saw her busy mind scrambling to cook up a plan.

In his younger days Uncle Boyko had fancied himself as a professional musician. But although he was accepted to study at the Sofia Conservatorium his grades were mediocre and his dream of playing in front of a sellout crowd never eventuated. Instead, the only instrument of sound that he played on a daily basis was the bell on the Sofia tram. Nevertheless, in his free time he had loved nothing more than to drag out the tuba, spark up the gramophone and play the "Russian Sailor's Dance" along with his chosen recording. However, despite his own musical shortcomings it was with much pride he made it known that Milan was his closest friend. He was the country's finest violinist, and for Uncle Boyko that was good enough.

I remembered the noisy occasions when our two families got together and enjoyed a meal with his famous guest. They were childhood friends who shared a common musical interest. And although Uncle Boyko could never be the child prodigy that Milan was, their friendship endured despite the separation. When Milan went to study with Moscow's elite, they wrote regularly and when he came to Sofia it was cause for celebration.

Louise was right. An opportunity was being presented. I would have to get a message out. It was crucial it go undetected. It must not have the potential to put anyone in harm's way. Perhaps I could give something to him. Something that only he or my family would know the significance of. There was no telling how it would be received but I had to try.

By the following morning I had come up with a plan. When I raised it with Louise her eyes sparkled and for a short moment I was conscious that perhaps her excitement would be too much for her to contain.

'If I tell you, promise me you won't tell a soul. It's life and death Louise. Understand?'

Her wide eyes lost their sparkle and she stared back at me. 'Promise,' she said.

'He's coming in eleven days. I'll buy two tickets for the Sunday performance. I think it's better than Saturday as the crowd won't hang around after the show. We could wait in the street and approach him before he's driven away,' I said.

'But how are you going to know where he'll exit? We could be waiting out the front and miss him. He could be taken out the back door.'

'Yes, true. Maybe we should go check out the State Theatre. Find out where the performers enter and exit.'

'Good idea. But do you think he'll recognise you?'

'Probably not. Last time I saw him I was twelve.'

With that said we both fell silent. If I did manage to make contact there was no way I could speak to him. He would be under close scrutiny. There had to be another way.

'Oh gosh! Look at the time,' said Louise jumping to her feet. 'We've got fifteen minutes to get to the ward. Sister Barrett will have our guts for garters if we don't get down to the ward quick smart.'

We slammed the door to our room, took off down the hallway straightening white stockings and clipping back curls. Throughout the day my mind was focused on a plan.

'Nurse,' said Sister Barrett with a tight mouth. 'A little concentration wouldn't go amiss around here.'

'Sorry, Sister,' I replied.

My eyes flicked over to the bed opposite. Next to Mrs Henderson's yellow rose arrangement, taking up most of the bedside table top was a stuffed toy Teddy bear. The kind the hospital florist liked to sell as an added extra. Around the toy's neck was a large satin bow. '

'What's the matter with you today?' snapped the sister. 'Stop daydreaming or you'll get double bed pan duty.'

For the rest of the afternoon I maintained my focus but during the break my thoughts raced. I could hardly contain my excitement when I finally had a moment to tell Louise.

'I've found a way,' I said.

'How?'

'I'm going to buy one of those toy Koala bears and give it to him. I'll write a message in pencil on the inside of a ribbon and tie it around the neck of the toy.'

'But won't they get suspicious.'

'Maybe. But if they do there'll be nothing to see, as the seams of the toy will be intact. If they did take the ribbon off all it would say is,"Uncle Boyko was right, you're the best. Lidia (girl in red dress.)"'

With our dress-circle tickets in our handbags and the toy tucked under my arm we climbed onto the Parramatta Road bus and headed for the State Theatre. Thirty minutes after the concert Milan stepped from the side entrance. He was dressed in a black tuxedo with a stiff white shirt giving him the appearance of a thin crow. The tails of his coat flicked backwards as he strode towards the waiting car. Two "minder", complements of the Russian Embassy, were at his side.

'Now,' I whispered to Louise and we both hurried on a collision path with him. The car door was open but before he could place his foot inside we rushed him. Louise, thrust the concert program in front of him with a pen ready.

'Milan… Please. Can you sign this?'

He smiled, took the pen and signed. I moved closer to him as Louise gushed enthusiastically. I was close, so close. My lips moved to his cheek seemingly to place a kiss but instead I whispered in my native tongue.

'Look under the ribbon.'

I handed him the toy koala bear with the large yellow ribbon. He shot a look straight back at me then stepped towards the rear door of the waiting car. With the toy tucked tightly under his arm and his violin case in his hand he climbed in. The escort slammed the door and jumped into the passenger seat alongside the driver. A few theatre stragglers stepped from the kerb just as the car was set to move off.

'Look at those rich bastards, you'd think their skinny legs could move a bit quicker,' scoffed the driver.

'Strange place Australia,' said the other. 'The rich are skinny and the poor are fat.'

I stepped back smiling and in my best English cried out. 'We love you Milan… We love you,' and I blew him a kiss.

He looked back through the rear window of the sedan. It was late in the evening but in the deserted street colourful shop windows were brightly lit and stocked with every imaginable enticement. The car sped off and we stood together at the kerb watching the amber tail lights turn into George Street.

'Do you think he understood?' said Louise.

'I'm not sure. I hope so,' I said.

CHAPTER 17

AT 11.30PM ON NOVEMBER 9, 1989 the Berlin Wall came crashing down. Suddenly Europe was filled with hope. On the front page of the *Sydney Morning Herald* a photo of East Berliners dancing infront of the Brandenburg Gate. It was accompanied by a report that other Soviet block borders were expected to follow suit.

As soon as I thought it safe I wrote to Mama but six weeks passed before it bounced back. Across the envelope in red: **RETURN TO SENDER.** I climbed the stairs to my apartment with the letter clutched to my chest. There was no alternative but to hold onto hope and so I wrote again, this time to Uncle Boyko. Every day I returned home impatient for news. Until one day it came.

I pushed open the wrought iron gate to the Art Deco building and walked to the rear of the letterboxes. Underfoot the path was slippery with the mush of fallen camelia flowers and the leftover rain dripped from overhanging tree branches. My cold fingers rattled the small letterbox key in the lock of number seven. I lifted the metal flap and reached inside. There was one quarterly electricity bill, one flyer for the new Italian restaurant in Harper Street and a council notification of a local road closure. But that was not all. I took a deep breath. A letter had arrived. It was all I could do not to open it then and there, but I needed to shut out the world, be in my own place, to take in what I needed to know. When I entered the apartment I switched on the light, flung my shoulder bag on the couch and sat down to tear open the envelope.

Dear Lidia,

It is with much sadness that I have to write this and my heart goes out to you. Your dear mother passed away on the 16th November 1964. She came to live here six months after you left and it was a comfort to have her with us. My father also passed away last year. Marko lives with his wife and two children in Stara Zagora but Mama and I are still living in the old apartment. I don't want to say much more in this letter but hopefully we will be able to meet in the future. It pains me to tell you this terrible news but we are also very happy to hear from you.

Love always, Yana.

I lay on the couch, one hand dangling to the side holding the letter and the other shielding the lamplight. I shut my eyes but when I sealed off the outside world an inner world rushed to the fore and grief overtook me.

I tried writing back but each time it got tossed aside and a month later I still had not written. A small part of me was saying get out of bed but it was cold and parts of the sheets not occupied by me held an unwelcome chill. I looked at the bedside clock. It was 7:05am and really no need to get out. There would be no more pulses to take, no drip bags to fill and no timetable to follow. I was going to miss being the ward sister but a month earlier I had handed in my resignation with an overwhelming desire to return to my roots.

Time as a nurse had given me a sense of community and working with longer-term patients I got to share a little part of their lives within the confines of the hospital walls. I reached over, gathered up the pile of cards on the bedside table and sat up in bed reading the farewell wishes from patients and staff.

I re-read Emma's card and smiled to myself. She was one patient who was particularly endearing. I met her when she was eight years old and critically ill. There was something about her that resonated in me. I often found myself spending a little extra time with her on the nights when she struggled to sleep. And there were times when I felt she would not get through her treatment. During her long stay in the ward we formed a close bond. I caught myself telling her stories of butterflies, Cinderella and her ugly blisters, and all the fairy-tales, with added extras that my father told me.

The tales would make us laugh and when it was her turn she would tell me her nightly adventures with her imaginary friend. She had a spirited imagination and an inner strength beyond her years. I felt sure it was the reason she won her battle. I hugged her hard and watched her leave hospital with a joyful anticipation that a second chance of life brings. I never forgot to send her a birthday wish and she never forgot me.

It was my birthday, the 11th of May. I was fifty-one years old and I was in a reflective mood. Not working can tend to do that. My mind went back to another time and another birthday, the day I turned seventeen.

I raised myself up from the bath and reached for the towel hanging on the back of the door. It was mid-winter but the residue of warmth left over from my long soak left my skin pink. I rubbed the towel across my back and leaned into the mirror to brush an eyelash away. Drawing my face closer, I stared at my reflection as a stranger would. My natural wave remained but peroxide had a tendency to turn hair strands to straw, and small capillaries were appearing at the corners of my nose.

I could not say the years had crept up on me because it had dished out its fair share of calamity, but the nursing profession had given me a sense of purpose. I took the kitchen stepladder into the bedroom and searched the top cupboard. I strained to pull forward the white plastic container lodged at the back. Carefully, I stepped down and placed it on the bed. I opened the lid and lifted the red dress out. The fabric had been folded for long enough that the creases appeared as a riddle of seams. I lifted it up, prised the pleats apart and fanned it out in front of the mirror. Age was drawing me back and I was pleased I had made the decision to book my flight home.

I stepped out through the exit of the airport arrivals door and into the late afternoon sun of a Sofia day. The taxi queue was long but the wait was short. A mustard cab rolled forward in the slow line until it stopped at the kerb. The driver got out, walked to the rear of the cab and sprung open the boot.

'Where to, lady?'

'Rakovski Street. Hotel Sofia, thank you.'

He heaved my suitcase up, tossed it in and I climbed into the back. The boot slammed shut. He opened the driver's door and manoeuvred his lardy layers behind the steering wheel.

'Where've you flown in from?' he said, turning down the radio.

'Australia.'

'Austria.'

'No, Australia.'

'How long were you there?'

'I wasn't on holiday. I live there.'

'Why leave paradise?' he said. 'Everyone struggles here, save for those turncoat bastards from the old regime, now wearing designer suits and doing shady business deals.'

I'm not sure what I was expecting but I was surprised by his negativity. 'I'm sure it will take time for the country to get on its feet,' I added but it did not appear to change his mood.

He shook his head. 'Not likely. It's as corrupt as it ever was.' He spat the ball of gum out through the side window and glanced back in the rear vision mirror. 'Why come back?'

'I don't know,' I said looking back at him.

'Do you have family here?'

'Yes,' I replied but his question took me off guard.

My stomach felt as if it was churning into a walnut shell. I had been in two minds as to whether to write to Yana but I held a deep mistrust of the authorities and preferred to arrive unannounced. Instead I had returned on my Australian passport, using my married name, thinking it safer.

'Will you stay in Sofia?'

'Not sure,' I replied.

'Darn lights,' he said, abruptly stopping the car a metre beyond the red light. 'They cause more problems than they're worth.'

I stared out the side window. In three decades the sprawl had made the outer suburbs barely recognisable but the closer we drove towards the centre the familiar rows of prefabricated units _worse for wear_ came into view. The old city stood in a maze of overhead tram cables, crisscrossed with wide boulevards. It felt as familiar as it ever had. The Sydney travel agent had recommended a small hotel but the shabby façade did not live up to its glossy brochure. Despite this, the bed was firm, the room clean and from the window I could see the distant snow caps of Mount Vitosha. I kicked off my shoes and lay down.

Next morning a honeycombed light shone through the lace curtains. I woke and peered several times at the bedside clock.

Jetlag had overtaken me and it was ten minutes to eleven. I headed down the hall to the common bathroom and turned on the shower taps. A loud hammering echoed through the pipes but it felt good to wash away the remnants of a twenty-four hour flight. I skipped breakfast and walked out through the hotel lobby with the curiosity of a tourist. Crowds of office workers weaved passed me as I made my way to Slavikov Street. It was busily upbeat. Gone were the ordered lines of people on corners ever hopeful the supply on offer had not run dry. Yanko's butcher's shop had been gutted and refurbished. The clunk of the cleaver on the chopping block had been replaced by the hiss of a coffee machine. The blue cow painted on the white tiles behind the bar was the sole reminder of its bloody history. I stood for a while and smiled remembering how the butcher's finger once graced my bedroom "museum".

Two blocks further down, on the opposite side was our old apartment. I took comfort that the sandstone exterior had seen little change. A wide median strip divided the street with the same large oaks I remembered. I crossed over and sat on the park bench. Three pigeons, the shade of tarnished silver, peeked through the remnants of a discarded lunch.

Time had lain to rest speculation of what would or could have been, and for a long while I could not bring myself to read my mother's words. I remember that winter day, alone in the Cabramurra house when I lifted out the old red biscuit tin. It was buried beneath Gabir's notes of encouragement and had taken me a year to open.

Dear Lidia,

I love you with all my being and it is with that love I pray every day that somehow you will have a better life. I am so very proud of you. Be strong and do not be sad for me.

Love everlasting,

Mama

In a public place I sat while scooters and cars carved their way up and down the street. It was all a blur to me. People went about their business and I went unnoticed, stuck in memory's grip.

A hundred metres from the corner of Doncova Street I gathered myself together and walked down the footpath. As I came closer my steps slowed and my heart hit a runner's pace. Aunty Iva sat frail and half asleep in a wheel chair with string shopping bags hanging off the handles. Yana's small frame and middle-age agility valiantly struggled to bounce the chair up the steps. On reaching the landing she wiped her brow and her flustered cheeks let out a forceful sigh. Suddenly I caught my breath and stood immobilised.

Then all at once I yelled, 'Yana!'

She turned quickly and Aunt Iva leant forward, straining to see what had grabbed Yana's attention. I removed my sunglasses.

'It's me... Lidia!'

She looked back squinting. Then at once her chin tucked, her hand flew to her mouth and her eyes popped. Both arms shot up and she almost forgot to put the brake stopper on the chair wheels.

'Lidia! Oh my God... It's Lidia!'

What she lost in height she made up in width and her hearty

frame clambered down the steps. She hitched her skirt and we ran at full force. Our arms flung tightly around one another. We hugged for a good ten seconds, until stepping back, hugging and stepping back again.

'Let me look at you. Tell me I'm not dreaming!'

'You're not dreaming,' I said.

The moment was almost too much to take in. We pulled away from one another and stood staring with hands to cheeks. Aunt Iva sat craning forward, with her bony fingers clutching the collar of her dress.

Yana turned back. 'It's Lidia,' she cried out.

Aunt Iva's head shook non-stop and her jaw trembled. Excitedly we linked arms and hurried back. As I came close she raised her hand up to me. I leant down and placed my arms around her twisted shoulders. For a moment I felt my own mother's face against mine but when I pulled back her face was riddled with deep lines across livid cheeks. She muttered something I could not catch. Her head shook incessantly as if telling herself that this was not happening, that this moment was not real.

Across the street a gypsy busker momentarily ceased playing and watched on. Then he tucked the violin back under his chin and resumed a more upbeat tune.

'Can you believe this?' said Yana with a teary smile. 'It's Lidia.'

'No I can't. It's a miracle.' She hugged me again.

'Look at the three of us. I can't believe it. Come inside. Come. Come!'

She opened the front door and I followed. In her excitement

she struggled to find the door key. We walked through to the sitting room where whiffs of a hearty vegetable soup lingered. It was not as I remembered because the peach coloured walls, net curtains and floral chesterfield couch gave the room a feminine feel but the mantel clock, the veneer wall unit and the hand carved Victrola gramophone still remained in place.

'I'm stunned to see you are still living here. This is wonderful news,' I said looking about.

'We'd been waiting to hear back from you but when no further news came we thought we'd lost touch again. What a surprise. How long are you here?' asked Yana.

'I haven't got any fixed time. I thought I'd just see how things panned out. I've left my job so I'm a free agent.'

'Wonderful news. We've so much to talk about.'

'Yes we have,' I replied and I picked up the framed photo of Uncle Boyko and traced my finger over the glass.

'He died of a heart attack,' said Yana. 'At least nature claimed him. We faired a lot better than you dear Lidia.'

I ran my hand over the timber top of the the Vitriola. 'I remember this,' I said.

'Yes, I told mother we should get rid of it. It only clutters the room but it was father's pride and joy and she can't bear to part with it. Remember how we use to gather around? We've still got the old vinyl records.'

She put her arm around me. 'Now come sit. We want to know everything, don't we Mama? Please, sit down.'

I moved the cushion and sat on the couch next to Aunt Iva. She looked at me with wet grey eyes, her head shook and her mouth quivered.

I took her crooked hand. 'How've you been?'

She nodded and Yana looked across.

'She doesn't hear very well, so don't be surprised if she gives you a wrong answer. She refuses to wear a hearing aid and the headscarf doesn't help'

Aunt Iva squeezed my hand. 'Malina. You... You're so much like your mother,' she said. 'God rest her soul.'

'I know,' I said and I leant closer to her. 'Yana wrote me, remember?'

She nodded but appeared as if she had not heard me.

'Your mother believed you had survived,' said Yana. 'But as time went by and with no news she went quiet. It was hard to say whether her heart stopped because of the embolism. Her last wish was to be taken back and buried next to your father.'

I drew in a slow breath. 'I tried sending a message via Milan. He came to Sydney. I never knew whether it got through.'

'Yes it did. He was unable to get to Sofia for four months but he found your message. He put two and two together but when he wrote to father he didn't mention it other than to say he had a successful trip to Sydney. It wasn't until he came to see us that he explained what had happened. He said at first he was really puzzled. He said you told him to look under the ribbon. When he got back to the hotel he untied it but couldn't see anything. He was about to cut the toy open when he saw your message on the inside.' She shook her head. 'Sadly the news was too late for your mother.'

I shifted in my seat. 'Tell me about her. What happened?

What did she say?'

Yana lit her cigarette and shook the flame from the match. She drew in hard. 'She said she knew you were leaving three days before. Not that you had told her or anything. It was just a mother's instinct. Then she found your little bag with your red dress inside and she stuffed the cigarette case underneath it. The night you left she went to bed early but stood at the window and watched you leave. The next day she locked herself in the house, afraid someone may enquire as to where you both were. But no one did. It wasn't until she returned to the factory after May Day that she learnt the news.'

'How?'

'The Darzhavna visited the factory. She was taken to the office. They handed her a brown paper bag with Raphael's bloody shirt in it. Evidently she collapsed.'

'Did they interrogate her?'

'No. When she gained consciousness the factory supervisor was with her. The officers had left. Raphael's fate was obvious but yours wasn't. She clung to the hope you'd survived because there was nothing of yours returned.'

Yana stood and walked out of the room. She came back with the martinesta and placed it in my hands.

'Your mother brought it with her when she came to stay.' Yana stroked my shoulder. 'Have you eaten?'

'No.'

'Good, I've made a pot of bean soup. Soup always makes you feel better.'

I held the little faded doll in my hands. After that we were quiet for a time. Yana set the table and I helped Aunt Iva into the dining chair.

'It seems strange to ask how you've both been, I said. 'So much has happened. It's hard to know where to start.'

'Maybe we start from the end,' she said as she ladled the soup into three bowls. 'Who knows it could be the beginning.'

I walked to the bench and carried a bowl to Aunt Iva.

'Thank you dear,' she said and her eyes never moved from me.

Yana wiped her hands on the kitchen towel and joined us at the table.

'Things have changed yet are still so familiar,' I said. 'All those childhood memories came flooding back when I was walking down the street.'

'Yes,' said Yana tapping the ash from her cigarette.

'Remember when Raph and I came to stay with you while Tatko took Mama to hospital with appendicitis and he mistook turpentine for Kerosene and turned the bedroom into a coal pit. I'll never forget his face when he emerged, he looked like an African. ?'

'That was a night to remember,' laughed Yana, barely able to get the words out. Aunt Iva looked on questioningly.

'You remember, Mama, when father poured the turpentine into the heater?'

Aunt Iva raised an eyebrow. 'Tut-tut,' she muttered. 'It took weeks to clean up all that soot.'

A heartwarming soup and a heartwarming story managed to lift my spirit.

'I passed the old apartment on the way. It was both

confronting and comforting all at the same time. I've so many
vivid memories of that place.'

'Yes, I still believe they relocated you because of that
apartment.'

'How's that?'

'A day after they took you away a party secretary moved in.'

'Really?'

'Yes. There was a rumour in the street that those
eavesdropping Lolovi's may have had something to do with it.
They became very friendly with the new occupants soon after.'
Her eyes flicked to me.

'A sign of the times I guess. You couldn't trust anyone
back then.'

I took another sip of soup and she continued.

'When we learnt of your escape Father travelled to Porgova.
He returned with your mother. She refused to walk past the
apartment... It upset her so much. Instead she'd go out of her way
to avoid it, always walking in the other direction when she went
to the shop.'

I placed my spoon down. 'I never got over the guilt of
leaving her.'

'I can only imagine,' said Yana. 'But you must. She would be
overjoyed to know you're here.'

'I'm so grateful to you both for having cared for her.'

'That's nonsense. We are family. That's what families do. Isn't
that right, Mama?'

Aunt Iva nodded. She leant across the table and patted my hand.

'Eat up, dear, your soup will get cold.'

'I will. It's delicious,' I answered, but as I raised each nourishing spoonful to my lips my need for nourishment was more inclined to learning what had happened since my departure.

'You said she had a stroke?'

'Yes,' replied Yana. 'But her health had gone downhill prior to that. After a time she seemed to retreat into herself.'

'What do you mean?'

'You probably don't want to hear this but seeing you asked. She started drinking. We told her it would kill her but all she would say was "that's ok." Then she started losing weight. It was a shock to see her that way. She had always been so particular. We were helpless. In the end I think she lost her will to go on. She collapsed at the tram stop. It was quick. She didn't suffer.'

Yana stood and put her arm around me. 'This must be hard for you to hear.'

'I need to know. I want to know everything. What about Raphael?'

'What do you mean?'

'Did anyone discover where his remains are?'

'No. We never did. We dared not look. We were all too afraid. It's odd how that never leaves you, even today. It drove your mother crazy, not knowing. Your friend Petar probably knew,' said Yana reaching for the salt.

I was instantly surprised to hear his name.

'He was killed,' I said.

Her eyes narrowed. 'No, that's not the case.'

I put my soup spoon down. 'What do you mean?'

She picked up her cigarette where she had left off. 'It was all very confusing really,' she said exhaling slowly. 'He was lucky. He was spared.'

'How do you know?'

'We received a letter from your friend. A girl called Anna. She promised your mother that if she heard anything she would write. Evidently there was a period of three years or so before Petar showed up in the village but no one really knew the full story. Anna said he had been captured trying to escape with you and Raphael and had been sent to a labor camp. He told the locals Raph had been shot and you had drowned in the river but as I said your mother refused to believe it. "I know my Lidia is alive she would say... I know she is."'

'Is he still in the village?'

'No he lives in Plovdiv now. Evidently he went back to visit his parents. And to the surprise of the locals he'd joined the People's Tribunal.'

I was shocked. It did not make sense. 'Why would he do that?'

She shrugged. 'Who knows? Probably fear of further persecution. Anyway, he's done pretty well for himself since the fall of the party. In fact if you turn on the evening news you could possibly see him.'

I met her look. 'How's that?'

'He's the Mayor of Plovdiv.'

'He's what!'

'Yes, I know. It's hard to believe he's had such a turnaround in fortune.'

My jaw dropped and I sat rigid in my seat. It was hard to digest. For no one expressed their hatred for the party more than

him. I could only imagine the terrible conditions he had endured
to change his heart with a broken spirit. My thoughts raced. I
needed to hear it in his words. To know how he suffered. To let
him know I had survived and all the things that had happened
in between.

'I must see him.'

Yana collected the empty bowls, walked to the sink. She
half turned to me. 'You probably can. He's been in the news a lot
recently. He's getting flak from the press. There's rumours about
the handling of the local election. I guess that comes with the job.
I'm sure it will all quieten down soon enough.'

The clock on the mantel chimed five-thirty. Time had passed
quickly and I rose to my feet. 'I'd best be off,' I said. 'Jet-lag's
catching up but I can't tell you how wonderful it has been to find
you both.'

She put her hand on my shoulder. 'You must come and stay
tomorrow. Stay as long as you like. It makes us so happy to know
you're still with us. It means a lot. Doesn't it, Mama?'

We hugged tightly. 'I'd love to stay,' I replied.

Aunt Iva nodded and held her arms out. We kissed once on
each cheek and Yana walked me to the door. The day had been
happy yet harrowing all at once, and I needed to be alone. Back
in the hotel I turned the television on hoping to see some news
of Petar but there was none. I turned it off and lay back on the
bed with my mind racing. Minutes later I turned it on again and
flicked through the channels but still nothing. With no chance of
putting my questioning thoughts at rest, I dressed and returned to
the street in search of a peaceful place.

The "Jewel of Sofia" was now proudly flood-lit in the city centre and its many domes appeared like golden onions. It was the first time I had ventured into the church. In my younger days it was a great source of curiosity for the local children and often warranted a dare. Though for those who entered for spiritual reasons it was an invitation for ridicule. We loved to peer in through the entrance doors, fascinated by the candles and gold-leaf icons. Miraculously it had survived a torrid history. The heavy entrance welcomed me. I crossed the stone threshold as so many of the faithful had done before and entered the sanctuary. I took three thin candles from the wooden stand to the flame and placed them amongst many others. In the semi darkness, columns of sculptured alabaster rose up like ghostly witnesses to the past.

The following day I returned to Donkov Street. Yana's cigarette glowed brighter as she sucked air in and leant back into the dining room chair.

'After you left yesterday I remembered something else.' She paused. 'It was not long after the collapse. About a year ago we received a visit from a Turkish man. His name was Gabir.'

'Who?'

'Gabir. Gabir Yilmaz. He told us he'd found you on the banks of the Tundzha.'

'That's right, but what was he doing here?'

'He told us he'd taken you to Istanbul for questioning but had lost contact when you left.'

'How did he find you?'

'He said your Sofia and Polgova addresses were taken during the investigation and he had kept note of them. He came here first thinking you may still have family in Sofia. He did some tracing of his own and found us. I told him we had an idea you were in Australia and he seemed very disappointed to know that. Oddly enough it was only a fortnight later that we received your letter asking about your mother.'

I looked at her dumbstruck. She got up and walked to the sideboard and rifled through the draw, then pulled out a small note book. Inside was tucked a folded piece of white paper.

'I was going to send it to you but then thought better of it. The country was transitioning and I thought it was best to be on the cautious side.'

She passed it to me. 'Here's his address and contact number.'

I took the note and unfolded it slowly, shaking my head in disbelief.

'He said if you ever returned to Bulgaria he would be very happy to meet you again. He had coffee with us and left. Seemed pleased to have at least found us and was hopeful that we'd be able to pass on his address.'

She hesitated then continued. 'I'm sorry I didn't, I guess old fears and suspicions take time to abate.'

'I understand,' I said folding it up and placing it in my lap. 'Did you say it was a year ago?'

'Yes, just over... wasn't it, Mama?'

Aunt Iva nodded, though it was hard to know whether it was a nod of agreement or due to some neurological disorder.

'He was very polite and appreciative. Said he'd been a widower for many years and had one son. We were surprised he spoke Bulgarian fluently.'

She stood, and sensing the note had deeply surprised me she took three of her best crystal glasses from the cabinet and a bottle of Rakia.

'I know it's only eleven thirty, but I think we could do with a drink.'

She poured the clear liquid into the shot glasses. A dribble of alcohol slid down the outer edge of the third glass. She spilt a little more onto the living room floorboards, as was the tradition, and raised the bottle.

'Here's to the departed souls of our beloved.'

We raised our glasses and downed the fiery liquid in one gulp. I placed the glass back down and looked at her.

'You know, I was meaning to go to Polgova to visit the graves but I might just stop off in Plovdiv. It would be good to catch-up with Petar. There's so much to talk about.'

'Yes. I'm sure he'll be surprised to see you, but what about the Turkish man? He seemed lovely,' she said teasingly. 'Edirne is only a day's trip from Plovidiv.'

I shook my head. 'I don't think so. It's been too long.'

She stood. 'What nonsense. That doesn't mean anything. The man has obviously gone to a lot of trouble to find you. You must mean a lot to him.'

Petar's survival and Gabir's visit had given me a restless night. I woke tired and packed a small suitcase for a few days travel. I still felt sure my nerves would get the better of me and a rendezvous across the Turkish border unlikely.

The vast hall of Sofia's Central Railway Station stood testament to Brutalist Architecture, with its imposing structure and hefty concrete shapes. Inside Cyrillic letters flickered across the arrival and departure boards. Crowds milled around the timetables while bewildered others trundled suitcases looking for the right platform. I stepped up to the ticket office window. 'A one way ticket to Plovdiv please.'

The woman behind the glass partition had enough chins to create a small staircase. She grunted and typed in the destination. The ticket shot out from under the screen window at speed. I thanked her and walked to the coffee shop directly opposite. My intention was to stay one night in Plovdiv. I sat down, looked up at the clock and gauged there was another forty-five minutes before departure. Enough time to mull over the events of the past two days. Sipping a second coffee I watched the comings- and-goings in the station.

The train slid into the platform accompanied by boarding chimes announcing its impending departure at eleven-fifteen. I walked through the entry gate and along the platform to the first class compartment of the not-so-new carriage. I was thankful to see the group of adolescent scouts headed for a weekend's adventure, push and shove their way past to economy. The train pulled out and it was not long before we were speeding away from Sofia and snaking through orange poppies, willow forests and pastures. The sun flashed on the broken glass of a dilapidated greenhouse, no doubt a leftover from a collective farm. A hawk flew high in the sky and beside me sat a priest in his late seventies in a black robe overflowing into the aisle. His tangle-free white beard stretched to the middle of his chest and fluffed up around his ears before disappearing under the tubular base of his hat.

The scenery was sending my thoughts backwards. The train skirted the river, climbed out of the valley and continued to follow the main road south east. Through the window an isolated house appeared over the rise. A large stork's nest poked from the chimney and I wondered about the red and white Martenista doll I had made for my mother. It had no doubt hung like a bloody snowflake throughout the winter. Mama had accepted abandonment but I wondered at what point she had given up believing I would return. Was that the moment that killed her?

CHAPTER 18

I WALKED INTO THE FOYER and up the marble stair case of City Hall. A brass plaque with a painted hand pointed to the first-floor landing. Along the red carpeted hall hung gilt framed photos and paintings of past leaders, considered pillars of society. I stopped and gave the door a small tap before entering. The Mayor's secretary looked up through eye makeup more suitable for a midday pantomime. She sat filing her sharp nails behind a wood-paneled desk stacked with an overflowing "in" tray. I made my way over.

'Can I help you?' she said.

'Good morning. My name is Lidia Ivanova. I would like to see the Mayor.'

'Was he expecting you?'

'No… but… '

'I'm sorry he is unavailable. You'll have to make an appointment.'

'Is he in?'

'Yes, but as I told you he is unavailable.'

'I understand, and I'm sure he is extremely busy. Is it possible to see him sometime today?'

'I'm afraid he doesn't see people who walk in off the street. You need to go down to enquiries. They'll be able to help you.' She looked me up and down then said, 'You're not one of those reporters are you?'

'No, I'm an old friend. I'm sorry I know my approach is a little unusual but I'm from overseas and I shall only be in town for one night. Could you just tell him that Lidia Ivanova is outside?'

She took a long sigh and turned to tap the button on the intercom. A hacking cough echoed through the speaker on the other end.

'Are you ok sir?'

'Er... Yes,' came the reply, then more coughing until a few seconds later it settled.

'What is it?'

'Excuse me sir, but Lidia Ivanova is here to see you.'

'Who?'

'Lidia Ivanova. She said she is an old friend of yours.'

There was silence and I leaned across the desk. 'Petar, it's me Lidia.'

'What!'

'I'm outside.'

'Christ!' he stammered.

Immediately the girl's demeanor changed and she sat upright in her swivel chair.

'Please be seated. Can I get you something to drink?'

'No, thankyou.'

I doubted I would be able to hold a glass of anything at that moment. I turned and sat on the couch adjacent to his office. I concentrated hard on the detailed plaster ceiling and took three deep breathes. My clammy hands were clasped tightly in my lap.

The office door flew open and suddenly he was there. I jumped up.

'Petar!'

'Lidia!'

He looked at me as if he had seen a ghost.

'I can't believe it. I'm shaking', I said.

He walked towards me with arms outstretched. On his face was a smile I remembered from long ago. His pallor was ruddy, his dark hair was grey, thinner more on the top than the sides but behind the glasses and his well clipped moustache stood a man accustomed to wearing the finest Italian cloth on offer. We hugged and kissed both cheeks then stepped back and we looked at one another in disbelief.

'What a surprise! I'm flabbergasted.'

'Me too,' I said.

'You're blonde. It suits you. Obviously the years have been kind.'

'I'm not sure about the years being kind,' I said.

'Well good genes, my beauty. Good genes,' he said. 'Let me hug you again. I need to know it's really you standing in front of me.'

With that he wrapped his arms around me and the receptionist sat still and staring.

'This is not possible. It can't be real,' he said. 'I thought you were... You were... 'His words petered out but he quickly composed himself. 'How long are you here for?'

'Till tomorrow.'

'That's not much time to celebrate. Why didn't you call?'

'I wanted to surprise you.'

'You've certainly done that.'

'It was a spur of the moment decision. I flew in a couple of days ago and my cousin told me you were here. I had to come and see for myself. I just couldn't believe it. It crossed my mind that perhaps there was some mix up. Perhaps it was another Petar Borev.'

'Yes it's me all right. Just different circumstances,' he added with a chuckle and he stepped back. 'My! My! Look at you,' he said and he kissed my cheek once more.

He smelt good, perhaps the scent of an Yves St Laurent aftershave.

'Izabela, I shall be out of the office till three o'clock,' he said and his eyes never left me.

'But sir, you have a meeting with a representative from Tsankov Urban Developments at one thirty.'

'Cancel. Tell him I have an urgent matter. Slot in another time.'

'Yes sir.'

He hooked my arm to his. 'Come, my lovely, let's eat... We've a lot of catching up to do. This is unbelievable.'

I could not help be impressed by the level of his success. We walked out through city hall as he acknowledged the greetings from the passing public. It was a far cry from the life of a lowly field hand. With my initial nerves gone we strolled towards the lunch queue outside Adriana's Fine Foods Restaurant. He gave a sharp nod catching the eye of the maitre d' and we were whisked through the archway to a secluded table at the rear of the dining room. My heart beat quickly.

'Where are you living?' he asked.

'Australia.'

'Really.' His eyebrows rose. 'I can't believe you're here. I can't believe you survived that night. It's a miracle.'

'You too,' I replied.

He looked over the top of the menu and for a moment seemed lost for words.

'So what do you do in the wild west?'

'I'm was a pediatric nurse.'

'That's impressive,' he said and he waved down the staff.

The waiter scooted past the other tables and headed to ours with his note pad in hand giving me the impression he regularly received a hefty tip.

'Sir, would you like to order?'

'The usual thanks and bring us a bottle of your best red,' he said handing back the menu.

The young man turned and hurried back to the kitchen.

'I thought you wouldn't mind if I ordered. I come here most days to be wined and dined by eager developers. I know the best choices.'

I eased back into the chair. 'I'm sure whatever you choose will be perfect,' I replied. 'You've done well for yourself. Plovdiv is a step up from Polgovo.'

'Yes, it sure is. Anyway where the fuck is Polgovo?' he said and he laughed out loud.

He still had the same self-assuredness and cocky sense of humour I remembered. 'What made you go into politics?'

'I didn't want to be known as just a small town kid. I got sick of being bossed around… Decided it was better to be the boss than the underdog.'

He grinned and leant across the table and took hold of my hand. 'My God woman, you're still beautiful.' He turned my hand over. 'No ring on your finger I see.'

'That's another story,' I replied and withdrew my hand.

He leaned back into the velvet-buttoned chair but his relaxed manner was interrupted by a sudden violent cough. It sounded as if his lungs were about to rocket out of his chest and it left him momentarily red-faced and breathless.

'This darn cough just won't let up. Sorry about that. Anyway enough about me, tell me about you. It looks like Australia has served you well. I'm sure your life has been very interesting.'

His eyes passed over me and I felt weak under his gaze. 'We never did make it to America. We would have been so good together. I don't think you ever realised how crazy I was about you?'

It was true. I never did. Back then I thought I was the one more out of control. The times we made love I could have counted on one hand but it wasn't the act that mattered. I felt safe with him, like nothing could touch me while he was around. Then the pregnancy happened and I feared he would leave me behind. I wanted to tell him about that loss. The one he knew nothing of but the words got stuck on my tongue.

The meal arrived and I was grateful for the interruption.

His comment had taken me by surprise and I suddenly felt self-conscious. 'Yes, I wonder if America would have lived up to your expectations?'

'Maybe not, but I know you did.'

I felt uncomfortable and redirected the conversation. 'I see you're married. You must have met the right woman?'

He rolled his eyes leading me to believe that his private life did not match the success of his public one. 'Yes a wife who spends all the money redecorating and two teenage boys who I struggle to communicate with.' He tapped open his cigarette case and lit up. 'Anyway that's enough of my family woes.'

It was surprising to see his level of success and I felt momentarily dumb struck. I leant across the table. 'I was certain you were dead.'

He cleared his throat, re-adjusted his seating position and slowly poured himself another glass of wine. 'They needed one to interrogate. They wanted to know who else may have been involved.' He stopped momentarily and shook his head. 'Let's not talk about that,' he said. 'Let's talk about brighter things.'

'No, I'd like to talk about it. I couldn't believe it when my cousin told me you were alive. I was stunned. What happened that night?'

He drew in a deep breath and sighed. 'It was so long ago, but it still remains so vivid in my mind... When I got to the top of the bank, I heard the shot. Before I knew it three men appeared from the bushes. I was knocked to the ground and had a pistol shoved in my ear.' He paused for a moment then continued. 'I was darn lucky. They fucking nearly killed me then and there. I broke down. In total disbelief... I'd lost you. It was the worst moment of my life.'

He stopped talking and took another gulp of wine. His broad shoulders slumped and he paused for a moment. I felt sure he had not spoken of this for many years or if he ever had, it was clear he struggled with the memory of it all.

'The regime was like that… Some lived some died… Never any logic to it,' he added.

'Do you know what happened to Raph?'

'They dragged him up the bank, dug a trench and tossed him in. Then they shoved me into a military vehicle. It was unbelievable. I thought I had the whole plan sewn up. God knows how they found out.'

'What happened after?'

'I was interrogated for a few weeks. Then they sent me back to Lovech for three years.'

I placed my cutlery together on the plate of half-eaten food and he sat shaking his head. The pain of that night obvious on his face.'Those bastards knew how to break your spirit.'

'But you've such a strong spirit, Petar, and you've proven that.'

'Yes, but there were nights that I thought I'd go nuts.'

With that said he picked up his napkin and patted his moustache.

I knew it was difficult for him but I needed to know so much.

I continued. 'What did you do after?'

'After what?'

'After your release?'

He took a deep breath and a long sigh out. 'I know this sounds strange but I was so scared I joined the party.'

He hesitated for a moment, as if waiting for me to comment but I had nothing to say and he leant over and touched my hand warmly.

'It feels so good to see you. I thought about you for years. Those times we were together. They were so special.'

An awkward moment intervened, and an amplified silence descended both sides of the table. He turned his face away and smoothed the table cloth with his right hand. His left reached for his silk handkerchief. Small beads of sweat salted his brow and he discreetly wiped them away.

'The pain of that day never goes. I would have done anything to save him.'

I pushed the piece of carrot around my plate in silence. He reached for my hand.

'I can't tell you about the years of guilt that followed. The times I mulled over how I had failed you and what I could have done. But there was nothing.'

Our eyes met.

'Didn't you ever think it was odd they let us get so far before picking us up?' I asked. 'They must have known our movements.'

'Why do you say that?'

'Because it wasn't as if we were in a populated area. We were in an isolated part of the countryside.'

'It could be they wanted to see how we intended to escape. Maybe others would follow.'

'But how did they conceal their vehicle?'

'What vehicle?'

'The one you said they took you away in.'

'How would I know?'

'Well you'd think we would have heard or seen it.'

'They were obviously waiting hours beforehand.'

'But in that exact spot where we were to launch the boat?'

'I'm not sure what you're trying to say, and anyway we could discuss this endlessly and never come up with an answer.'

'I guess you're right,' I said and I rubbed my hand across my forehead. 'The food was delicious but these last few days have been rather hectic. I think it's all starting to catch up with me. Would you mind if we paid the bill?'

'Of course not,' he said and he beckoned the waiter with an authoritive wave. 'It's been wonderful to see you again. Where are you going from here?'

'I'm catching a bus to Polgovo tomorrow morning. Then I may head south to visit a friend in Turkey.'

He reached across the table and took my hand. 'If you're ever back in Plovdiv call me and I'll organise something special.'

'Thank you,' I replied. 'The lunch was lovely. I'm so pleased we could meet.'

He placed his business card in my hand, kissed me and walked off in the opposite direction. Amidst the office workers returning from lunch, I stood watching him walk across the square until he was masked by other pedestrians. I slowly walked back to the hotel. I dumped my shoulder bag on the corner chair, slipped off my sandals and propped my shoulders against the bed head.

My mind was a muddle of questions.

CHAPTER 19

THE DINNER MENU slid under the door but I was in no mood to eat. I preferred the comfort of the hotel room despite the television's poor reception. But morning brought with it a change of mood and I walked through the dining room doors and joined the small group of Russian tourists at the buffet. Room eight's occupant stacked her plate as if she had never seen a breakfast. Two hours later the same woman joined the bus queue carrying a bag full of rolls and a large chunk of cheese for the journey north.

The bus was parked amongst a line of other vehicles ready for trips to various locations within the province. Drivers loitered at the front of their vehicles, scratching crotches and joking, with an occasional spit full-speed to the gutter.

With my five lev ticket bought I strolled along the gum-spotted pavement studying the bus numbers until I reached number forty-seven. It was an old Russian Liaz, parked with its radiator cover propped against the right front tyre and a red stripe down the length of its beaten body, giving it the appearance of a spent tube of toothpaste.

'Sorry, the bus will be delayed another thirty minutes,' said the driver. 'Give me your case and I'll put it in the baggage compartment.'

Nineteen people milled about but once the hole in the radiator was repaired and the vehicle was declared roadworthy, chaos reigned. The casual crowd surged forward with menacingly sharp elbows to claim the window seats. With a twist of the ignition key and a number of engine coughs the bus juddered into action and the journey to Porgovo commenced.

We raced along the twisty road as if the driver had won tickets to the afterlife. Two miniature soccer balls dangled from the rear vision mirror seemingly dancing to the tenor voice bawling from the dashboard cassette. As we charged ahead, beet fields replaced the wheat and it was with a mounting apprehension I saw the orange roof tops of the old village. Compressed air hissed from the hot brakes and the bus edged to the kerb. I stepped down. The driver was close on my heels eager not to lose more minutes from his timetable. He shifted some of the luggage aside and with a vigorous tug removed my case.

'There you are, lady,' he said and he turned quickly and climbed aboard.

I stood with my suitcase at my feet. As the bus pulled away a smile crossed my lips. In the back window of the emergency door a freckled-faced boy waved to me with his nose firmly pressed to the glass.

I stood still and looked about. It was not as if the day wasn't perfect. It was not that the things looked different. It was an all-encompassing sense of loss that dug deep. Further down the road an old man with leathery skin and leather cap appeared atop of a horse-drawn wagon piled high with hay. Together they ambled past and he acknowledged me with a nod. It was as if the village had stood still though the town hall no longer dominated the square, and all that remained of Lenin's statue was the plinth where it once stood.

There was no sign of the fat boy with the vacant stare sitting outside the store and I felt sure my childhood friend Anna had long since moved on. I picked up my case and walked over. The bell tinkled above the entry door but it appeared the store was empty. It was stocked with all the basic necessities, saving the locals a trip to Topolograd. I failed to see the middle-aged woman with her floral headscarf busily knitting white booties and gnashing her jaw in time with her needles. My mouth was dry and I walked to the end of the aisle where cartons of mineral water were stacked in no logical order. I never remembered the store so stocked. I took a small bottle of water and was about to call for assistance when I noticed the shopkeeper.

'Dobra den. Just the mineral water thank you.'

The woman appeared surprised I spoke Bulgarian and I felt like a foreigner in my own land.

'So, you're not from these parts,' she said.

'I am actually.'

'Really…Where?'

'Right here.'

She looked puzzled and she squinted as she thoughtfully summed me up. 'When was that?'

'Thirty or so years ago.'

She put down the knitting needles and leaned on the counter. 'Is that so... I know everyone in the village... I must know you then,' she said, scrutinising my face. 'What's your name?'

My heart quickened. 'Lidia Ivanova.'

Her eye brows rose as if to take flight, dragging her hooded eyelids with them. She jumped up and let out a shriek. 'Lidia!.. It's me, Anna!'

In an instant my spirits lifted. She knocked over the three legged stool in an effort to get to me. Country life made her appear older but ten years disappeared in seconds with a smile. Few surprises happened in the village but this was a day to remember.

She jigged up and down with excitement and flung her arms around me. 'Lidia! I can't believe it. This is amazing!'

I hugged her tight.

'Good God I thought you were dead.'

'No, still here,' I replied laughing.

'Where've you been all this time?'

'Australia.'

'Australia! Who'd have thought. Your mother was right. You survived!'

I stood back. 'Look at you,' I said. 'You still have that wonderful smile.'

'Hmm, my face looks like an old boot. Not like you,' she said with a wide grin followed by a joyful laugh. Her hands went up and tapped the sides of her head repeatedly, as if the moment was scrambling her wits.

'This is amazing,' she said. 'This is the best day! And Australia… who would have thought you'd have ended up there. It's a miracle.'

She grabbed my hand and led me through the beaded curtain hanging at the back entry to the shop. 'Come meet my family.'

She pulled me behind her and struggled to get words out fast enough. 'This is my daughter Svetlanna and my son-in-law Grigor.

Her daughter held out her hand to shake.

'Svetlanna, Lidia has come all the way from Australia. Can you believe it! Australia! She's my oldest friend. We went to school together. The same class.'

Svetlanna was heavily pregnant, barely twenty and obviously the reason for Anna's furious knitting. She nodded and smiled back but Grigor remained oblivious. He sat on the edge of the couch in a green and white football jersey watching the Saturday morning tele broadcast of the match between Ruse and Stara Zagora.

'Huh, a bomb could go off and he wouldn't notice,' she scoffed. 'Svetlanna, mind the shop.'

We walked through into the kitchen. The once-skinny girl who had stood at the front door of our broken-down house with offerings from her mother's shop was now heavy-hipped and thick- waisted. But her warm heartedness remained. The sweet coffee brewing on the stove was poured into two cups and she grabbed a packet of unopened biscuits and tipped half on a plate.

'What a surprise. How long are you staying?'

'I was only intending to stay a few hours. I came to visit the cemetery.'

'Why leave so soon?'

'I have no particular plan. I thought it would be easier to get accommodation in Ruse.'

'That's out of the question. You will stay here. I insist. It's meant to be. Yuri's gone hunting this weekend. He's my husband, so if you don't mind sharing the bedroom then that's that. You must stay. We've so much catching up to do.'

'Are you sure it won't be too much trouble?'

'Of course not. And tomorrow we'll go to the cemetery and I'll show you your old house. You won't believe what it looks like now.'

Shop business was slow but the hours passed quickly, interrupted with an occasional tinkle from the bell, barely audible above the roar of the soccer game in the sitting room. She took the foldup bed from the laundry. Clean sheets were fitted and my temporary bed was set up in the corner of her room.

It was years since I had heard the sound of a rooster at dawn and I lay wondering whether it was from the same gene pool as the one that crowed proudly over our old house. We rose early, showered, and ate breakfast. Anna prepared a morning snack to take and found me a pair of ankle-length boots more suitable for a walk in the country. It was 8:00am when we stepped out into a perfect summer's day. It felt strange walking across the square with my best friend from long ago. We made our way along the main road. We waved a greeting to a local woman beating the grit from her prized tiger-print rug and she waved back with a look of curiosity.

'Give her ten minutes and the whole village will know I have a visitor,' said Anna.

We stood at the rusty gate of the old school where weeds poked through the asphalt of the yard.

'Do you remember the group exercises before class. We'd be struggling to do a few star jumps now,' she said digging me in the ribs.

The scent of the harvest was in the air and bees from Levski's apiary were up early sucking the sweet offerings from the clover. We reached the laneway to the house and it stood as before, isolated and hemmed-in by fields.

'It was empty for years after your mother left but finally it has new owners.'

I felt no connection to it but nevertheless it drew me back and I wandered around the perimeter. The vegetable patch and chicken coop were gone but the branches of the old pine still splayed across the yard. Now the sound of a renovator's hammer echoed from the kitchen walls.

Less than a half a kilometre south of the village was the cemetery on the hill. Before continuing further we sat down on the bank where overhead lichen clung to the underside of the old bridge. Anna opened the canvas bag and pulled out the thermos of coffee. I looked about, taking in the green fields and the stillness of the countryside.

'Things look the same.'

'No, life here is different,' she said.

'How's that?'

'The young people are leaving for higher-paying jobs. The garment factory no longer exists. You can't blame them. There's nothing here,' she said with a sweeping wave of her arm. 'The only ones left are the old living off their vegetable patch and chickens.' She laughed to herself. 'Who'd of thought democracy would trap us in poverty.'

'Maybe given some time things will get better,' I suggested looking up at the bridge.

'I hope so.'

'Had you ever thought of leaving?'

'No, I'm the main attraction in the village. No one would buy the store. Besides, I belong here.' She put her arm across my shoulder and smiled. 'What are you thinking?'

'I remember crossing this bridge with Petar in that rickety cart.'

Instantly her back stiffened. 'That bastard... we were pleased to see the back of him,' she said and her mouth tightened.

I was somewhat shocked by the venom with which she said it. 'Why?'

She stopped kicking the dandelion and looked up. 'He was a snake. Nobody liked him. That's why people avoided him.'

'You never told me you felt that way.'

'It wasn't my business to. Besides, I had a feeling you had a soft spot for him.'

There was no telling where the conversation was leading and I was beginning to feel more uncomfortable as she continued.

'Folks around here knew his family and his background but the likes of you and the other deported never did.'

'Why was he so disliked?'

'You know him, he thought he was a cut above.'

'Yes, that's true but that's not the worst of someone's character. Surely he could be forgiven for that.'

'Ahh, there was more to him than that. You never knew what he was thinking. We didn't understand why he came back. When he first left the village he said he was going to Ruse to attend university. Then something happens and five or six years later he's back here driving the tractor. It was just before you and the deportees arrived. The next thing we know he runs away with you. A couple of years later he's back saying he was sent to Lovech.'

She pulled the head off a dandelion and looked across to me. 'You know all about those camps. Very few came out of there with their sanity intact.'

With that said she poured the coffee into the screw top cup. 'I put sugar in. I hope it's not too sweet,' she said as she handed it over.

'No, it's perfect,' I replied. 'But keep going I want to know more.'

'No you don't want to hear about that bastard. He's not worth the time of day.'

'Yes I do. I'm interested to know why you feel that way.'

'Well, all right then. When he returned we heard he'd joined the party. And blow me down, to cap it all off the regime gets the boot and he's now the Mayor of Plovidiv for Christ sake.'

She stopped there and the look on my face was enough to have her appologising.

'Sorry, Lidia, I shouldn't have blabbered on about it. You don't need to to know this stuff.'

'I do actually. I need to know these things. He could have been taken away. Maybe it did all happen.'

But by the look on her face I knew my argument held little substance. All I ever knew was what I had been told, and my memories of him were taking a battering. She went on. All that needed to be said was coming at an unstoppable rate.

'I know him. He's cunning and ruthless. He has no remorse. That never happened to him,' she said folding her arms.

'How can you say that?'

'Because I saw what he was capable of. I learnt that at seven.' She stopped talking and took the sandwiches from the bag.'Let's not talk about that moron. Come on let's eat.'

'No, tell me. It's so long ago it doesn't matter anymore. What happened?'

'I'm not sure whether I should. It's not going to help anybody to know these things.'

'Please, Anna, tell me.'

'Well, all right then. As I said I was seven at the time. I was playing in the back field behind the shop when I heard this low muttering. I could see him in the shadow of the oak and he was with Rasheed... Anyway, I moved closer to see. They seemed to be arguing. He was angry... really angry. Had this crazy look about him. I couldn't hear what they were arguing about but suddenly he grabbed the collar of Rasheed's shirt and twisted it till the veins in his neck stood out like the tendrils of a grapevine. The boy's face went from red to purple and when Petar let go Rasheed collapsed.'

She hesitated and her eyes rose up to the church on the hill. 'You couldn't say he was out of control. He knew exactly where he aimed his boot and by the time he was finished, not a cry came from the wreck that was Rasheed. I never forgot that day. I was paralysed with fear.'

'Did he know you saw him?'

'Sure did.' She nodded. 'The gate to the backyard seemed an impossible distance away. I shrunk down into the long grass close to the fence with my eyes firmly shut. Thought I'd gone unseen, but when I opened one eye he was striding towards me with determination. I squeezed my eyes shut again. Then he leant down with his face real close "Get Up!" he said. I was shaking and he pulled me up on my toes and slammed me up against the fence. The sheer terror of the moment kept me still. "Poke out your tongue," he said. My tongue shot out of my head and his bloody fingers grabbed it." Now listen carefully," he hissed. "You so ever tell anyone what happened, you shall never wag it again. I'll cut it off." He let go of me and disappeared in seconds... I never did... I never told a soul.'

With every disclosure my heart had stalled in my chest and I sat open mouthed. 'That's shocking.'

'Yes. It was. Rasheed was found staggering around the village without any recollection of what happened to him. From that day on he could only carry out the simplest of tasks. Maybe you remember the dribbling boy that sat outside the store. No one questioned what had happened. People minded their own business and the authorities had little regard as to the welfare of a Turkish boy.'

She leant forward and picked up the small rock in front of her feet and tossed it hard. It hit the water with force and sank then she looked away beyond the stream.

A taste of acid rose from my gut and I dared not tell her about my shared meal with him. 'I had no idea,' I said.

'Yes, the Mayor of Plovdiv,' she scoffed. 'I guess he had the right qualifications for that job.'

We both had lost our appetite and the sandwiches remained untouched. It was with a sense of urgency we climbed the path to the cemetery. Threatening clouds gathered to the south and black thoughts percolated in my mind.

'You know,' she puffed. 'This day is not dissimilar to the day your mother was buried. Your Aunt and Uncle probably told you it was her wish to be here.'

We were both a little breathless on reaching the top of the hill. We wandered through the corridors of monuments and in the back corner of the graveyard we arrived at a humble marker which read: MALINA PETROVA IVANOVA. Beside my mother was an unmarked grave and a patch of wild sunflowers. I walked over to the flower patch and gently pushed aside the dusty stalks. Anna stood back watching. The petals and leaves twisted in my wake as I bent down.

A small glass jar with its rusty mottled lid tightly welded onto the glass rim stood upright on the earth. The vermillion colour quivered inside and I held it towards the sky. It was as if the creature contained had been touched with a millisecond of life, for its wings pivoted as I held the jar. The iridescent wings of my freedom butterfly, etched in black. As brilliant as the day I had found it.

Anna made her way over. 'What's wrong?'

'This is where my father lies.'

Anna took my hand. There was no formal prayer. It was not something we knew. But together we knelt with our heads bowed amongst the yellow. A moment passed till I eased myself up on one knee and offered her a hand up.

'I'll be over there,' she said and she wandered about the headstones leaving me with my private thoughts.

Swallows darted about. I sat between the graves and looked down the valley, past the line of poplars used as a wind barrier. Further down, the crease in the tree line ran down towards the river. Amongst the flattened marble and sporadic urns of lavender sat a brown-eyed rabbit with scissor ears parting. He did not move a whisker but his round eyes reflected my every gesture. His downy white tail turned and he quickly joined the chorus of dandelion heads taking flight on the breeze pushing up the valley. Light rain followed and it was not long before the white marble angels were turning shiny grey. I kissed my fingers, touched my mother's name then hurried to rejoin Anna sheltering under the oak. When the shower passed we linked arms and left.

'What a mess! Our lives were ransacked and for what?' I said as we walked down the hill.

'Exactly,' she said. 'But you owe it to them to be happy.'

We hooked arms. 'What are your plans from here?' she asked.

'When I met up with my cousin she told me the Turkish soldier who found me when I escaped had visited them in Sofia.'

'Really?'

'Yes. It was a year ago.'

'Why would he do that? What did he want?'

'According to Yana he wanted to know where I was. He thought I may have returned to Sofia. He's still living in Edirne.'

'What are you going to do?'

'Yana did her best to convince me to get in touch with him.'

'I wonder what he wanted?'

'I don't know, but he was very good to me at the time. In fact if it hadn't been for his visits I think I would've gone crazy.'

'That's it then, you have to call him.'

'I'm not sure. It's been too long. Besides I wouldn't know what to say.'

I could tell she was not listening. She stood with her hand on her hip. 'Do you have the number?'

'Yes, but I'm not calling,' I replied.

When we got back it was clear she was not going to let it pass.

'Come on, lets ring,' she said teasingly raising her eyebrows. 'You've got nothing to lose. It'll be fun.'

I opened my purse and pulled out the slip of paper. Slowly my index finger turned the dial of the old red phone, jammed between the clutter on the shop counter. But after two rings I hung up when I was ambushed by a sudden dry mouth.

'This is crazy. I can't do it.'

'No it's not... If you don't, I'll call him myself,' she said pulling aside the beaded curtain in the doorway. I swallowed hard and redialed. I gripped the receiver tighter and waited for the next ring and the next.

'Hello,' came the voice at the other end.

'He... Hello, can I speak to Gabir please?'

'Yes, your're speaking to him.'

He sounded a little taken back to hear a Bulgarian voice at the other end of the line.

'Gabir, this is Lidia,' I said holding tight to the receiver.

'Who did you say you were?'

'Lidia Ivanova.'

Three seconds of silence passed.

'WHAT! Lidia... I don't believe it.'

I burst out laughing. It was the happiest of moments. A tangle of questions and replies rushed down the wire.

'Where are you?'

'Bulgaria.'

'Oh my God. I have to see you. Where abouts?'

'In Polgovo.'

'I've got to see you! You must come to Edirne. Or of course I could come there.'

'I will... I will. I'll come to see you. I'm on holidays and I have time.'

'When?'

'I was going to leave here tomorrow. If that's ok, I could go on from here?'

'Yes,' he laughed. 'Oh my goodness, now I won't be able to sleep.'

'That will make two of us,' I said.

'There's so much to talk about. I'm so grateful you called. It's unbelievable. I've been trying to find you for years.'

'You probably won't recognise me. I'm different from the last time you saw me,' I said.

'Me too, age has embezzled my crop of black hair. It's all snowy around the edges.'

Anna eagerly thrust a bus timetable in front of me.

'I've got the timetable here. There's a 626 bus leaving Elhovo at 3:30pm. Is that ok?'

'Great. If you could be on that one I can meet you at the terminal on Mimar Sinan Street.'

I could almost see him standing at the end of the line, though it was an image from long ago. I hung up in disbelief. It had been a good ending to the day.

Anna came out from the kitchen holding two glasses of Slivovitz. Across the table laments and laughter were all rolled up in an evening made merrier by the sixty percent alcohol content of her homemade brew. The next morning I repacked my case. The connecting bus was due to come through around 10.30a.m. but I was told the local driver had a habit of sleeping in. Still I was in no particular hurry. The time spent with Anna had shed new light on matters needing to be resolved.

Rain spotted the short strip of tar-sealed road running through the village and we sat in the bus shelter keeping dry and agreeing to meet again soon. From a distance we could hear the bus approaching.

'Follow your heart,' she said and she hugged me warmly.

I climbed aboard, the door closed and I turned to wave through the side window. She waved back in the rain. Her smile faded as the bus drove down the main street past the white-painted trunks of the old oaks. Soon the road turned to gravel and mud splashed the bushes bordering fields primed for harvest.

CHAPTER 20

WHEN I THOUGHT ABOUT Gabir waiting at the terminal my nerves almost got the better of me. If not for Anna's excited insistence I would have returned to Sofia.

In Elhovo I boarded another bus packed with Bulgarian and Turkish faces. As we sped towards Turkey semi–trailers and traders vied for position, each intent on delivering early loads in order to return home by nightfall. Wrinkled gullies and clumps of forest slid into the valley leading to the border and my memories resurfaced.

We pulled into the village of Radovets for a fifteen-minute refuel and a welcomed break. The smell of diesel greeted me along with the gluey remains of bugs having ended their short lives in a splat and a fry on the hot radiator. It was the last stop before Edirne. Soon the muscle-bound driver settled into his seat and we were back on highway seven, headed for the border.

Times had changed. There were no machine-gun toting guards pacing the steel mesh on an overhead cat walk. The checkpoint appeared as a remnant of a macabre theme park and a hundred metres away an old man idly rummaged through a rusty pile in search of scrap metal. We moved across at a halting pace. Below, the calm yellow-blue of the Tundzha River reflected back. By now my head ached. I cupped my chin in my hand and looked out through the window where a rising film of heat quivered out of the tar seal.

A Turkish customs officer stepped aboard to check our passports and shortly after we were moving. Distant villages turned to suburbs and the sienna-blue haze could soon be seen hovering above the Selimiye Mosque. I reached into my handbag for my compact mirror and makeup. Another dribble of wet made its way down my back leaving damp patches in the tucks of my blouse. I patted my cheeks and neck with a tissue and hoped orange lipstick would improve my sticky appearance.

The bus terminal was on the outskirts of the city and had a steady influx of travellers intent on filling their empty bags with weekend bargains from the markets. We were ten minutes ahead of schedule and we stopped alongside a bus load of people coming in from Greece. I grabbed my tartan travel case and stepped up under the covered walkway. All around me was a mass of unfamiliar faces. Suddenly I felt foolish that perhaps my decision to come was a rash one.

Slowly I turned full circle scanning for a picture that matched my idea of him now. To one side of the terminal entrance a man on the other side of middle age, stood furtively looking about. In his hand he awkwardly clutched a bunch of tulips with their red blooms facing the pavement. He was behind the glass panel of the walkway but had not seen me. I trundled my small suitcase behind until I was in full view. Eyes straining, breathless, we caught sight of one another and were transfixed on the pavement. It was the same, our hearts inexplicably hooked. The absence of years rushed past like an unstoppable train. And then we both called out.

'Lidia!'

'Gabir!'

I dropped the suitcase and ran to him. We collided in the middle of the pedestrian crossing. He flung his arms around me while hanging tight to the tulips. Our world stood still, surrounded by a world of timetables and motion. A sharp interjection from a Volkswagon's horn caused us to break apart. We hurried off but I had left my suitcase on the other side.

'Wait, I'll get it. Here these are for you,' he said and he handed me the flowers.

My eyes took him in as he quickly walked back. I did not view him then as I viewed him at that moment. His kindness had never wavered despite knowing my time spent in the Istanbul "guest house" was limited. He wheeled the suitcase across the road and grinned widely.

'I'm thrilled. I don't know what to say.'

'Same for me. I'm surprised you recognised me.'

'Yes, you do look different but blonde suits you.'

As for him his hair had given way to grey but his eyebrows and lashes still clung to the dark colour of his youth. Nestled in the middle of his chin was an indent, like the finger print of a sculpture's afterthought. The combination of sadness and joy was imprinted on his face, with his sagging cheeks in contrast with the smiling corners of his eyes.

A late model Citroen was parked as if the driver had jumped from the car in a hurry. He pulled out the keys, unlocked the boot and a metal tool box was pushed aside to make way for my case. Then he rushed to open the passenger door and I climbed in. He turned the key and we started with a jerk.

'I can only blame you for that,' he said jokingly. 'You make a man lose his concentration.'

He restarted it and we entered the round-about and drove out onto the main road headed for the city. The Beatles song blasted out "I feel fine" and the speakers above the back window did a good job to camouflage our mutual awkwardness.

'It's so good to see you,' he said glancing over. 'I often wondered what happened to you.'

'Tell me about you,' I said. 'My cousin told me you have a son.'

'Yes, Adem. He's my pride and joy.'

'And a wife?' I enquired.

'No, I lost her when he was born. She developed an infection and died three weeks later.'

'That must have been hard.'

'Yes. We have been a father and son kind of team. He's a good boy and worth a hundred others.'

'I'm sure you're a good father.'

'I did my best. And you? Did you marry?'

I glanced away. 'Yes briefly but it was a case of me wanting to belong and he needing a wife.'

An awkward moment filled the cabin and his eyes briefly left the road.

'You never met anyone else?'

'No,' I said and I rolled the window down, with a sudden need for air.

He looked over at me, and was momentarily distracted. A motorcyclist with what appeared to be his entire household contents strapped to the pillion seat, cut us off. I grabbed the edge of the seat and he slammed on the brakes but the oblivious cyclist motored on.

'Welcome to Turkey,' he said and he jovially slapped the steering wheel. 'Here we've got a different set of road rules. Go and stop and no in between.'

We laughed and a moment later he turned the music down.

'This is a fabulous day. I'm glad we managed this reunion.'

'Yes, I couldn't believe it when Yana told me you had turned up at her door. What made you seek me out?'

'Unfinished business I guess. Your leaving happened so quickly. Even after all those years I couldn't but wonder what became of you.'

'I gather you're not still in the army?'

'I left after Adem was born. I wanted to be around for him so I started a small auto repair shop not far from home. I was lucky really. My mother lived with me up until she passed away and my friend Josef helped. Do you remember him? The soldier that was with me when we found you?'

'I think so.'

'He suggested I take you to the Kirkpinair oil wrestling championship tomorrow. I thought it might be great for you to see. It probably sounds a strange thing to take a girl to but it's a major annual event here and a real carnival atmosphere.' With a short hesitation he continued. 'Of course we don't have to go if you would prefer to do something else?'

'I'd love to,' I replied.

Dappled light through cedar trees filtered along Orta Bayir Street and he drove into a shady parking spot. Across the street an old man dressed in a waistcoat sat with his friend smoking a pipe outside his store. He tipped his cap and muttered something amusing to his friend. Gabir smiled and we walked on past the row of timber houses.

'Gossip is rife here. I think Josef's loose tongue has been active. I'm sure half the neighbourhood knows of my Australian visitor.'

From behind the house shutters, I could almost feel eyes taking me in. We arrived at a two-storey timber home jammed between a row of others. It was situated in the oldest quarter of the city.

'Welcome to my home,' he said and he swept his arm to one side.

It had mud brick walls on the ground floor and cedar cladding on the second. Along the pitched roof a row of pigeons eyed us like street vigilantes. A balcony with a wrought-iron railing was suspended over the front entrance and behind an iron gate was a pathway bordered by an unattended garden bed.

'Mind the step. There's a loose chip of marble which I've been meaning to fix but haven't got around to.'

He opened the front door and led the way through to a room opening off the sofa room.

'I'll put your suitcase in here. It's Adem's room which explains the pictures of our local football team. He hasn't lived with me for a year. He's studying engineering at university. He's only just returned to Istanbul last week from spending his summer break with me.'

I followed him in and looked about.

'It's a shame. I would've liked for you to have met him.' He placed my bag on the rug beside the bed and smiled. 'Maybe you will someday. Now the bathroom is the second door, left of the kitchen. You're welcome to have a shower if you like. Have you eaten?'

'Thanks, I've had a sandwich but I wouldn't mind washing my face and changing out of these sticky clothes.'

'Sure. I'll be in the kitchen if you need anything.'

I sat down on the divan next to the window. The room had a rustic feel with exposed timber beams on the ceiling and whitewashed walls. In the corner was a tall chest of drawers and on top of it a framed photo of a young man with his arm slung over his father. I rubbed my hand over the multi coloured bed cover. The pink pillow case was new as it still had the packaging creases and on top of the clean folded towel was a box of Turkish delight. I smiled to myself. Not a speck of dust could be seen on the sunny floor boards and a subtle lemon fragrance hung in the room. I stood up and hauled my case onto the bed and unzipped it.

It felt good to wash away the grit and slip into my clean cotton dress and it felt good to see him again. I was glad I had made contact. When I walked into the kitchen he was standing by the stove. He looked up and cleared his throat.

'I'm sure you feel better now,' he said.

'Yes, much, thank you.'

Next to his legs was a small pug with a crinkled forehead and two bulging black eyes. It looked at me and let out a low growl.

'Tilki,' he said and he gave it a nudge with his foot. 'Sorry, she's not used to female company. But guaranteed in half an hour she'll be your best friend.'

He pushed her curly back end out the back door. 'Please sit. My neighbour makes the best baclava. She bought me a plate full this morning so please help yourself.'

We sat at the table in the sage coloured kitchen, drinking coffee and telling our stories. He told me how he had tried to find where I had gone but to no avail and how he had felt on the last day we spent together.

'I returned to Edirne happy. I never forgot the moment when I caught sight of you running across the yard with a flash of a red skirt under your coat. I felt reassured that you would be ok. Then the next time I came down you were gone.'

He shook his head.

'I thought they'd have told you,' I said.

'They did but not until I got there weeks later. I knew nothing. I asked that woman in the office. Remember her? The one that raced back and forth behind the counter on her office chair, with the speed of a formula one driver?'

I laughed. It was lovely to witness a less serious side and a far cry from the previous time our paths had crossed. Back then I had been a screwed-up girl under the wing of an angel. He smiled at me then his expression changed.

'I was so angry that day. I tried making enquires but each one met a dead end. I could never have imagined you'd have been sent half way round the world. That must have been difficult?'

'Yes, it was a bit.'

'Are they your parents?' I said looking at a framed photo on the bookcase.

'Yes, I took that in Bulgaria. It was on their wedding anniversary. Just before we came here.'

'Had you ever thought of going back?'

'No. The only reason I went back was to find you. And I did. Or rather you found me,' he said with a warm smile.

Outside the rival calls to prayer bounced across the roof tops and clouds gathered over the suburb.

'Let's walk,' he said and he pushed the chair back from the table.

I stood up and stretched.

'That would be great. I've been sitting all day.'

We walked the streets and bazaars of the old city and when the crowds ventured out to take in the evening, coloured lights flooded the fountains and minarets.

'This is my favourtie spot to eat. Not that I come here very often. It's more Adem's and my birthday venue.'

I caught the vague scent of him as he placed his hand on

the centre of my back and guided me through a bright doorway. We sat on the terrace of the riverside restaurant where the black syrupy waters of the Tundzha threaded away through the arches of Meric Bridge. 'Mezze' plates and cooling dips were ferried past us at speed. The Rakia flowed and the cloudy white liquid caused my pale skin to colour.

'For years I had nightmares about this river,' I said.

'I'm sorry, I wasn't thinking. Maybe it was a bad choice to come here.'

'No, not at all... I don't feel that way now.'

We looked at one another for a moment. It was different but the same. Age had a way of rearranging youth, but what I remembered of him were his eyes and his warm-hearted squint. He had a serenity to him. A deep inner resolve.

The last of the diners left and with the clanging of plates and chair reshuffles it was apparent that the staff were eager to leave. As we left the sky opened and the rain poured down sending alley cats scampering for cover between ancient stones and us to the shelter of a tailor's doorway. When it eased we locked arms and walked along the cobbled street together in silence with no need to fill in the gaps in the conversation.

Next morning a steamy day awaited and soon the large shadow of Josef's shoes squeezed under the front door gap. He pushed the doorbell a number of times. When he entered he winked at Gabir, gave him a friendly slap on the back and on seeing me thrust his ample hand out.

'Pleased you to meet again,' he said in schoolboy English.

His smile revealed a gap in his front teeth like a twenty cent slot in a pinball machine.

'You too, Josef,' I said. But I had no memory of him.

By the time we arrived at the Sarayici Stadium I was well informed about the game and caught up in my friends enthusiasm.

'So what's the history of the game?' I asked.

'It all came about when the Sultan offered his leather pants to two men as a prize to whoever won the wrestle,' said Gabir clearly eager to tell the story. 'They fought all day and into the night but the next morning they were both dead from exhaustion.'

We climbed the grandstand steps, where the women were outnumbered twenty to one. A sea of oily masculinity marched into the arena. They slapped their thighs and knelt to kiss the earth. The whistle blew and with brute strength, couples lunged and locked arms. Hour upon hour bodies slammed to the ground until the sudden death play-off ended in a high pitch whistle. It was late-afternoon when we left.

Josef shook my hand and smiled warmly. 'Nice to meet you,' he said .

He patted Gabir's on the shoulder and disappeared down the street through the market stalls.

We walked the bridge and stood above the arch. Gypsy music wafted across the slow-moving water. Gabir turned to face me. Moths fluttered in the golden haze of the bridge light as he placed his hands on my shoulders. I raised mine to meet his wrists and the rain hung in the sky.

'This is a very special day for me.'

'For me too,' I replied.

Nothing more was said. Nevertheless it was a heart to heart and arm in arm we walked back.

It was pitch black when I woke. A wisp of balmy night air was causing the wooden end of the blind cord to tap against the window frame. The street was silent save for the occasional bark from Gabir's dog. I lay uncovered on the bed with the day's events at the forefront of my thoughts. Early adulthood had slammed into me and scuttled all that had gone before. I had arrived at life's crossroad without choice but this time the choice to return had been the right one. He was the only one left who knew me whole heartedly, who had pulled me back from the brink. And for reasons far beyond my understanding he had stuck by me. This time the circumstance in which I found myself standing above the waters of the Tundzha could not have been more different. But the subtle scent of wet mud on the river's edge remained with me.

Memories hidden under the shallows of history bubbled to the surface, together with a gnawing suspicion. I lay there with Anna's comments now playing havoc in my mind. Her story about Petar had been a staggering revelation. I struggled to make sense of how our opinions of him could have been so opposed. Yet she was there before me and she was there to witness that which I knew nothing about. With each rotation of the ceiling fan memories dragged me back to that dreadful moment. Like the surge in the tail of a cyclone, a horrific realisation charged in. I lay in the darkness with a mind alerted to the puzzles of the past.

The smell of fresh coffee filled the kitchen. My head was foggy and the sleepless night had left me jaded though I did my best to feign bright and breezy. Gabir looked up and appeared not to have suffered any effects from the night's indulgences.

'Did you sleep well?' he said placing the dog's water bowl on the floor. 'I hope Adem's bed is comfortable for you.'

'Yes it is, very, though maybe I shouldn't have had that last glass of Rakia, my head's aching a little.'

'We did give that bottle a bit of a nudge. Can I get you something for it?'

'No, but coffee would be great.'

I pulled the chair away from the laminated table and sat down. Steam billowed from the small jug on the stove. He reached into the overhead cupboard and pulled out two cups. I couldn't help notice how his skin changed colour from tan to pale olive under the short sleeve of his shirt. He smiled and his head turned back to me.

'I thought I'd show you the markets. God willing, the sunshine will stay with us.'

'I'm in your hands,' I said. Then I laughed. 'I guess I always was.'

'Yes, and I no longer have to wonder what happened to you.' He beamed across the table at me but his expression quickly changed.

'Is there anything the matter?'

'You look so serious.'

'I'm ok. It's just that I woke up last night and couldn't stop thinking about what happened. I spent most of the night mulling it over.'

'I'm sorry. Did I do something wrong?'

'Not at all. It was the river. It brought up memories.'

'Maybe it was a bad choice to go there after all.'

'No. It's just that there are things I find puzzling. Things I need to find out.'

'What?'

'Do you remember during the interrogation I mentioned a man called Petar Borev?'

His chin receded. 'It was so long ago,' he said.

'He was the other man. The one who organised our escape.'

He cleared his throat and I couldn't help notice he suddenly appeared uncomfortable. 'What about him?'

'Well I thought he had been shot too, but instead he survived.'

My eyes met his but he didn't comment. 'I met Petar before I came to see you. Can you believe this, he's now the Mayor of Plovdiv.'

He shook his head in disbelief and I continued.

And then when I saw my friend Anna in Polgovo, she told me things about him which I found completely contrary to who I thought he was. It doesn't seem to make sense. Last night I couldn't get it out of my head.'

I looked straight at him. 'Did you know if he ever crossed the river because it's hard to remember the details of what happened?'

He rested his chin on his clenched fist. His mouth was down turned and with a minimal shake to his head I took it to mean he knew nothing. I hesitated then continued.

'When I met with him he said he hadn't made it but instead he had been arrested at the border. It just doesn't add up. I'm so confused.'

Gabir moved his hand across the table towards mine and took hold. 'I think it's time to put the past behind you, Lidia.'

'But I can't. I couldn't sleep last night. I feel there's a missing piece to this. I'll never gain peace of mind until I find it.' I squeezed his hand. 'Did you ever hear anything? Something that was maybe said during my interrogation?'

'What can I say? I was only a soldier. It was so long ago. That sort of information would be hard to access now.'

'What information? '

For a split second I could tell he was grappling with a reply.

'Let it lie. I don't think it will do any good to pursue this.'

'You know something, don't you?'

He took my hand firmly. 'Walk away from the past, Lidia. It can only poison the future.'

'No, if I don't find out what happened it will never go away.'

At that point he realised by the tone in my voice I was not prepared to let the matter rest.

'All right then. At the time of your interrogation nothing was revealed. Husni never let me in on any background information. I was aware there was a Greek report but had no idea what it contained. I assumed the Greeks had been informed of the possibility that bodies may have washed downstream. But now I have information. I wanted you to know but I wasn't intending to give it to you so soon into your stay.'

'What?'

'A magazine article. I came across it a few years after you left. At first I wasn't sure if it was him but I believe it was.'

My heart began to thump. 'What article?'

'Just a minute.'

He stood and left the kitchen. I sat with my back rigid, my mind racing and anxious. When he returned he held a newspaper cutting. He handed it over along with two sheets of translation. The headline screamed at me. I read it and looked straight back.

'Where did you get this?'

'In my efforts to find you I made enquiries about him. It proved fruitless until three years later and purely by chance I came across that article. I was completely confused but I knew you were innocent. I translated it then and there thinking if I mannaged to find you I would show you. I now realise it was probably a bad decision. Looking at you now I wish I hadn't.'

The wake of desolation had long passed. Time had seen to that but a riot of anger coursed through my veins and I read the article for a second time. I had been an innocent pawn in a treacherous game. Slinking into the night, treachery had been hidden behind the smile of a lover. I covered the news clipping on the table with my hands and looked away speechless.

I took a deep breath. 'I'm going back,' I said.

'Why, what will you do?'

'I'm not sure but he's going to know I know about this.'

'But it will serve no purpose.'

'I don't care,' I said.

'He'll have you thrown out of the country, or worse. He's capable of anything if you confront him. For what? You'll mess up your life again.'

Suddenly the mood of the morning was transformed. 'I never

messed up my life. Others messed up my life.'

'No, that's not what I meant. I'm afraid for you. I truly am. Please don't do this.'

I stood. 'All my life I've been afraid. Afraid of consequence. Afraid of hidden messages. Afraid of what lies around the corner. Fear no longer has a place in my life. It's because of fear that people like him flourish.'

He stood, too, and we faced one another across the table.

'Then let me go with you.'

'No... I have to do this alone.'

He shook his head and muttered something under his breath in Turkish.

'What does that mean?'

'It's nothing, I shouldn't have,' said it.

'Tell me'.

'It's just an old Turkish proverb.'

'Tell me.'

'"He who gets up in anger, sits down with a loss."'

We drove in silence to the bus terminal and I pulled the suitcase from the back seat of the car before he had time to help me. He walked to the passenger side door and grabbed my arm.

'Don't go,' he said.

But I'm sure my weak smile sent a message that there would be no return. He kissed my cheek and I boarded the bus. I closed my eyes and my head rested into the seat next to the window. Outside car horns tooted. I wished I had not left so abruptly but I was overtaken with anger and an overwhelming need to confront. Every kilometre passing fuelled my mind as to what I would do once I got to Plovdiv.

I looked at my watch and knew by now Gabir would be home. He would have read my letter. I felt pangs of guilt at the way I had reacted. It had nothing to do with him. I knew he was worried but nothing would stop me and I was pleased I had writen him a note. I had propped it against the mirror of the dresser hoping he would understand my actions.

Dear Gabir,

I know you are upset that I have left so abruptly. I can't explain the power of this anger that drives me to confront the violations of the past. But I must. I cannot say whether I shall stay on in Bulgaria or return to Australia, for I am torn, having never really found that place I could call home.

But what I can say is that your generosity of spirit and the short time spent with you was wonderful.

Thank you so much for making me feel welcome.

Yours affectionately,

Lidia.

The bus crossed the river and I was racked with wretched thoughts. My former memory of the event was not the same as my current recollection. Thinking back there had been no rapid gunfire. There was only one single shot. It all made sense. It was something I had dared not think about until now. Everything fell into place.

The road leveled out at the foothills of the Sakar Mountain and amongst the fields, hot and sweaty men and women toiled under the last of a brilliant blue sky. Towards the west, steely cumulus clouds layered one upon the other threatening the distant skyline. By late afternoon I saw the old city of Plovdiv appear on top of three hills, and an hour later we arrived at the bus terminal.

Hotel Krasimir had served me well on my first visit and I was greeted warmly by the manager who recognised me from my recent stay. Not many tourists came to the hotel carrying an Australian passport and she was eager to engage me in idle conversation.

'Follow me, madam. I have a well-appointed room down the hall with a small balcony which has a beautiful outlook. I'm sure you will be happy with it. The kitchen is open for meals at 6:00pm and if you require anything, don't hesitate to ring.'

She pulled the brocade curtains aside and opened the French doors. The room instantly freshened. When she left I kicked off my shoes and poured myself a drink from the water jug on the shelf next to the writing desk. I stepped out onto the balcony and took a few deep breaths. Below, steep cobbled streets led off in a myriad of directions. The picturesque town stood defiant amongst a neighbourhood of multistoried apartments that spread out to form the country's second largest city. Across the street workmen were packing up trowels and shovels. They flushed the remains of gritty cement water down the gutter as the afternoon light rapidly slipped behind the Rhodope Mountain. I walked back inside and paced the room wondering how I would confront him.

Next morning I dialed out.

'Mayor's office, can I help you?' said the voice.

'Good morning, this is Lidia Ivanova speaking. I was wondering if Mayor Borev is available.'

'No, I'm sorry he is not in today.'

'I'm his friend from Australia and am really eager to see him before I return home. Is there any chance you could give me his home number?'

'I remember you,' said his secretary. 'Actually he isn't at home either. He took ill two days ago and has been undertaking treatment at the St Georgy Hospital on Vassil Aprilov Boulevard. He's in Room twenty-three and I believe he is seeing visitors now. They seem to have his breathing under control.'

I thanked her and gathered my things.

The elevator door opened at the first floor and I stepped out. Large linen baskets were stuffed against the walls with medication trolleys stationed outside each room. The sound of squeaky soles on polished floors could be heard as purposeful staff exited one room and entered another. Room twenty-three was situated thirty metres further down the corridor to the right. I entered through the swing door but there was no one in the well-made bed and thinking I had been given the wrong room number I walked back to the nursing station.

'Excuse me. I'm looking for Mr Borev. I think I may have the wrong room number. I was told he was in twenty-three but no one is in there.'

The young nurse looked up. 'Yes, that's his room but he's in the gardens taking in some morning sun. I've not long taken him down there. If you come to the window I'll point him out.'

We walked over.

'See the man with the burgundy robe in the wheel chair to the right of the elm tree and towards the rose garden. That's him.'

My eyes scanned the garden and there seated in the sunlight was the monster.

The nurse smiled. 'If you take the lift to the ground floor you will see the exit to the garden adjacent to the pharmacy.'

The elevator groaned its way to the ground floor then paused before the doors slid opened and I walked out. When I reached him his head was tilted to one side and a flurry of toxins rhythmically bubbled out of a mouth that hosted a macabre grin. He was sleeping. My shadow crossed his face and I stood before him scanning his mustard pallor with distaste. It was comforting to see his good looks had deserted him. I decided the visit would not be short so I crossed the lawn to the row of plastic chairs. I picked up one and with determination I walked back and set it down in front of him. A catheter snaked out of his nose and met in a y-shape at the base of his gullet. My fingers reached forward and I tugged. The clip fell from his nose and into his lap. Instantly he jerked forward, sucking in air as if it was his l ast breath.

'What is it? Who is it?'

He strained to see me standing in front of him, silhouetted against the sun.

'Lidia,' I replied. 'Here, you must have pulled this from your nose,' I said lifting the tube out of his lap and handing it back to him.

He was more than surprised to see me standing before him.

'What are you doing here?'

I gritted my teeth. 'I bet you didn't think I'd be back.'

He struggled to straighten and he pushed up on the arm rests of the chair. 'No I didn't. How nice of you to come. Shame I'm not in the best of condition. They say I have to stay here for a few days before I can go home. I say that it's nothing a good drag on a fag couldn't cure.'

His attempt to make light of his predicament turned nasty and it took a round of serious coughing before he could gain some control. It gave me pleasure to watch him struggle to clear his airways.

'What brings you back so soon?'

'Unresolved matters.'

'Really? What's that? It must be important considering it's interrupted your holiday'

I moved closer to him. Close enough that to others seated in the sunshine it appeared as a kiss to his forehead. A smile crossed his face and he raised his chin a little in anticipation. Our eyes locked together.

'Betrayal,' I said.

Then I sat back and watched him fight to catch his breath.

'What?'

'You know very well what I'm talking about.'

'No, I've no idea,' he spluttered.

On his face was a look as if he had been summoned to Hell's gates, and he ground together a tight jaw.

I sat forward drawing my breath slowly. 'Look at you. Low life, living the high life.'

He tried to raise himself higher in the wheel chair. 'What's got into you?' he said and his eyes narrowed. 'I've no idea what this is about. Are you deluded?'

'No, that's one thing I'm not. Delusion is more akin to you. You'd stomp on anyone to get to the top.'

He dragged his handkerchief out of his dressing gown pocket and violently coughed up a clot of muck. The pungent remnants of a life supply of nicotine bubbled in his chest and his eyes were wide and fixed on me.

'What's got into you to speak to me like this. If it wasn't for me you wouldn't have gained your freedom.'

'Tread carefully, Petar. You're on shaky foundations. Your reputation is built on a lie.'

He wrestled to right himself. 'How dare you insult me. I'm well respected. I've done nothing wrong. I've no idea what you're talking about.'

'Maybe this will jog your memory.'

I opened my handbag and pulled out the newspaper cutting. I waved it in front of him, holding it firmly in my grip.

'How am I expected to read that, it's in fucking Turkish,' he scoffed.

'Consider yourself lucky,' I replied. 'I had it translated.'

He raised his arrogant chin and looked away. 'I don't have my glasses.'

'Very well, I'll read it for you.'

I held the article stiffly out in front of me. '"SOVIET SPY REVEALS ALL". Does that ring a bell?'

He did not budge. Every muscle, including his struggling air sacs froze but his eyes randomly volleyed within their sockets as his brain sought a reply.

'That's not like you, lost for words. Did you hear me or would you like me to say it louder?'

He turned his head and looked towards the glass door entrance and he raised his arm. 'Nurse,' he called feebly.

She looked back, but I sprang up and headed to meet her.

'Beautiful day isn't it? He's having such a nice time,' I said and I looked back at him. 'Mr Borev wants to know if we can go a little further towards the trees? We haven't seen each other for many years and we have such a lot of catching up to do. It would be great if we could have some privacy. Being well known can have its drawbacks at times,' I added.

'Certainly,' said the nurse. 'Lunch won't be served for another hour so you might as well make good use of the sunshine. It's the best thing for him.'

His flaying arm flopped to his side and he sat with a look of desperation. As I walked away I turned back to her. 'Life can be so unkind,' I said. 'I'll make sure to wheel him back for lunch. Thank you.'

I walked over and took hold of the wheelchair handles. With a forceful kick of the brake lever the wheels slowly pressed two narrow tracks into the lawn. With determination I pushed him past the rose garden. No one paid much attention as we made our way across the grass. We arrived at a clump of trees situated on the northern boundary. The wheelchair bounced across the uneven surface at the base of the Rhododendron tree and I hit the brake.

We were screened from the other visitors, who sat with their loved ones doing their best to cheer and comfort. I slammed the plastic seat down in front of him but remained standing. He stared off into the distance chewing on his top lip and steadfastly refusing to look at me.

'What do you say,' I said shaking his shoulders hard till eventually he cleared his throat.

'Christ, why are you so agitated? I don't see what that's got to do with me.'

'It has everything to do with you.'

'What makes you think that?'

I pulled up the seat and began to read Gabir's translation.

'Ok, if you can't read it. I'll read it or you,' I said taking my glasses from my handbag. I sat back on the chair.

He turned his head away, raised an eyebrow and his mouth turned down on his droopy jaw. I cleared my throat and began to read.

"'Eric Chapman Former Soviet Spy died at his family home in Pottsdam Berlin at the age of 85. Since his capture in 1962 and release in 1980 he had never disclosed the identity of the other key member of the soviet operative. But in a

recent interview with reporter Wolfgang Kohler from the Deutsch Tagesnachrichten Chapman opened up.

According to Chapman the other man was a Bulgarian national by the name of Petar Borev. Together they devised a way of passing information under the guise of a chess game, to Chapman's Walthamstow address in London. Their mission was one of the most ingenious in Cold War history..."'

I glanced over. He sat defiant with his arms tightly folded but the coughing flush that coloured his complexion moments before was gone and his cheeks appeared bilious and bloodless. He refused to look at me and I continued.

'Let me see. Where was I?' I said as my finger followed along the line and I picked up where I left off.

"'In 1959 Borev turned up on Greek soil claiming to be a bona fide refugee. He was resettled in West Germany and took a job for the Bulgarian branch of the Radio Free Europe where he was given a desk within the Bulgarian Audience and Research Department. But unbeknown to his collegues, his mission was to identify defectors and disgruntled individuals who bad mouthed communism and offered up state secrets.

The information he gathered was sent to Chapman who in turn forwarded it to the Bulgarian Secret Service. Chapman had been under M15 surveillance for ten months. When arrested he was found to have in his possession numerous post cards sent from a West Berlin post box. But until now the indentification of Borev was not known.

"He was a brilliant bastard,'said Chapman. Cunning as all hell. He made it through Check Point Charlie with minutes to spare using the identity of Raphael Ivanov...'"

I paused for a moment. 'Does that jog your memory?'

He exhaled carefully through pursed lips, trying to keep his airways from closing off. I had seen it before, advanced emphysema. He gave a short little cough followed by cacophony of thick undertones. Suddenly he lunged at me but was thwarted by his nose clip. 'Give me that! '

I snatched the paper away and pushed him back with a flat palm to his chest.

'That's a fabrication. No one will believe you.'

'If you think the people of Plovdiv won't believe me, the people of Polgovo will surely give you a character reference.'

'What are you talking about?'

'Rasheed, the young Turkish boy you assaulted may have had his memory pulped but there are others in the village who can punch a hole in your pristine public persona.'

'Where did you get that?'

'Never you mind where I got it. The fact is I have it.'

'Give it to me!'

'For a boy from Polgovo the offer of a position in the secret service must have been thrilling... Am I not right?'

'Fuck you!' he said.

His defiance quickly disappeared when I slapped him hard across his Rosetta crazed cheek.

'Shut your filthy mouth,' I replied.

Again he tried to call out but his voice was feeble and his cough swallowed up his words.

'Don't waste your breath, no one is going to help you, they can't hear you. And don't think for a moment that when I leave here you'll be able to get one of your cronies to "fix me up." The news about the Mayor of Plovdiv will spread like a virus. In fact I hear you're already in a bit of strife over the election. If this gets out you'll be the Mayor of Nothing'

The anger in his face caused his cheeks to turn purple.

'Just for safekeeping,' I said. 'The original article is in the hands of a friend living outside of the country. If he doesn't hear back from me this will be sent to the papers.'

I held it out of reach and my other hand gripped the tap on the oxygen tank. Horror spread across his face. Beads of sweat leaked from his brow and his eyes were like marbles set to pop from his head.

'How easy it would be to turn this tap off,' I said. 'But then again that would be too quick. Better still I could turn it slightly and starve your lungs a little at a time. If I feel you are not telling me the truth I could turn it tighter. If I feel you are co-operating your lungs will be rewarded.'

He sat ramrod stiff in his chair. 'Don't. I beg you.'

'Beg… I never thought I'd hear that come out of your mouth,' I said and his eyes flicked from me to the tank and back.

'It's good to see you sit up and take notice.'

My voice was low but it was all I could do to stop from wrapping the plastic tube tight around his throat. I glared at him then slowly moved my attention to the page. I folded the article up and placed it back in my purse.

'There's no words to describe how much I despise you. You murderer! Shame on you.'

He turned his head away and his skin stretched tight across his mouth. The man who relished an audience, the man with the trimmings of greatness, sat lost for words.

'Your game playing is over. You get to lose. You have nothing to look forward to. I've been a nurse long enough to know what's in store and it gives me great comfort. Your reward is a slow, agonising death. Each day will be worse than the day before.'

I pushed out my lower lip. 'Why the sad face? It's not entirely out of your hands. You'll still get to make decisions.' I paused. 'Will I eat or will I breathe?'

My eyes drilled into him and his shoulders slumped. 'Now for once in your rotten life, do me the courtesy to tell me the truth.'

I looked down at the oxygen tank and my fingers clamped around the tap. He wheezed a breath in. His barrel chest pushed against his satin dressing gown. Terror crossed his blotched and swollen face and to my surprise he answered.

'What do you want to know?'

'The truth.'

'All right I'll tell you, but you leave me alone after.'

'It's not your place to bargain. One turn of this will loosen your tongue.'

'And if I say nothing you get nothing,' he scoffed.

Straight away I twisted the tap and in a split second his mouth shot open. His liver-spotted hands clung to his collar bones as if to pry them apart. It was all he could do to squeeze the words out.

'Ok... ok.'

I turned it back, his shoulders collapsed in. I sat watching him struggle.

'Tell me the truth in your own words. I want to know why you did what you did. And don't even think of lying because I'll have you know, I've done my homework and I know everything there is to know about you.'

To my surprise he did not call my bluff. For the first time in his deceitful life he revealed what had come to pass. He took a deep breath and began.

'It's not what I wanted. It was what they wanted. I had every intention of studying science but my language skills were such I was given a place at the Institute of Foreign Languages.'

For a brief moment he appeared to forget where he was and a slight grin tugged at the corners of his mouth. I stared back with a flat expression and he continued.

'Turned out I was good, better than they thought. The next thing I knew I scored a job in State Security. Studied communication and surveillance. When I graduated they sent back to the village in preparation for my mission.'

He cleared his throat and looked up at me.

'It's not something I'm proud of but that's how it was. Besides, for once in my life things were good. Who wouldn't be seduced by all that?'

'I can think of plenty,' I said.

'Yeah, well you can say what you like but if it wasn't for

me you'd still be pulling up beets. You can't tell me you weren't reaching for the stars when you ran away.'

'You played me for a fool with all your lies,' I said. 'That story about your murdered friend, I suppose that was all part of your sick little plan to reel me in.'

He looked straight at me. 'Some of it was. Some of it wasn't.'

'You never went to Belene, did you?'

'You've done your homework,' he replied .

I jumped up and leant over him.

'You twisted piece of shit!'

'Do you want me to tell you or not? 'he said.

A fleeting grin passed his grey lips as he sensed he had the upper hand. I slammed off his oxygen and suddenly there was no breath out only a heaving suck in like the forceful hiss of a coffee machine. I held it off long enough to see the blood vessel turn the whites of his eyes crimson. When the air rushed in, his spent lungs struggled to regain rhythm and I sat back waiting for him to get himself in order.

'Don't try that again. Now talk. I want to know where Raphael and I came into your plan?

'He was not to be part of the plan. That was your idea if you remember rightly. As for you... I was attracted to you. You were so fucking headstrong and I liked that.'

'So that was part of the plan?'

'What do you mean?'

'To seduce a girl and use her to legitimise your escape.'

'What better cover,' he said. 'Two lovers running to freedom.'

The word lover made me sick to my belly. I grabbed him by

the shoulders. 'You killed him!'

'I didn't fucking kill your brother. The Darzhavna killed him.'

'How dare you deny it! May you rot slowly before you reach Hell!'

The slap to his face embedded the catheter well into his right nostril. His head reeled back and his chest swelled as a crippling surge of air tore through his gaping mouth. Never could he have imagined the memory of that night would return with such vicious potency. I thumped his shoulder. His head turned back. He massaged his brow and his head hung low. I leant into him and no amount of expensive aftershave could conceal the scent of his decay.

'Look at me,' I demanded.

Slowly he raised his head and barely audibly he whispered a reply. 'Believe me, I never meant to kill him. It was an accident. They told me I was to shoot him in the legs and they would collect him. I tried to pull him out of the water but he was fucked. It was pointless.'

His hands trembled, his cheek twitched but his eyes remained dry. 'I don't blame you for wanting me dead,' he said clasping his chest.

'How could you do that to us! What sought of monster are you?'

'I was young. They made me do it. You know what it was like back then. I was just a nobody. You know that. There was nothing I could have done... Nothing, he said patting his forehead with his handkerchief. 'Honest to God... That is the truth.'

I folded my arms. 'Yeah, well you never did believe in God Petar.'

His demeanor was pathetic. The once cocky man was desperate to wash away his deceit but his head never hung like someone shamed.

'Where's his body?' I said.

'I don't know,' came his flat reply.

My head throbbed and slowly he turned to me.

'Money can't replace what I did,' he stammered. 'But it can make life better. You name your sum. I have influence. I can set you up.'

'Set me up! How dare you… You set me up all right. I spit on your every word.'

A wad of mucus flew from my mouth and hit him just below his left eye. It slid over his ruddy cheek and down to his jaw, where it hung fat and juicy. His mouth fell open, exposing a tongue like a dry block of pumice. The tubing crossing his neck appeared like a hangman's noose and my eyes were fixed on it. I leant in close and hissed the words into his burning ear.

'I wonder how much air is left in that tank.'

I took a deep breath, turned and walked away. The wards were quiet and the garden was empty. I strolled in through the doors of the hospital lobby and out the other side, onto Vassil Aprilov Boulevard and I never looked back.

CHAPTER 21

THE HOTEL RECEPTIONIST looked surprised to see me.
I gathered it was unusual to see a guest return to the small hotel
so early in the afternoon. The day had dished up a hefty serve of
emotion. I felt exhausted. I fell asleep on the bed only to wake
in darkness. It was 7:20p.m. I swung my legs off the bed and
walked to the phone. I called Yana to tell her I would be catching
the morning train back to Sofia then I showered and climbed
into bed. Every few minutes from afar I could hear the distant
thunder rumble closer as a storm rolled in. I lay in the dim room
with my eyes open, rifling through childhood memories. Raphael
always had an answer. When night thunderclaps came and my
childish fear caused me to crawl across the dressing table and
climb into the safety of his bed he would laugh and say.

"God is busy beating the dust from the clouds, Lidia. You'll
see, in the morning the clouds will be white," which at the age of

seven was a perfectly reasonable explanation. However at the age of eighteen and for years to follow, one crack of thunder could turn me to stone. Now a peacefulness was threading its way into my mindset and I fell asleep.

Yana's warm arms were welcoming and it was a comfort to return and put my case in her room.

'Come, tell me what happened,' she said fussing.

In the lounge Aunt Iva sat in an armchair by the window in a strip of yellow daylight. Coffee was brewed and I proceeded to tell them the events of the past week.

'We always felt there had been foul play,' said Yana. 'Didn't we, Mama?'

My Aunt nodded and Yana continued. 'I believe your mother knew as well but we were powerless. I am happy he now suffers. It's a wonder you didn't turn off the tap on his oxygen tank.'

I leaned over. 'It did cross my mind but then I figured he was best left to suffer. It felt good to walk away.'

'You're right. He will get what's coming to him,' she replied with a disdainful nod.

'So what next?'

'I've decided to return to Polgovo.'

'Why?'

'I need closure and I was hoping you might come with me?'

'What for?'

'A little commemorative ceremony. I'm going to get in touch with Anna. She can have a word to the local priest. Perhaps he can oversee it. I was thinking perhaps on the 15th August.'

'On Dormition Day,' said Yana.

'Yes, Mama's... Name Day. If Aunt Iva is well enough maybe we could take her too?'

'I'm sure we can manage it.'

'So would you mind if I stay a little longer?'

'Of course. Stay as long as you like.'

It was Thursday the 28th July when I heard the news. I had spent the day organising a brass plaque to be taken to Polgovo and had just walked in through the front door of the apartment when Yana met me in the hall.

'Lidia, he's dead!'

'Who?'

'Petar. It's all over the news. He died this morning.'

I dropped my bag and sat down on the hall seat with my back against the wall. She fell silent beside me. I raised my eyes up to the ceiling. All that had come to pass. The disquiet that had accompanied me on waking and falling asleep was no more. The painful years had far outweighed any physical blow. No longer would memories and perilous thoughts send me to that dark place. A significant change had come about. A calmness. A renewal.

It was a busy time for the clergy but on receiving the phone call Anna agreed to visit the priest the following morning. Armed with an assortment of delicacies from the top shelf of the store Anna paid him a visit. His shaky hand pencilled the date for a 9:00am service to be held at the old cemetery on the hill.

On a Baltic Day with an August breeze tugging at our skirts, we solemnly followed the short priest through the cemetery. Either side of me stood Anna and Yana. Aunt Iva was seated in front of the equally-elderly priest. Somehow he had survived the purges, which must have verified in his mind that he was one of God's chosen.

The brass plaque was mounted on a thin slab of granite the size of a shoebox lid. It was pressed into the earth where my father lay and beside it the jar with the butterfly. I stepped back and looked on. They were no more than names.

The epitaph read:
In memory of my beloved father and brother,
Alexandra Yordanov Ivanov and Raphael Alexandrov Ivanov.
Beneath the sunflowers lie the dreams of two good men,
taken for no good reason.

"He who falls while fighting to be free, can never die"

Poet Hristo Botev

Mid winter was causing me to reminisce. It was summer on the other side of the world and the ceiling fans in Sydney would be working overtime. February's weather could be punishing at times.

Since the commemorative service I had returned to Sofia and stayed on at Yana's insistence but as the months went by I was becoming restless.

A young girl skipped past the tram stop with her school bag and plaits bouncing on her back, evoking in me memories of a previous time. I thought, too, of Emma and wondered how she had fared. My young patient had never ceased to surprise me.

'All your wishes have come true,' I said to her the day she left the hospital.

'Yes,' she said. 'And I've made another one, Lidia.'

'What's that?'

'That all the sad people will find their sparkle,' and her head turned back to me as she walked out of the hospital with a wide, wide grin.

As I sat at the tram stop, I smiled. I decided to drop her a postcard and tell her that the stars now shone bright in this eastern sky.

The cables bowed and bounced as the tram turned into the busy city street and stopped. Passengers in heavy coats hustled to climb aboard, eager to seek shelter from the wind. I sat on the seat and placed the string bag of groceries on my lap. Directly opposite an elderly couple sat. They never spoke during the journey and seemed only to communicate with a nod, a smile or a flick of the eyes. Time had given them a common understanding and a bond that did not require speech.

I sat solo, glancing discreetly in the couple's direction. Their shoulders rubbed together with every turn in the road until two tram stops further down they got off. The bell rang and the tram continued on.

Gabir began to occupy my thoughts. Lately I dreamed of him and if I didn't, I tried to. It was with him that I felt at home. It was with him there was no need to fill in the silence. He was like a blanket of warmth silently enveloping me. I remembered having asked over dinner why he had bothered with me and his reply was curious.

"Like a carpenter finding a fine piece of furniture tossed aside, it's the nicks and chips that endears it to the one lucky enough to discover it."

And sitting on that crowded Sofia tram I made the decision. I was the last one standing but I no longer accepted a life of loneliness. It was with him I had to be.

I never called him, never wrote but stood on the threshold with a thought I could never have imagined. I was walking into his life.

The last bus to Edirne from Sofia had pulled into the terminal at 7:00pm. on an early spring evening and I had taken a taxi to Orta Bayar Street. I paid the driver and wheeled my suitcase up the short path to the front door. The dog growled low then leaped from its padded fruit box in the corner of the kitchen. It tore off down the corridor before I had time to press the doorbell.

'Tilka. Stop it!' came his muffled voice.

As his footsteps approached he called out.

'Coming.'

The porch light flicked on and I held my breath. The door opened. His hands immediately went to the sides of his head then his arms fell open.

'Lidia!'

I smiled at him with tears of happiness.

He was flabbergasted.

'I'm lost for words. I don't know what to say.'

'There's no need to say anything. Can I stay a while?'

'I can't think of anything that would make me happier.'

He kissed me lightly on the cheek and bent down to take my case. 'Let me put this in Adem's room.'

The door closed on our previous lives as we entered a world almost forgotten by one and never known by the other. A place of enchantment and intimacy. I followed him in.

'I've been so worried about you. Oh my goodness this is such a surprise. You must be hungry, I'll cook you something.'

'No, it's ok ,I've eaten.'

'Come then we will have a drink to celebrate.' He handed me a glass of wine. 'I'm sorry if I pressured you when you were here. I was afraid for you.'

I reached across the table and placed my hand on his. 'It's alright,' I replied then hesitated. 'He's dead.'

His back stiffened. 'How's that?'

'It's ok, don't be concerned. I didn't cause his rotten heart to stop. He brought that on himself.'

For a moment we looked at one another in silence.

'Are you ok?'

'Yes. He's in Hell and I get to rest in peace.'

'What will you do now?'

I looked back at him and sighed. 'I have no idea. Life has

been a series of hurdles and tumbles but finally I feel I walk on level ground.'

'I'm pleased to hear that. You must be tired.'

'Yes I am but I wouldn't mind taking a shower, if that's ok?'

'Of course, I'll get you a towel.'

He returned shortly and stood in the doorway of the bedroom with a clean towel. 'I can't tell you how happy I am to see you.'

I smiled at him.

'Is there anything else you need?' he said.

My hand rested on the suitcase zip. I stopped what I was doing. It was the first time in my life I understood the full meaning of freedom. I looked up at him. 'Only you.'

He took a backward step and his breath momentarily halted. Outside the world was silent. We were both struck by a moment of awkwardness.

'You. Before I sleep.'

Tangled somewhere between passion and shyness he walked gently towards me, his soft eyes never straying. He placed his hands either side of my face. His lips met mine. Mulled claret lingered on the edges of his tongue and he pulled me into him.

'You can't imagine how I dreamt of this.'

'I know,' I whispered.

'Come, I'll run a bath for you. '

He took my hand and I followed. I watched as he poured a ribbon of oily essence into the tub. The steaming water hissed and danced into a frothy web.

'One moment,' he said stepping out from the bathroom.

Seconds later he returned holding a lantern. He placed it on the shelf above the towel rack and opened the small metal door. The candle quivered into life as a lacy amber light shone through the metal cut-outs. Nothing was said. We stood in the half-darkness unwrapping the gift of one to the other. His kisses slipped down onto my collarbone and the cocoon I had spun around me for years fell away. I held his gaze as I buttoned him down. Stripped bare he stood in the darkness almost afraid to breathe and I knelt before him. He stiffened in my hands and my lips brushed the crown and the length of him. I rose up and he kissed my throat, the soft part between my shoulders and the crease under my breasts. We bathed till the milky water cooled.

Behind the bedroom door darkness shied from the moonlight. My hips rose to meet him as his fingers followed every curve. They glided between my soft thighs, lower deeper, then passed the folds that lead to the source of my desire. There his fingers lingered, stroked and pulsed. An eager tightness formed in my belly till I could no longer wait. He moved into me and our rhythms matched. Pale skin on olive ebbed and flowed as the delicious tremors of the night gave way to the salty taste and musky scent of love. He rolled away and pinheads of sweat glistened on the fine hairs of his chest.

'I thought I'd never see you again,' he said stroking my head and I cried in his arms for the lost years, and I cried for the blessing of the love of this man.

'Don't cry,' he said and his rough hand caressed my cheek. 'Why these tears?'

'Fear.'

'Fear of what?'

'Fear that when you love you lose.'

He held my face in both hands. 'That's not so. I've loved you for decades and I haven't lost you.' His chin nestled into the bridge of my nose and he kissed my forehead. 'You are my weakness,' he said and we slept.

The following morning I woke to find his thigh crossing mine and his eyes watching.

'I'm not going to ask you to stay. I believe you know where you belong,' he said.

CHAPTER 22

THERE WAS NO HARD DECISION MADE. Somehow it had fallen into place and I stayed in his little house. You could say life began later than sooner. It was rich in its simplicity and it was perfect as it was.

The years moved on till eventually we became old lovers living the life of the elderly; breakfast at 8:30am, lunch at 1:30pm and dinner at 6:30p.m. Sometimes we would catch the bus to the river until the lights came on in the old town. At night we would climb into bed with tired bones, me with my head tucked under his chin and he with the armholes of his singlet skewed. He was there to walk me back into life and he was there to walk me out.

October 16th 2011

Our Russian Blue cat sat purring and preening on the sunny spot on the rug. My head rested into the back of the reclining chair. The illness was taking its toll. Along with a combination of coloured drugs and fatigue most of my day was spent positioned in the warmth of the sunroom looking out on the small back garden. As my eyes closed I wondered whether the small parcel I asked Gabir to post would have arrived in Sydney. My mother's ring no longer fitted my finger and time saw it placed in the silver ring box on the dressing table. There were no children to pass it on to and I had deliberated for some time over it, until one starry night when it became clear. I remembered Emma, the child I had nursed in the year I left Australia. Twenty-two years was long but I knew somewhere in my old address book I had kept her parents address. With a bit of luck they would be living there and could pass on my gift. I lay on my side with the bedside lamp on. As Gabir slept on I valiantly battled to concentrate due to the heavy dose of painkillers.

In the morning I asked him to send the ring, together with my letter.

> *Dear Emma,*
> *I am lying here looking out at the stars, or as you use to call them "The SPARKLES."*
> *I was thinking about you today. Last night I had a dream not unlike those which you so often told me about.*
> *You were an inspiring young girl as I'm sure you are today. My mother gave me this ring the night I escaped Bulgaria and it would give me great pleasure to know you wear it.*

I like to think of the ruby hearts representing two kindred spirits and the surrounding seed pearls the stars.
Goodnight Emma,
Love Lidia

The coloured tea glass shimmered an amber light across the ceiling and the afternoon sun commenced its descent behind the domed silhouette of the local Mosque, like a black cutout in an orange sky. Gabir sat down beside me and placed the apple tea on the brass table. He clasped my hand in his. 'Are you awake…I've made tea?'

I stirred and my elbows dug into the worn upholstery of the armchair as I struggled to gain an upright position.

'What were you dreaming about?'

'I was thinking of Emma. I wonder if she has received the ring?'

'The woman in the post office said delivery to Australia takes nine to ten days. Emma may well have received it today.'

I smiled and sipped my tea. He shuffled out to return the tray to the kitchen. The lace edged curtain wafted inwards on the whispering breeze. Something caught my eye.

A blue butterfly appeared on the window ledge and fluttered to my bed.

END

The After-words

MY OWN FATHER passed away on the 16th October 2011.

There was no telling where my loss was to lead me. The very thought of not having him around was inconceivable. As the days ran out I told him this but he placed his big hand upon my back and he said.

'It's not so bad. A couple of weeks and you'll be back on track.'

It was four weeks before his death I concluded the story, albeit a rough draft. I printed it as a hard cover book and gave it to him but in truth it was his gift to me.

I learnt a lot more about Murrae than I had ever known. Our quiet moments were equally important and discussions deeper than the day-to-day events. He was not a religious man but I asked him one day what he believed in, and to my surprise he answered.

'Reincarnation.'

'What do you want to come back as?' I asked.

'A duck,' was his reply.

We sat and laughed and he told me the joys of life as a duck.

At his funeral I was determined to make a speech despite a fear of public speaking. He was a popular man and many came to see him off. I stood on the podium and for the first time fear was not with me and I recounted his desire to return as a duck.

Over sandwiches and cups of tea two old men approached. Prior to Dad's illness, the three of them had been restoring a 1920's bus in the shed on the hill above the Albany Lake Reserve. In the morning on the day of the funeral they were working on it. The doors were wide open, and in the sunlight, something never seen before happened.

A duck walked into the shed.

Acknowledgements

There are many people who have helped me on my writer's journey.

Yana Shopov who offered first hand knowledge of life growing up during this dark time in Bulgaria's history.

Matthew Richardson who went out of his way to advise and encouraged me to pursue my dream as writer.

Robin Brass, Denise Bosnic, Ricardo Avellanal and my mother Joan Henderson for their enthusiastic support. As well as friends who put up with my endless chit-chat about this project and my lack of social interaction in order to finish it.

Julie Postance whose guidance through the self publishing quagmire has been invaluable.

Amanda Spedding for her keen eye and detailed edit.

Edel Duffy for her valuable marketing expertise and encouragement.

And lastly, Lidia Doncova-Macri who's unfailing support for this story, her love of Bulgaria and her readiness to answer my questions made it possible. Without her I would never have travelled to Bulgaria, been introduced to her wonderful friends and family, and have had the resources to research this book.

Sources

https://en.wikipedia.org/wiki/Bombing_of_Sofia_in_World_War_II

https://en.wikipedia.org/wiki/Martenitsa

https://pressroom.rferl.org

http://www.hoover.org/research/voices-hope-story-radio-free-europe-and-radio-liberty

https://www.youtube.com/watch?v=GtJwbBWwJDc

http://www.novinite.com/articles/172899/Bulgaria%27s+President%3A
+CommunistEra+Officials=Still+Wield+Influence

http://www.marines.mil/Portals/59/Publications/Bulgaria%20Study_4.pdf

https://en.wikipedia.org/wiki/Bulgarian_coup_d%27%C3%A9tat_of_1944

https://en.wikipedia.org/wiki/Bulgarian_Communist_Party

https://en.wikipedia.org/wiki/Georgi_Markov

http://www.decommunization.org/English/Testimonies/Svideteli.htm

https://en.wikipedia.org/wiki/Forced_labour_camps_in_Communist_Bulgaria

https://www.awesomestories.com/asset/view/Belene-Bulgarian-Forced-Labor-Camp

http://pametbg.com/index.php/en/memorial-places/belene/49-belene-concentration-camp

http://beleneisland.org/dt_gallery/belene-concentration-camp/?lang=en

http://www.bonegilla.org.au/

https://en.wikipedia.org/wiki/Bonegilla_Migrant_Reception_and_Training_Centre

http://www.naa.gov.au/collection/a-z/bonegilla.aspx

http://www.migrationheritage.nsw.gov.au/exhibitions/somuchsky/

https://en.wikipedia.org/wiki/Shoulder_dystocia

http://www.thefamouspeople.com/profiles/hristo-botev-5649.php

Susan Mimram has spent most of her working life as a graphic designer and technical illustrator but she has always been a storyteller. However it was not until her father was diagnosed with a terminal illness that she discovered a love of writing. As she puts it, telling her father this story had shades of a modern *Arabian Nights*. Three weeks before his death she completed the story and had the first draft bound. She gave it to him as a gift but it was more his gift to her. By encouraging her to write, he had taught her the power of imagination.

Susan grew up in New Zealand but has lived in Sydney most of her adult life. *Someone's Listening* is her first novel.

www.ingramcontent.com/pod-product-compliance
Lightning Source LLC
Chambersburg PA
CBHW030645260626
47157CB00007B/2500